PRINCE CHARLIE'S BLUFF

Prince Charlie's Bluff
by Donald Thomas

THE VIKING PRESS   NEW YORK

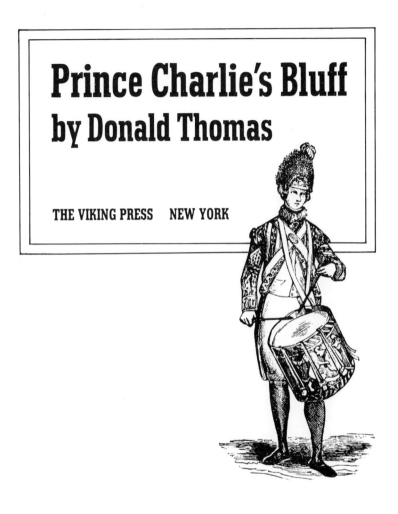

Published in 1974 by The Viking Press, Inc.
625 Madison Avenue, New York, N.Y. 10022
SBN 670-57615-8
Library of Congress catalog card number: 73-16829
Printed in U.S.A.

CONTENTS

'Annapolis, Annapolis! Oh, yes! Annapolis must be defended. To be sure, Annapolis should be defended. ... Where is Annapolis?'

Thomas Pelham Holles, 1st Duke of Newcastle
(Prime Minister of Great Britain and First
Lord of the Treasury 1754–1762)

PRINCE CHARLIE'S BLUFF

THE AUTHOR

In the closing years of his long life, the Hon. Edward Fraser turned again to those papers which he had assembled during his tenure of cabinet office and his period as Secretary of State. From these documents he proposed to complete his great, unfinished history, *The Annals of the Kingdom of Virginia.* Unhappily, his energy had been exhausted by half a century of public service. The great history of Virginia was never completed.

Yet in 1915, less than a year before his death, Edward Fraser had prepared for publication an edition of the remaining fragments of the journal of his grandfather, Lovat Fraser (1732–1821), reputed the natural son of that Simon, Lord Lovat who was executed in 1747 for his part in the Jacobite uprising of two years earlier. Lovat Fraser, undeterred by the fate of his father, was one of the first of his clan to join a new Jacobite plot, after the Quebec fiasco of 1759, for the restoration of the Stuart Kings in the Province of Virginia.

Lovat Fraser's journal relates the fortunes of the Frasers and the Stuarts during the lifetime of Charles III, the so-called 'Bonnie Prince Charlie'. The manuscript of the journal is bound in the same volume as a collection of letters, which do not form part of the present edition, written from London by Lovat Fraser in 1819–1820 while his son, Balmerino Fraser, was Virginian envoy at the time of the English Revolution and the government of Sir Francis Burdett.

Other volumes of the Fraser papers included a French journal of the Mississippi War for 1811–1814 and Edward Fraser's political memoir of his own life in the Kingdom of Virginia during the years 1846–1870, covering the Regency of the Lord Casimir and the reign of Richard IV. Fraser lived to do little more than complete this memoir, and to put in order the papers of Lovat Fraser, his grandfather. On his death, the documents were found with a note, entrusting them to 'that paragon of humane learning, Woodrow Wilson, President of Princeton University, who, had the circumstances of history been altered, might also have been President of the United States'.

THE KINGDOM OF VIRGINIA

Of the three kings, a queen and a regent who ruled the sovereign state of Virginia, one died at the hands of his assassins and the others, more surprisingly, survived their term of life and died a natural death.

The first of these rulers, James III, was King of Great Britain and of Virginia. Yet he was king only in title and never set foot in his American territories. Two of those who held power after him were idealists, though with scarcely an ideal in common. Two more were fools, but for all that they brought the benefits of peace more abundantly to their people. Yet wise or foolish, knaves or heroes, there ran in the veins of them all the blood of the Royal House of Stuart.

Charles Edward, 'The Young Pretender', as the Hanoverians sneeringly termed him, remarked when he landed in Virginia as his father's representative that the Stuarts brought only independence from George II of England as their dowry. During the twenty-seven years of his reign as Charles III, he behaved publicly and privately with the grace and charm of a guest. How probable it seemed, when he first landed, that he would indeed be a guest, and one whose stay would be of short duration!

Hardly had his elder daughter succeeded to the throne as Queen Henrietta, when the bullets of republican assassins threatened the very existence of the tender plant of monarchy on the North American continent. How strange it seems, therefore, that Henrietta's reign should have spanned that half-century in which Virginia became the greatest nation of the western hemisphere. A girl of twenty-six, Henrietta lacked the charm of her father and the intelligence of her royal brother-in-law, Lord Louis de Johnstone. It was well said of her that she would have made a better farmer's wife than a queen. She left politics to her ministers, as she left the care of her linen to her laundress. If she did her duty as those ministers commanded, it was because she had neither the inclination nor wit to do otherwise. Yet Henrietta and her successive administrations gave Virginia fifty years of peace and growing wealth, interrupted only by the Mississippi War in 1812.

At her death in 1846, Queen Henrietta left her kingdom as a nation whose peaceful territorial expansion embraced an area greater than that of any European state apart from Russia. She was more sincerely mourned than either her father or her nephew, Prince James Edward, who had predeceased her and whose infant son was her heir. Virginians felt a particular loyalty towards her as the first monarch to have been born upon the American continent, and as a Queen whose reign had brought them a European degree of prosperity. Henrietta had been the symbol of Virginia's stability, while war and revolution made Europe and the Americas tremble.

Her younger nephew, the Lord Casimir, who became Regent of Virginia during the infancy of Richard IV, was fifty-six years old at the time of her death. I remember, though not in its details, the funeral procession of Queen Henrietta as it passed through the streets of Williamsburg to her burial place in the Royal Chapel, in Bruton Parish. I recall, as though I could see it now, the face of Lord Casimir at the opening of one of the first sessions of Parliament during the Regency. It was the face of a debauchee on the body of a sprite. Gluttony and lechery had shrivelled, not fattened him, until he looked like a fragile old man. Though he was the uncle of Richard IV, he might more properly have seemed his grandfather.

The Regency of this feeble profligate in Virginia is as notorious for its misfortunes here as was the reign of George III in England. But neither that unhappy King nor the Regent of Virginia lived to see the awful harvest of his misdeeds.

How quickly the power of government under Lord Casimir's Regency passed to McAlistair and his 'patriots' is well enough known. Territorial disputes and the system of black slavery had long been fruitful topics of dissension between the Kingdom of Virginia and those Republican States to the north, which had won their independence from George IV of England in 1820. But it was left to McAlistair to improve upon these disputes. He was in no way restrained by the Lord Casimir but only by a fear that the English might come to the aid of the Republican States before either the French or the Spanish could support Virginia. Then, after the disasters which overtook her in 1856, the English Republic was of little consequence in the world's affairs. Well might their poet Wordsworth write his most famous political sonnet on *The Coming Extinction of Britain's Imperial Power*, 'Once did she hold the gorgeous East in fee.' With this poetic prophecy fulfilled, McAlistair's generals marched north, sure of freedom from English intervention and, therefore, certain of eventual victory.

Half a century after the tragedies of New York and Philadelphia, the consequences of that American war are still the bitterest of all historical memories. For four years after the Armistice, the Lord Casimir remained Regent and McAlistair was his minister. The coming of age of the infant King in 1862 then brought to our throne Richard IV of Virginia and Great Britain. (For, in their titles, the Stuarts never abandoned their claim to the British crown.) This young man seemed to combine, for the first time, the most admirable qualities of his Stuart ancestors without their grosser failings. He showed the courtesy of his great-grandfather, King Charles III, and a liberal-mindedness which sharply distinguished him from his uncle Casimir's ministers.

King Richard IV abhorred the system of black slavery, as it then existed, while the denial to free-born Virginians of political rights commonly enjoyed in Europe appeared intolerable to him. Yet it was, most of all, in his youth that men saw the promise of the future. Some regarded him as the saviour of the new world, who would at last give substance to the dreams of the first colonists who had left Europe to follow the hope of liberty and justice in the Americas.

No man who was not alive in 1862 can imagine the general feeling of expectation and promise throughout Virginia, and perhaps most of all in the vanquished Republican States. How that promise was fulfilled, and how the political despotism of McAlistair played its part is a matter of common knowledge. To many observers, these were merely the last of the political convulsions which had shaken North America since that day in 1759, when young Lovat Fraser and 12,000 more of General Wolfe's force sailed from England to attack the great French fortresses of Louisberg and Quebec.

EDWARD FRASER

1

THE PLAINS OF ABRAHAM

By 1756, the guns of the French and British armies were engaged on three continents, and those of their navies across two oceans. In the Mediterranean, the British lost the island of Minorca. In their attempted invasion of France, they were beaten back both at Rochefort and Cancale. The King's son, the Duke of Cumberland, fought a disastrous campaign in Hanover. The news from India was dominated by the horror of the deaths of British captives in the 'Black Hole of Calcutta'.

Nowhere were the misfortunes of war more apparent than in North America. French armies, striking south from their Canadian strongholds of Montreal and Quebec, seized Fort William Henry in 1757, opening the way to Albany and New York. They thrust so strongly towards New England that rumours circulated of Boston itself being taken and burnt. Worst of all, Indian tribes, in the service of their French masters, swarmed across the Ohio valley and fell upon the undefended farmlands of Virginia and Pennsylvania. The victims of these raids were found dead by the burnt ruins of their homesteads, mutilated beyond all description, often being left with their entrails crammed in their mouths.

Neither in the Virginian capital of Williamsburg, nor in London, could men at first believe the story that a fully equipped British army, under General Braddock, had been routed by a horde of Indians. When the story proved true, the despair in the American colonies began to grow into panic. Braddock was dead, his soldiers killed, captured, or put to flight. The eight women of the column were taken by the Indians. His own mistress, after being put to uses of which decency forbids the description, was stripped, riddled with arrows, boiled and eaten.

The Virginian settlers showed little spirit for warfare of this kind on their own farmlands. Many were for making peace on whatever terms the French offered. Indeed, the resources of the Royal Navy were largely employed to prevent trading with the enemy, for the Virginians continued to smuggle sugar and rum from the French West Indian islands throughout the period of hostilities. British attempts to raise a militia from the colonists were met first by apathy and then by resistance. The colonists protested loudly at being involved against their will in the hostilities of two European powers. They had no wish to be the uncomplaining instrument of Britain's military power. 'What is the glory of the British constitution more than that of the French, but Liberty?' asked the New York Gazette on 8 November 1756. 'But if once Liberty is lost, there will be no difference between an English and a French government.'

Lord Loudoun and his commanders were soon obliged to post strong picket lines round New York to check the flow of deserters from the regular British forces. In Virginia itself, the British Lieutenant-Governor, Robert Dinwiddie, cursed the colony's traders for 'a set of abandoned wretches'. In England, as Horace Walpole observed, 'The partisans of the ministry damn the plantations, and ask if we are to involve ourselves in a war for them.' The colonists, in their turn, denounced the government in London for spending their taxes to hire mercenaries for the protection of George II's Hanoverian dominions, while leaving his American subjects to the mercy of the French and the Indians. It was small wonder that an English officer, in a letter to his family, remarked that these colonists had grown so fearful of the French and the Indians that the enemy 'might take all Maryland and Virginia simply by going there'.

In England, the government led by the Duke of Newcastle seemed on the point of collapse. His enemies quite expected him to be ousted by the dismissed Paymaster-General, William Pitt. They reckoned without the inveterate hostility of George II towards this grandson of 'Diamond' Pitt, the trading Governor of Madras. At the critical hour, moreover, Pitt was at Bath, taking the waters for a crippling attack of gout. He returned to London to find that it was the astute and wealthy William Murray, later Lord Mansfield, who had lent his powerful influence and judicial brain to support Newcastle's administration. When Charles Townshend too was made a member of this cabal, Pitt, unable to suppress his bitter sense of exclusion, hissed at his enemies across the floor of the House of Commons, ' I wish you joy of him !'

Confronted by a succession of military defeats, the new administration summoned the advice of its soldiers. Newcastle, in his lisping and indolent manner, insisted that something must positively be done. He did not himself know what they might do, but he was certain that something must be done. Presently, as if finding an inspiration, he demanded that the war in North America should be continued by the colonists themselves, who must be made to find men and money to fight the French. Yet it soon appeared that there was no time to organise such a scheme.

Brigadier-General James Wolfe and Brigadier George Townshend (the brother of Charles Townshend) offered rival plans for the same bold offensive stroke against the French. A British army of 12,000 men, escorted by a naval squadron, must cross the Atlantic to seize or blockade the French fortress of Louisberg, guarding the mouth of the St Lawrence River. With this done, they must then sail up the St Lawrence with as little delay as possible and take Quebec in the same summer, before the formation of ice in September or October should make the river impassable. With the fall of Quebec it would be a mere matter of routine (in this view) to march overland upon Montreal, and so destroy the base of all French power in Canada. With its roots torn out, the growing might of France in the Ohio valley would wither and die.

This scheme for Canada was first opposed by Lord Mansfield, who demonstrated that there were scarcely enough troops for the European campaigns and that 12,000 more must be impossible to find. George Townshend answered him by proposing the raising of a number of new regiments from Scotland and Ireland, as well as from the counties of England. Two were to be raised by Simon Fraser, son of Lord Lovat, the Jacobite leader beheaded in 1747. Newcastle disputed the wisdom of raising two such regiments from a clan which had fought to a man for 'Bonnie Prince Charlie' hardly ten years before.

'Why, sir,' he said pettishly to Townshend, 'the Earl of Loudoun raised such a regiment in 1744. And what did he see, sir? His entire regiment deserted to the Pretender's son not a year later.'

Lord Mansfield, however, played the lawyer with his busy mind, showing by what exact laws and cunning statutes it could be ensured that the regiments would be shipped to Canada as soon as raised and not allowed to return until they were disbanded and disarmed. Newcastle hummed his fears to himself until they were quieted at last by the Captain-General, the Duke of Cumberland, victor of Culloden and the 'Butcher' of the defeated Jacobites.

'Believe me, sir, you will find little taste for rebellion in men who are soldiers in a strange and hostile land many thousands of miles from their own. Yet if you still think them to be rebels, why let us send as many of them as we may, and let them form the vanguard of our attack. Then, if two thousand rebels are sent, you may be surprised if you see as many as two hundred of them return!'

In March 1759, General Wolfe's force, including two regiments of Fraser's Highlanders, sailed from Portsmouth. Among those on the transports was Simon Fraser, son of the executed Lord Lovat. On a separate ship was a young officer of the Highlanders, Lovat Fraser, whose name reflected the belief of many of the clan Fraser that he was the natural son of Lord Lovat and, hence, half-brother to Simon.

During the weeks of the Atlantic voyage, the 27-year-old Lovat Fraser decided to keep a journal of the events in which he was *soon to be involved. He was erratic as a diarist and never regarded himself as a man of letters. On some days he would make an entry covering many pages, in his careful and upright script. At other times he would allow weeks to pass without making any entry at all. He confessed that on some occasions he carried events in his memory and wrote them down after a considerable interval. Yet the part played by Lovat Fraser in the history of Virginia is carefully recorded from the first entry of 31 May 1759, when General Wolfe's armada engaged the French guns of Louisberg.*

31 May 1759. Thirteen weeks after leaving Portsmouth, and hardly a week after touching at New England, our squadron dropped anchor within sight of the French fortress of Louisberg. The foul weather, which had favoured us ever since we entered the open sea, continued for the period of our riding at anchor. Reconnaissance parties were all that put out towards the shore in the landing boats, and one of these we lost as it was returning to the fleet through a heavy groundsea. When the boat was overset, the men were neither swept away upon the flood nor sank to reappear, but were snatched down from our sight for ever as if by some terrible and invisible force.

On the last day of May, General Wolfe commanded the Highlanders and the Grenadiers to enter the landing boats for the debarkation, which was planned in a rocky cove to the north of the fortress. The storm had fallen and the grey ocean moved in a long swell, pitted with raindrops like the small pox. This constant drizzling hid from us all but the shadowy prospect of a dark and precipitous shore, whose hills and cliffs seemed as steep as the walls of the French fortifications. A little after nine o' clock in the forenoon, the word was passed to our men, who had been sitting in their craft since before dawn, and our own landing boat was pushed out with the rest from the lee of the wooden hulk which had carried us from England.

As our boats pitched and heaved in the full Atlantic

swell, sending us this way and that, the sailors bent their backs to the oars, pulling hard to make their way against the tide. Not far from us, Brigadier George Townshend, a man of vast parade, called to his sailors in his drawling English manner.

'Pull bravely, my boys! What need we fear from God-damned frog-eaters and a party of savages in their arse-clouts?'

The Grenadiers in his boat gave him three rousing huzzas, as the long oars cut the surging water and the drummers in the stern beat the stroke. Yet our Highlanders shivered under their plaid shawls, perhaps calling to mind how many of their clan, womenfolk and babes at the breast, had been put to the sword as 'savages' by their English comrades a few short years ago. No voice was raised in our boat as the tide and the oars of our sailors bore us through the rhythm of the drums. General Wolfe, whom some called 'The Duchess' for his fair skin and woman's face, was in a landing boat at a little distance off. In the view of many, his was a woman's heart also, exhibiting a spite and vindictiveness peculiar to female nature.

We were borne towards a little cove, where pine trees had been felled among the dunes to form redoubts which the French defenders might occupy. Yet all seemed as silent as if we were approaching an uninhabited island. No sound of guns nor movement of men came from the steep walls of Louisberg on our left nor from the wooden barricades of the shore. A long swell gathering behind us drove our boats pell-mell towards the rocky cove, where we could clearly discern the surf breaking and boiling over the black stones.

Captain James Ogilvie, a gentleman of many accomplishments and dark appearance, much prized by the fairer sex, sat next to me in our boat.

'I promise you,' said Ogilvie, 'there will be no going

through such a surf as that on a lee shore. The boats will be dashed to pieces for a moral certainty.'

Our Highlanders pulled their shawls tighter round their shoulders and huddled away from the drizzling rain. Three or four of them were playing at dice for a fine dirk, under the cover of a shawl.

The storm of war broke without the least warning. A volley of shot fell among us like driven hailstones, whipping spray from the sullen surges of the water before we could hear the crack of the Frenchmen's muskets or see the smoke. Our men knew that they were fairly caught on the open sea by the French sharpshooters, yet this was a danger in any such attack. Several of our sailors seemed to pause, their pigtails glistening from the rain and foam, expecting when the order should be given to sheer off. For all that, the order was to go forward. We were hardly twenty feet closer to the shore when a roaring, as if the iron gates of hell's furnace had been thrown open, assured us that the guns of the fortress of Louisberg had begun to play in earnest upon our fleet of landing boats. The thunderbolts from their cannon threw up such waterspouts as overset any landing boat within several yards of the impact.

Men who had sat upright, their grounded muskets forming a grove of steel in the boat's centre, now vainly sought protection by crouching below the level of the wooden sides. Soon after, one of our sailors caught a French musket ball in his belly, and fell back, crying out that he was a dead man. So he was, for his intestines being swollen with a hearty breakfast there was no hope that the ball would pass between them, and he died this evening after much suffering. No sooner had a tall Highlander seized the vacant oar than a French salvo threw up two monstrous plumes of water to our left, tipping the boat to its side and sending us all in a helter skelter. The craft righted itself before any man was lost, but around us in every direction were other soldiers in the water, whom sailors tried to pull to safety with their oars. We saved some by pulling them to our own boat but a dozen more sank beneath the turmoil of the water, their hands lifted in a last vain prayer, before we could assist them.

The wily French had held their fire until we were almost within hailing distance of them, and having lured us so far they now inflicted the most terrible execution upon our men. Looking again to our left, I saw Brigadier Townshend who still urged his sailors forward as if they rowed for a prize, beating his hand on the boat's side in time to the drums. Far behind us, the British ships of war lay at anchor with their sails furled. Their gunners did not dare to engage the French batteries, for they feared that their salvoes, falling short, would fall among us.

On either side of us, men thrown from their boats were dragged down by the weight of their uniforms and equipment. A sudden volley of musket fire found out General Wolfe's landing boat, which was among the nearest to the shore, cutting his flagstaff in two pieces. At this, the order was given to sheer off and abandon the attempt, for there would have been no landing alive on such a coast through the high waves and the fire of the French. Yet the command was easier to give than to obey, when the first boats were not a hundred yards from the shore and being driven hard towards it by wind and tide. Our own sailors were sorely tested to turn the landing boat against such a flood. Even as they swung us round, we offered a broad target to the French marksmen, who took the lives of three Highlanders and one more of our sailors. General Wolfe sat coolly with his glass to his eye, surveying the hostile cliffs, and it was a wonder that he had not been one of those whose life was lost.

I doubted then that we should ever escape the perils of that coast, for try as we might every wave seemed to drive us back to the hands of our enemies. Yet the oarsmen carried us away, an inch at a time, until if we were not beyond the range of the French guns we were at least beyond the skill of their sharpshooters and their masters of ordnance. After such a currying we were glad enough to reach the shelter of the transports, having lost five men in our boat. Two soldiers, one shot through the head and another through the breast, were already dead, as was a sailor, likewise hit in the breast. Another soldier and sailor, mortally wounded, were to die before nightfall.

3 June 1759. Great discontent is felt by our men, who grieve at so many brave comrades lost to such little purpose. Our plan being revealed to the French by our first attempt, a second invasion would meet with little more success than the first. In any event, there is no time for a second assault upon Louisberg, for General Wolfe's orders must be to take and secure the great city of Quebec.

'I will tell you what I know, though I may not say *how* I know it,' said Captain Ogilvie to me last night. 'It was never intended to take Louisberg, but only to skirmish with the French so that their ships and army must be held there to protect it. Those who are closest to General Wolfe will tell you that Quebec is the only prize.'

He later told me that if Quebec were to be taken the thing must be done quickly, for by September the winter ice would oblige our ships to leave the St Lawrence River. So says Captain Ogilvie, a man of much information.

Today at noon, the greater part of the naval squadron, under Admiral Boscawen, was left to entertain the *mounseers* of Louisberg with a little cannon music, while our transports and the remaining ships of war weighed anchor and sailed northwards, towards the St Lawrence River.

A little before darkness the wind freshened and our ships were scattered over a wide surface of the ocean. Our own transport being caught in conflicting currents not half a mile from the rocks of a deep bay, our crew of New

England sailors missed their tack. The sea began to drive us towards a rocky ledge, where we should, of a certainty, have been dashed to pieces. The master of the vessel, whom I had long taken for a canting fanatic, fell to his knees, crying out, 'What shall we do? I vow, I fear we shall all be lost! Let us go to our prayers! What can we do, dear Jonathan?'

As for the said Jonathan (as pious a hypocrite as most of his tribe), he stood in the bows, shaking his head and muttering, 'Do? I vow, Ebenezer, I don't know what we shall do any more than thyself.'

While these preaching enthusiasts were on their knees, loudly begging pardon for their sins, Captain Ogilvie, who had served several years on board a ship before ever he was a soldier, heard and saw the helpless state of mind which our New England men were in as the ship drove towards the shore.

'Why, damn your eyes and limbs,' he shouted in a mighty rage, 'down with her sails and let her drive arse foremost! What the devil signifies your praying and canting now?'

Ebenezer quickly took the hint and, abandoning his prayers, called to Jonathan to lower the sails.

Everything necessary was instantly done. Captain Ogilvie gave the directions and, seizing the helm, we recovered our position, cleared the rocks, and drove into the bay stern foremost, where we anchored securely to await a change in the tide.

'I vow,' said Ebenezer, 'I believe that young officer's advice was very good. Yet I could wish that he had not delivered it so profanely.'

5 June 1759. Nothing would do but General Wolfe must find out and punish 'cowards', who robbed him of conquest at Louisberg. It is not to be wondered at that he should look for these in the Highland regiments, where his hatred has so many years been fixed. One man singled out is Andrew Forbes, a great booby with more taste for shearing the wool of his sheep than the heads of the French. Five days since, while his comrades prepared to assault Louisberg, this wretch found his bowels so moved with terror that he must conceal himself on board the transport, where he eased nature the length of the battle in a makeshift privy. There he was discovered by the picket guard, bloodless and quaking, while the French guns played upon his fellows in their landing boats.

For this cowardice, General Wolfe would have seen him hanged as an example. Yet the witty Brigadier Townshend (ever an enemy to all the General's schemes) advised some mercy.

'You will find him no braver for hanging, sir,' said the Brigadier. 'Damme, I should not wonder if the cowardly wretch did not loose his guts over all our heads the moment he swung free.'

It was my chance to be retained as escort to Forbes, a lumbering Highlander with matted hair and a plaid shawl. He was brought to the great cabin in the stern of General Wolfe's ship, the *Sutherland*. Here the General, Brigadier Townshend and Brigadier Monckton had formed a court of summary jurisdiction for dealing speedily with defaulters, of whom there seemed to be a large number.

The General sat between his two brigadiers at a draped table, all having their backs to those windows in the stern of the vessel which lit the great cabin. Behind them, a crowd of junior officers from the English regiments stood or lounged, watching as if it were a kind of sport. When our Highlander's turn came, he was brought to one end of the table, while at the other end the sergeant of the guard stood and described, upon his oath, the nature of the cowardice of which Andrew Forbes was accused. Then our culprit was instructed to ask such questions or make such petitions as he might. He had little enough to say for himself beyond falling on his knees on the bare boards and begging loudly for his life from the officers who judged him. This display moved the admiration of some of the onlookers, who smiled wisely at such a devilishly fine spectacle. When the man was silenced, the court-martial found him guilty, as he was, and after a short consultation pronounced their sentence.

'It is the opinion of this court that the prisoner is a notorious coward. They sentence him to ride the wooden horse half an hour a day for six days, with a petticoat on him, a broom in his hand, and a paper on his back, bearing this inscription: "Such is the reward of my merit." '

The Highlander was then marched away by a sergeant and two troopers of the 47th regiment. With tears, he acknowledged 'their honours' goodness' towards him, for he had expected nothing less than a rope from the yard-arm. I remained with the other onlookers, close to the table, to take further instructions. I was just behind Brigadier Townshend, who had devised so apt a punishment for Andrew Forbes, and saw him drawing something upon a sheet of paper. (The Brigadier was an accomplished caricaturist, and his contempt for the upstart General Wolfe ensured that he never lacked a subject for his art.)

Vastly delicate in his humour, the Brigadier's pen now represented General Wolfe spying down a latrine with his eye-glass and exclaiming, 'I thought I had seen the last of those poxed Jacobite knaves, but I find I am mistaken!' It was impossible that General Wolfe should not see this, sitting as close as he did, and this was without doubt the reason for the sentence of five hundred lashes awarded for insubordinate conduct upon the young trooper who was then before the court. When the proceedings were done, I heard General Wolfe say to the Brigadier, in his manner of quiet fury, 'You shall answer for such insults as this, sir, when we are returned to England!'

'Your humble s-a-a-rvant, sir,' drawled the witty Brigadier.

The General, however, still smarted from such lampoons and sought a subject for his anger. He rose from his chair, turned his back upon his adversary and, ignoring my presence, he favoured those officers before him with his opinion of the Scottish nation, whom he had assisted to butcher after the uprising of 1745.

'Depend upon it, gentlemen, they are a people better governed by fear than by favour, and for my part I dislike 'em much. They are civil but treacherous. Their women,' and some of the English captains grinned knowingly at this, 'why their women are coarse, cold, and cunning. When they followed their Pretender's rebellion, they gave no quarter to our soldiers but put prisoners and dying alike to the sword. Oh, you may be sure, gentlemen, we took our revenge for that! When their turn came, we made no prisoners among 'em. Our cavalry did their business for 'em with wonderful spirit, and we completed our victory with much slaughter. Had certain of our commanders there not been in their dotage, we might have sent half a regiment to take their rebel leaders. Why, they would have resisted, and so much the better, for then we might have massacred their entire clan. You think me vindictive, gentlemen, but I have lived long among 'em, and I think I know how to treat a Scot. Our own brave lads shall make sure that this morning's cowardly Highlander does not sit easy in his saddle.'

While General Wolfe addressed his officers in this manner (for there was much more of the same stuff) I fixed my eyes on the rising and falling horizon beyond the wake of the *Sutherland*, and I bit my tongue not to speak. With so little compunction would our 'brave' and 'gallant' General have wet his sword with the blood of our poor womenfolk and innocent children! I puzzled my brains why I or any of my people should be fighting the

25

battles of a Hanoverian king like George II, and risking our lives for the glory of a commander who would have murdered us all without a qualm a little while before. It was our poverty and the loss of our lands which had brought us to this. Otherwise, what greater hatred should we have for the French than for King George and his generals? What greater harm had the French soldiers ever done the Scots? For France was ever the old ally of Scotland. Yet all these questions came too late. The bows of the *Sutherland* already cut against the tide with a roaring of water like a mill race, as we drew near to the estuary of the St Lawrence River.

At noon, the young English trooper received his five hundred lashes before the other men of his regiment. Upon being released from the mast, he turned, to the amazement of all, and performed a somersault in mid-air, to show (as he said) that he was 'game to the backbone'. We hear that General Wolfe repents of his spite towards the man, who was a tumbler before he turned soldier, and has privately made him a gift of two or three guineas by way of amends. Whether this is true or not, I cannot tell.

7 June 1759. A melancholy sequel to the sentence of the court upon Andrew Forbes. He was to taste 'their honours' goodness' to him on the lower deck of the *Sutherland*, where he might be the spectacle of the marines and the sailors' women. There was a great throng of spectators, so many that the quarters, for all their open ports, stank like a set of stables rather than human lodgings.

All decency was done away with. The sergeant and the guard stripped Andrew Forbes naked as a baby, and hoisted him astride the instrument of penance. Several of the women tore off a shift from the youngest of their number, on whom the lot had fallen. She, a very fair-skinned girl, had drunk too good a ration of rum to protest much and laughed as hard as any while she ran to hide herself from the press of people.

The shift was pulled over the head of the Highlander as he sat astride the sharp wood, the paper was pinned to his back, and a broom forced into his hand. The sailors' women, more than the men, were vastly amused to see him in this predicament, fastened there with a cold perspiration breaking out on his forehead. They asked him jeeringly how he liked his commission in the wooden cavalry, and one of them ran forward to pull at his legs and make him cry out. It seemed that his loins must split or his limbs be pulled from their sockets, and it was a wonder that he was not ruptured. The guard were told off to prevent the women but it appeared as if the blood had left Andrew Forbes's face, for he was white and his cheeks seemed to shrink.

The sign proclaiming his cowardice fell to the deck. When the sergeant of the guard pinned it to the cloth again, he asked Forbes if he would play the coward another time, and Forbes cursed him for the son of a whore. This angered the mob, making the women spit upon him, who had been content to laugh before. Several of the men goaded him in the ribs with sharp sticks, until they were ordered back, and he roared at them like a tormented bear.

When he was at last let down and his hands freed, he still talked quietly and distractedly to himself in his own Gaelic tongue, which was perhaps a deliberate deceit. However, once he was at partial liberty, he seized a sharpened stick where it had fallen, and rushed like a giant upon his enemies. The mob pushed back from him, but those in front were unable to escape his thrusts before he was taken again by the guard. There were cries from the women and a scream which all at first thought to be a woman's. Yet it was an English sergeant whose hands were clapped to his face and whose eye had become a

27

great welling of blood, where the Highlander in an unlucky stroke had pierced him to the brain.

Not four hours afterwards, the body of the English sergeant was weighted and buried in the sea. Andrew Forbes could hope for nothing from the witty Brigadier, who must leave him to the mercy of General Wolfe.

Captain Ogilvie swears to the words that passed between Forbes and the General, and which are now known to all throughout the Highland regiments. Once the story of the tragedy had been told, the General asked the Highlander if he had risen early that morning to attend to his duties.

'Yes, and so please your honour.'

'And did you see the sun rise, sir?'

'I did, your honour.'

'Very well, for I promise you that you shall not see it set.'

Our fleet rode at anchor in the late afternoon, the masts and rigging of every ship blackened by the outlines of the men, who had all been ordered to climb and take their places there. A single gun from the *Sutherland* announced that Andrew Forbes had been swung into eternity, witnessed by the men who manned the rigging of the fleet. For an hour, his body hung against the glimmering light like a dark omen, and there was a great silence over the entire squadron. Then he was cut down, the ships unfurled their sails and we weighed anchor.

On the transports which carried the soldiers of the clans, this example which had been designed to strike such fear into our men only moved their anger and resentment. Many a Highlander now recalled the slaughter of his people a dozen years before, when women, children and aged parents had fallen to the swords of General Wolfe and his gallant followers. So, by the genius of the same General, a cowardly trooper was become a hero to his comrades.

19 June 1759. Last night I was seized with a sickness

and a griping, which has affected many on our transport. By Captain Ogilvie's advice (who is well taught in all such matters) I took a vomit and this morning found myself marvellously restored and in good spirits, for which I thank God.

Not a week after the melancholy death of Andrew Forbes, we sighted land to the south-west which was the southern shore of the St Lawrence River. Soon afterwards we came to a place where the river was not twenty miles across, and now we pass between a peaceful landscape on either side. There is not the least mark of war to be seen and no Frenchmen have yet appeared to bar our progress. Yet after our long voyage from England such pastoral scenes as these appear as the Paradise of Eden itself. Stone houses, windmills, and watermills are neatly built near the river's banks, their crops of wheat and barley being carefully enclosed by wooden pales for better protection from marauders of all species. The air of the river seems clear and fresh, while the great hills in the distance with the mist upon them remind us of our own Highlands.

At a council-of-war in the great cabin of the *Sutherland,* where I was aide to my Kinsman, Colonel Fraser, General Wolfe was pleased to give us his judgment upon those American subjects of King George who are to be our allies in the coming battle against the armies of France.

'Why, gentlemen,' said the General, 'the Americans are for the greater part the dirtiest, most contemptible, cowardly dogs that you can conceive. There is no depending on 'em in action. They fall down dead in their own dirt and desert by battalions, officers and all. Such rascals as those are rather an encumbrance than any strength to an army.'

As he said this, the General looked, like a peevish old maid, at me. It being evidently required that I should say something, I ventured a comment that the Royal

Americans, whatever their faults, were excellent marksmen. Their men were exercised in a different manner to our own. At this, some young Lord Caesar, who had quit the dragoons to join General Wolfe's staff, inquired, 'Exercised in a different manner, sir? Now, how may that be?'

'Why, sir,' said I, 'their whole training and exercise is to load quickly and to hit the mark when they fire.'

'What?' asked my lord. 'To take deliberate aim at an enemy, sir?'

'Good aim, sir, or else they will not fire.'

'So, if an officer were to appear, twenty men shall aim at him together! Absolute murder!'

'It is war, sir,' said I.

'Oh, it is war, sir!' said he. 'Your servant, sir! Heroic indeed!'

And with this my lord smiled wisely round at his companions, as if to say that none but a treacherous Scot would approve so cowardly a design. This is the contempt which Highlander and American alike receive from their commanders.

26 June 1759. Today we are close indeed to that fortress which we must soon take or lose our lives in the failure. The ships of our fleet are anchored off the wooded isle of Orléans, which divides the river in two no more than seven miles or so downstream from the citadel of Quebec. Our men are already debarking and their white tents are set up on the nearest point of the island in preparation for the siege. The river is the width of a mile on either side of the island, and there are to be camps on either bank. On the northern bank, General Wolfe is setting up camp not six miles downstream from Quebec, while Brigadier Monckton is to make his camp on the southern bank, no more than a mile or two across the stream from the city.

For all that the French have done to confuse our navigation by moving their floats and buoys, our pilots have brought all our ships and the entire army safely up the St Lawrence River to this point. The French batteries at Cap Tourmente and on other promontories fired upon us as we passed, but to little effect.

General Wolfe has issued a proclamation to the farmers and the villagers of the area occupied by our troops, informing them that if they are obedient to his commands they shall be spared, but that otherwise they shall be put to the sword. The issue is to be entirely at their own choice. Some of our own clansmen might tell them that the choice shall be to supply General Wolfe with the necessaries of life until his victory, and be put to the sword afterwards for all that.

10 July 1759. Being at Brigadier Monckton's camp this morning, which is on the heights that look across the river to the city, I had my first prospect of Quebec. From the position of our batteries on the southern bank, it appears a fine town and an admirable fortress, being built on a promontory with sheer cliffs and water as its defence on all but one side. We may bombard it, indeed we may, and we may sit here until we or they be starved into submission, but there seems little likelihood of taking such a citadel by storm.

Captain Ogilvie, who also accompanied our party, reports that when General Wolfe first saw this same prospect of Quebec he shook his head and remarked to his officers, 'Gentlemen, I cannot flatter myself that we shall be able to reduce this place.'

Whether the General truly believes this, who can tell? Perhaps it was said so that his achievement in taking Quebec, if it should happen, would afterwards appear to be all the more glorious.

The great buildings of the city, tall and in the French

style, stand on the heights. Through my glass I could easily make out a steep road connecting them with the humbler buildings of the lower town at the water's edge. There is little enough comfort to be had from the knowledge that we may be obliged to take such a fortress by crossing the river and scaling those sheer cliffs in full view of the French gunners. That would be to repeat the affair of Louisberg. In conversation with Captain Ogilvie and Colonel Simon Fraser, we agreed that a wise general might advance on the flanks of the city, so far as he could, before committing himself to such an assault. Yet such a plan cannot be delayed, since the battle must be won before the ice of these regions compels our navy to withdraw in September.

20 July 1759. It is said that General Wolfe is deadly sick and has been let blood. As to that, any man can tell that hundreds of our soldiers are sick, feverish and trembling, their bowels loosened. We are plagued by flies that swarm like a black carpet over the outside of our tents and often inside them as well. Some of the marines and a few of our soldiers have crossed the river from Brigadier Monckton's camp and deserted to the enemy, in hopes of finding a better lodging. Two of the French have escaped from Quebec and today threw themselves upon our mercy. Their trials differ from ours, for though they are as yet free from sickness our batteries firing across the river have worked much destruction among their grander buildings as well as among the poorer houses.

The worst news for General Wolfe comes today from his admirals. On the advice of his pilots, Admiral Saunders has told the General that his ships must begin to think of weighing anchor in six weeks, whether or not Quebec be taken, for otherwise the fleet may be trapped by the winter ice and we shall all perish for a certainty.

If the fleet goes, General Wolfe will have no salvation but in going too, and there is an end of Quebec and Canada. It seems a moral impossibility that General Montcalm in the city can be driven to submission in six weeks, unless it be by the perilous means of a direct assault upon the fortress.

Last night, after a reconnaissance to Brigadier Monckton's camp on the southern bank of the river, I was taken with an alternate sweating and trembling as the boat carried us back again. I took ten drops of saffron in hot water and was much improved this morning, I thank God.

2 August 1759. We have had our first battle, and little enough thanks for it from either our General or his brigadiers. Judging that it was impossible to take Quebec without first reducing its outposts, General Wolfe determined that the Highland regiments and the Grenadiers should seize the advantage on the northern bank of the river, four or five miles downstream from Quebec, and open a new way to the city from that quarter.

On the northern bank, some five miles downstream from the city, the waterfall of Montmorency forms a great natural curiosity, for it pours in a torrent over the wooded cliff and falls to the river below. If it were possible for our army to establish itself upstream of this watery barrier, said our General, why there would be little enough to prevent our marching to within a mile of the city itself.

General Wolfe intended that the Highlanders and the Grenadiers should be rowed across the river from the Isle of Orléans to the northern bank, and should land upstream of the waterfall. They were to debark at the foot of the cliffs on a muddy shore uncovered by the ebb-tide. The French gunners on the heights above would be hard put to it to direct their fire downwards at so steep an angle, and so our men would be securely lodged.

A second force of some three regiments of British

troops would advance up the northern bank from General Wolfe's camp, and would cross the falls of Montmorency by a ford on the muddy shore, where the fallen waters flowed more gently into the river. The two expeditions would then unite speedily and establish themselves at the foot of the steep cliffs. The French batteries above were then to be the subject of so fearsome a bombardment by the guns of our ships that they must be prevailed upon to withdraw. The brave Highlanders and Grenadiers would mount the cliffs and seize the abandoned position, while the *mounseers*, having no stomach for such a fight, would flee towards Quebec.

At nine in the forenoon, the Grenadiers and the 78th Highland Regiment were ordered into the landing boats, in preparation for being ferried across the river to assault the northern bank. It was more than an hour before all the men were embarked, though by then General Wolfe himself was present to watch the success of his plan. Some of our boats, including that in which Captain Ogilvie and I were carried, had orders to row here and there to mislead the French as to where we intended our landing, and to induce them to think that we aimed at a point much farther upstream. Our instruction was that the Grenadiers should debark first, and that our Highlanders would follow them. In the meantime, the sailors in our boat found it warm work as they rowed us to and fro, for the sky was clear above us but the heat of the day soon caused a mist to gather near both banks of the stream. We strained our eyes, trying to see if the other force which was to advance up the northern shore from General Wolfe's camp had yet given combat, but we observed nothing.

From the level of our boats, the wooded heights occupied by the French gunners appeared to rise like a mountain range into the warm sky. Before us, Captain Mantle's *Centurion*, a frigate of 64 guns, rode at anchor, the tall wooden walls overhanging some of the landing boats. We watched the sailors who watered and sanded the decks in preparation for the action, while others rolled the cannons forward through the open ports. On all our ships of war the drums were now beating to quarters.

A little after eleven o' clock, our Highlanders began to point excitedly to where the first white cockades of smoke rose slowly against the blue sky. In an instant we heard the distant vibration as the batteries of General Wolfe's camp began to play upon the French positions. Then, with a fury that left us almost deaf, the guns of the *Centurion* and the other ships close by us opened a rolling cannonade against the French redoubt. Such mighty salvoes caused the ships that fired them to swing hard at anchor. The swell of water rocked our army's boats, while the smoke of the guns drifted away across the glittering river. Two of our smaller transport vessels, bearing a score of cannon, tacked close in towards the French shore, so that they might be grounded there when the tide fell and might serve as batteries to assist our landing.

We saw the French guns flash like signal-lamps on the heights, and their smoke too curled like summer clouds above the woody slopes. Some of their salvoes threw up muddy waterspouts from the clear river, yet the distance was too great for them to bombard us with much effect. Indeed, I did not see that we lost a single man in all their firing upon us.

Looking through a spy-glass towards the low strand where we were to debark, I observed that the enemy had constructed two redoubts close to the water's edge, and it was these which our armed transports had engaged in fight. The general cannonade continued on both sides till well past noon, while our men in the landing boats grew warm and impatient for the work they were to do. Yet Captain Ogilvie, from his knowledge of the sea service, advised us that we must be patient for a while longer, remarking, 'There will be no landing on such a shore as that until the tide is at the ebb. The speed of the stream is so great otherwise that there could be no holding the boats to their landing but all would be swept past and carried out.'

I asked him how long it might be before the ebb, and he swore that it could not be less than another hour.

'However,' he said softly, turning to me with his dark brows drawn, 'I wonder that General Wolfe did not postpone the embarking of his men in these boats, rather than to tire them by being cramped so many hours in this fashion. Surely he must know the rise and fall of the tide as well as any man.'

The afternoon soon grew warmer but was overcast with such clouds as if the cannon might indeed be the sound of heaven's thunderbolts. A swarm of small black flies plagued our men, who slapped and cursed them as the boat swung in the tide. We all rejoiced when our sailors at last received the order to row us to the northern bank, where we were to debark. As we crossed the broad river, I saw that the current of the stream was slacker, as Captain Ogilvie had foretold, yet it still moved with some speed.

General Wolfe, who stood upright in one of the first boats, had given the command to attack, though he was not to land himself. The Grenadiers as usual received their order with a mighty cheer. Yet from our position we saw that the force of the current was still carrying the first boats away from the landing and bearing them towards the mud spits that ran out by the waterfall. The sailors in some of these boats managed to regain the strand but other craft made a sad sight. Caught by mud and tide, they were borne from the shelter of the cliffs and stranded in full view of the French batteries and sharpshooters. Several were so exposed that it would have been death to their comrades to go to their aid. Many a man was cut to pieces by grape shot and canister, while others were obliged to wait the slaughterers' attention like to many patient cattle. A number attempted to escape in the water, only to find that they could not swim for the weight of their equipment, and were dragged down by the current in the sight of their friends.

Our own landfall was more successful. The Grenadiers were first ashore on the muddy flat, some of the Royal Americans accompanying them. These foot soldiers gave a rousing huzza as they jumped from their boats and straightway charged across the sedge to take the two French redoubts on the low strand. In an instant, our redcoats were mingled with the white and grey uniforms of the enemy. Yet we heard no more than a few shots fired and the last cries of several men put to death by the sword. Then, as our own boats with the 78th Highlanders grounded, the fighting died out along the foot of the cliffs and the muddy shore, at least, was in our possession.

We were hardly out of the boats when Captain Ogilvie plucked me by the sleeve, saying, 'By God, Fraser, they are climbing the cliffs!'

A light rain had begun to fall as our boat grounded but it was plain to see that the Grenadiers and some of the Royal Americans were indeed pulling themselves with great labour up the muddy slope, climbing between the trees which grew precipitously there. Captain Ogilvie hailed them but hardly a man noticed him.

'They have the wrong orders,' he said hurrying forward, 'or else they choose to disobey the right ones. No man can take the French position in this manner until our fleet has silenced their batteries.'

A Lieutenant of the Grenadiers was ordering the unloading of a small keg of powder from a boat.

'You, sir,' shouted Captain Ogilvie angrily, 'order those damned fools back! If they climb higher, they must infallibly come into the view of the French marksmen at the top. Order them back, I say!'

'As to that, Captain,' said the Lieutenant in a surly manner, 'they have officers of their own with them to give commands. Ask for yourself.'

Even as he spoke, the French sharpshooters began their work, their muskets spitting and crackling above us like dry wood in a fire. Our Grenadiers continued to struggle upwards, not doubting their success against the French if they could once reach the crest of the bluff. There was no longer any means by which we could make them return, indeed all our efforts were required to prevent the 78th Highlanders from charging up the slope to join them.

The storm grew, rain falling more heavily and the mud underfoot becoming more treacherous. Though some of the powder was dampened, the volleys of the French muskets came as fast as ever and we moved our Highlanders closer to the foot of the cliffs for their protection. The bodies of one or two of the Grenadiers came slithering down the muddy slope, arms and legs askew, and fell almost at our feet. We heard the cry of men higher still, and looking up we could see that many of the redcoats were, in truth, dead where they lay. All the shouts of triumph that came to us were from the French. A few minutes had proved enough to turn the day's victory into defeat, the fortunes of battle having altered with a speed which forms cowards of most men.

To make matters worse, the guns of the *Centurion* and several other ships of our fleet began to bombard the cliff, their salvoes being directed against the French batteries but also blowing up parts of the neighbouring slope on which our men lay. Presently this cannonade ceased, for word was sent that the Grenadiers had advanced too precipitately and must be destroyed if this firing continued. Then there was an hour of disorder and uncertainty on the muddy shore, every man expecting an order from the General or his brigadiers, yet no order being given.

At last the command was brought to withdraw and our drummers beat the retreat for those men who could still hear them, calling back any who might be left alive on the slopes above us. The French had ceased their firing but hardly a man had come back safe from the muddy cliffs. It seemed impossible that so many could have been lost in so short a time. General Wolfe had now instructed the Highland regiment to save the wounded and guard the evacuation. The Grenadiers were to be taken off in the boats, while the Highlanders were to follow the withdrawal of Brigadier Townshend's force which had set out from General Wolfe's camp to march along the shore and join us. They had stopped short at the Montmorency falls and had already been commanded to return the way they came. No man talked any longer of victory at the heights of Montmorency, but only of such measures as might prevent a worse disaster.

The 78th Highlanders were told off to fetch as many of the wounded as might be to the landing boats. By this time all the French guns were silent, having had their fill of slaughter and their powder being also dampened by the rain. Our hardiest men went forward up the slope to carry back any who were still living. In company with Sergeant Innes, a bearded and swarthy clansman, I climbed almost to the highest point reached by the Grenadiers, for I was curious to inspect the scene of the defeat. Our way was strewn with the bodies of the dead, their limbs racked into every posture and their faces set in every expression of death. They seemed like figures on a frieze or statues on pedestals in the gardens of men of grotesque and singular taste. I noticed how some of them had striven to hide the wounds which had killed them, and how one Grenadier, whose breast had been opened, had died crouching on his knees with his head to the ground, both hands pressed to him as if to hold life in.

We saw among the trees, not a hundred feet above us,

that the French soldiers were stripping the bodies of our dead, seizing the small spoils of war, even to the clothes of the men. There was no help for that but I gave instructions for the evacuation of several Grenadiers yet living and followed them down the slope, where it was hard enough to keep one's feet for the incline and the mud. When we returned up the slope a second time, it was to find that a party of Indian savages belonging to the French side were killing our wounded who remained, despite the expostulations of a French officer who endeavoured to prevent them. Indeed, several of the French officers accompanied us down to the shore and spoke kindly to us in their own tongue, as though we had not been mortal enemies but an hour before. Captain Ogilvie and I took up our position on the slope, where the path was easiest to carry down the wounded, and seeing a party of four or five savages sneaking down the cliff, their knives between their teeth, we fired upon them and killed the two leaders. Their companions ran off speedily enough, but when we came to where the two dead savages lay we saw the most remarkable thing. The rain had washed over their faces, and to our great amazement one of them was a white man, almost as naked as he came into the world, except for the dye with which his whole body was painted. If ever there was truth to the horrid stories of Canadians who led the savage bands, it was here.

It is our shame that we owe it to the humanity of the French officers that more of our wounded were not barbarously hacked to death by the Indians before the Highlanders could carry them to the boats. We moved as many as we could, except for those whose wounds were so deep that they implored our men not to lift them. It was impossible, in the nature of things, that they could have lived more than a very little while.

On the muddy shore there were at last more Frenchmen than of our own army, for it was left to Captain

Ogilvie and me to be with the last company of Highlanders to march away along the river bank towards General Wolfe's camp. As we ordered our men for the departure, I was much struck by the sight of a tall French officer of some superior rank who spoke to a number of our men, and whose tone I could have taken for Lowland Scots. He was elegantly dressed and showed little enough marks of battle. What was more, he looked in my direction as though he might have known me. We never spoke and it was a moral impossibility on my part to believe us acquainted. Yet I bore in mind the impression of his fresh complexion, clear eyes, and nobility of demeanour.

There was little enough else to remark. It is now confirmed that our Grenadiers were never meant to attack the cliffs in such a manner, and that they did so without orders of any kind. General Wolfe has blamed the Grenadiers with a ladylike resentment, worthy of a dame school.

'Gentlemen,' he said, 'such impetuous, irregular, and unsoldierlike proceedings destroy all order and make it impossible for the commanders to form any disposition for an attack. Nay, they put it out of a General's power to execute his plans.'

When an officer of the Grenadiers endeavoured to make some apology, General Wolfe grew waspish.

'The Grenadiers, sir, must not suppose that they are to beat the French alone.'

Brigadier Townshend, however, has freely given the officers in his division an opinion of General Wolfe's own plan of attack.

'Such an attack', says the Brigadier, 'was a monstrous contradiction of the advice and opinion of every officer. Damme, when things are come to such a pass as this, you may judge what we are to expect for the future.'

And with this he cocks his hat as fiercely as any highwayman and walks off. No one dares to confront him in such a temper.

6 August 1759. Our losses at Montmorency are computed at 400 or 500 men dead, which is the loss of an entire regiment, and many more wounded. Yet I cannot find that all our cannonading killed a single Frenchman. It is told as certain truth in all the camps that our three brigadiers, Murray and Monckton, as well as Townshend, have sent a letter to General Wolfe. They complain that his orders have not been sufficiently precise, which must reflect on his handling of the late attempt at Montmorency. They also protest that they are no better informed than any common soldier who hears those public orders which are read to the army at large. Those who witnessed the General's anger in his cabin on the *Sutherland*, after he had read this letter, report that he damned two of his brigadiers for cowards (Murray and Monckton) and the third (Townshend) for a villain. We hear that the said villain has already sent messages to London, where his friends have great influence and where his brother Charles is likely to be (if he is not already) Secretary-at-War. It is said that Brigadier Townshend has urged no less than a House of Commons committee to inquire into General Wolfe's misconduct of the whole campaign.

15 August 1759. General Wolfe is to be seen nowhere at all, and is reported deadly sick. Yet Captain Ogilvie, who once designed to be a surgeon, gives it as his opinion that it is a stone in the bladder and no more.

'Why,' says Captain Ogilvie, 'in such a state, the General is sure to offend both parties, for he will neither recover nor die.'

Yet we hear that his physicians have ordered him to be let blood again, and that he is in such a lamentable state as to make it doubtful that he should plan or execute any further attack upon the French.

24 August 1759. The doctors who despaired that General

Wolfe might die are in better heart, and it is only Brigadier Townshend who now despairs that the General may live. Such a recovery of health must snatch from the Brigadier the possible glory of taking Quebec himself.

On being restored to health, General Wolfe first issued orders more strictly forbidding the troops to rob the houses of the farms around our camps or to offer violence to their inhabitants, and particularly to those of the gentler sex. This must go hard with such as Sergeant Innes. The very day after the attack on Montmorency, I observed the Sergeant offering an insult of a most delectable kind to a firm-fleshed girl, not a quarter of a mile from the tents. I was possessed for some time afterwards by the memory of her long white legs as he toiled at her, while her feet, which she drew a little off the ground, seemed to beat of their own volition, like a pair of Cupid's wings. Her eyes were indeed closed but the violence which she suffered did not seem, at that moment, unwelcome to her.

General Wolfe's concern for the farmers does not extend to those who may feel some sympathy for their countrymen in Quebec. Our patrols have been out each night and have fired those houses where the farmers have offered food or arms for Montcalm and his soldiers in the city. Indeed, one of our expeditions was zealous enough to cut down a priest and eighty of his congregation who neglected their loyalty to General Wolfe.

9 September 1759. Admiral Saunders and his sea captains have given General Wolfe their terms, allowing him a week to make his attack.

'Sir,' said the Admiral, 'we dare stay no longer. The thinnest ice must soon appear in the gulf of the river, though we shall know nothing of it until our ships reach the estuary.'

'Yet we see no ice here, nor any likelihood of it while the days are so warm,' said the General.

'No, sir,' said the Admiral, 'for, as our pilots will tell you, it closes the river's mouth first. Once the mouth is closed, we are imprisoned as fast in this river as if there were a field of ice about us at this moment.'

'We might starve them out, if we stayed another month,' said the General, though he was not in earnest.

'Aye, sir,' said the Admiral waggishly, 'so we might. And for the satisfaction of doing that, we should then starve ourselves, for 10,000 of his Majesty's soldiers and a great part of his fleet would be at the mercy of a bitter winter.'

So the General gave his word readily, attempting the appearance of having agreed with Admiral Saunders from the first, and only having been put in doubt by the opinions of his three brigadiers.

11 September 1759. This evening, not an hour ago, I was one of the party to accompany General Wolfe and Colonel Simon Fraser on a dark reconnaissance of the shoreline at the very foot of the heights of Quebec. Three of our ships have now got up river above the city, and it seems determined that we are to take the heights by storm tomorrow night and the city itself on the following day. A little upstream of the city is a point of land called the Anse du Foulon. Close by, a narrow path winds up the cliff from the shore, just wide enough for a gun carriage to pass, though devilishly steep. We spied it out this evening after dusk, taking our little boat in as close as we dared. At the top of that path begins what they call the Plains of Abraham, an open stretch of country on the only side of the city not protected by the river. If our men might get quietly ashore, without warning the French, the daybreak would reveal 5,000 of General Wolfe's army drawn up before the city, cutting off Montcalm and his men from all other support. Then, says General Wolfe, Monsieur le Marquis de Montcalm must fight us. And then we will play him such a set as shall win us Quebec.

The success of this plan is uncertain, and much must depend on our landing unobserved. To move such an army in silence, even across water, is no easy manœuvre, yet we are hopeful that a French flotilla of provision boats may be in the river tomorrow night and will conceal our own movements. General Wolfe instructed that I should accompany the reconnaissance for my acquaintance with the French language, having spent some years in that country. When our attack is made, I am to be in the first boat, so that if we should be challenged by the French sentries in the darkness I may reply in their own tongue and attempt to deceive them, that they may take us for a party of their own soldiers.

As we made our inspection of that muddy strand, our sailors rowed so gently that their oars dipped with hardly a sound. We spoke softly, though a single craft of such a kind might be of little enough consequence to the French pickets. My kinsman, Colonel Simon Fraser, and I sat close to Brigadier Townshend and at some little distance from General Wolfe. As we pulled away from that shore and cut the tide towards our own ships, a silence settled on us all. It is not to be wondered at if our thoughts were engaged by the prospect of the battle which must follow our next visit to that coast. While each of us was thus silently occupied, I became aware of a strange voice speaking as if from the darkness of the waters.

'The boast of heraldry, the pomp of pow'r,
    And all that beauty, all that wealth e'er gave,
Await alike th' inevitable hour:
    The paths of glory lead but to the grave.'

By the end of the verse, we perceived that it was General Wolfe himself who declaimed these lines in his most sententious manner, having lately conceived a passion for Mr Gray's *Elegy Written in a Country Churchyard*. Yet the recitation was greeted by no other comment than the General's own.

'They are noble lines, gentlemen,' he said, 'and noble sentiments.'

'Noble, indeed, sir,' said a junior officer hastily, who was sitting close by him.

'Gentlemen,' said the General, 'I can only say that, if the choice were mine, I would rather be the author of those verses than take Quebec.'

This monstrous parade of cant was too much for the witty Brigadier, who said in his most supplicating voice, loudly enough for even General Wolfe to hear, 'Only take Quebec, sir, and let Mr Gray answer for his verses.'

14 September 1759. The dice are thrown that must decide the future of all the Americas, yet how many of the bones of our men and of the French lie on the Plains of Abraham is beyond any reckoning. Indeed, though I saw as much of the battle as any there, I am hard put to it to record the extent of the conflict.

It was ordered by General Wolfe that the Highlanders should have the honour of leading the attack, their men being well used to climbing steep and awkward paths. Once at the summit of the path, they were to cross the plain to the far side and take up their position at General Wolfe's left when the army turned into line to face Quebec. Each man was issued with such provisions of hard biscuit, cheese and water as should last him for two days. Then at nine in the evening our soldiers entered their landing boats opposite to the foot of the cliff, where the path ran upwards to the Plains of Abraham.

Our spies had informed us that the greater part of the French army under their General Bougainville were still near Montreal, so there was no question that if our men might be got safely ashore we should be more than the number of Montcalm's troops in Quebec.

The landing boats hung in the tide until halfway between midnight and dawn, while the decks of the transports were crowded with men who waited to occupy our places in the boats once the Highlanders were ashore. When the tide was at the ebb, General Wolfe commanded two lights to be shown in the topmost shrouds of the *Sutherland*, which was the signal for the attack to commence. This order was flashed from ship to ship by dark lantern. For all that, our flotilla of landing boats moved with such stealth that the Captain of the *Hunter*, one of our sloops, took the first boat for a party of French attempting to slip downstream. A musket shot echoed over our heads and we were so close that we could hear the guns on the *Hunter* being run out to engage us. Several of our men called across the water to the sailors, until ordered by General Wolfe himself to be silent. Then the General hailed the sloop and prevented a further attack.

We scanned the cliffs earnestly to see if all these sounds had betrayed us to the French, but we could discern no movement. In this we were aided by the guns of Admiral Saunders's fleet which opened fire five miles downstream in a thunderous bombardment on the French positions there. By this we intended them to think that, if there was any attack that night, it would be against the heights of Montmorency again. Meanwhile our sailors rowed us softly past the dark outline of the Anse du Foulon. We were approaching our landfall when the sentries on the point called after us, having heard our oars. One cried, '*Qui vive?*'

It was now my turn to answer, being in the first boat with General Wolfe and his officers. I leant towards the shore and replied in a loud whisper.

'*La France!*'

'*A quel régiment?*'

'*De la Reine!*'

Our sailors kept their oars poised and our guns were ready, though it would have been a blind skirmish. There was no certainty that we had deceived the guard for I could hear two of them speaking together. Then one, whom I took to be the captain of the post, called to me.

'*Pourquoi est-ce que vous ne parlez pas plus haut?*'

'*Tais-toi! Nous serons entendus!*'

Having thus assured him that to speak loudly was to be overheard by the English sailors, I added that we were a party of French carrying certain provisions to the lower port. For all our caution, we had already been fired upon by a marksman from one of the *bande de cons* (meaning the English fleet) anchored in the river.

Our interrogator seemed content with this. Our little fleet of twenty-six landing boats drifted down past the point and into the cove, where the bows of the first craft soon grounded in the mud.

General Wolfe, Colonel Simon Fraser, Captain Ogilvie, and I landed almost together, while Fraser's Highlanders swarmed from the other boats and ran pell-mell at the cliffs. The General was pleased to commend me on my use of the French tongue and then, looking up at the heights, which were more precipitous than we had imagined, he observed, 'Gentlemen, I know not by what means we are to get our army up there, but, gentlemen, we must use our best endeavour.'

It was a tortuous path indeed, so steep that at times we were obliged to grasp at the branches of small trees or bushes to keep our footing on the slippery mud. Some of our boats had come to rest at a little distance from the path, and the track itself was too small to take all our men. Yet there was nothing for it but to reach the Plains of Abraham before the dawning day should reveal us to the French. The work went on in silence, those of our Highlanders who were some way off made their own paths up the cliff. In their dark kilts and plaid they covered the rough slope over quarter of a mile's length.

Captain Ogilvie and I, who were in the first company of the regiment, reached the crest without so much as seeing a Frenchman. As soon as sufficient of our army had reached the top, orders were given for the pipers to sound the gathering, in order to assemble our scattered clansmen under Colonel Simon Fraser. We stood in a field of damp corn and, before we could move from there, the batteries of the French fortress and the English fleet opened a general cannonade. Each salvo rang out like the clatter and clanging of iron shields in the heavens, while the flames lit the dark sky so vividly that we could see by their light to pick our way forward.

The infernal glow of the cannon's flashing was soon eclipsed by a colder but steadier light as the day began to break in the sky above Quebec, whose walls lay on our right while we marched. The skirl of the pipes and the brave tattoo of the drums beat for the Highland regiments as we strode forward, three abreast, in a column that was quarter of a mile in its length. At our head, the men sang the songs of their clan to the rant of a piper, while to the rear of the column our soldiers sang psalms as they marched into battle. Yet no man sang such songs as when the clans marched with Prince Charles Edward to Falkirk or Culloden, for the old music is forbidden them. Nor did any man wear the tartan of his clan, for that has given place to the plain dark kilt worn by those who are the soldiers of King George II.

The sky was almost fully light when we reached the road running from Quebec to St Foy, which was to mark the further flank of General Wolfe's army. The regiments were halted and wheeled into line of battle, facing the enemy three ranks deep. Soon, the English regiments to our right in their scarlet coats and white leggings had extended the line. Indeed, our front was so long that we were soon obliged to deploy our army only two ranks deep to close the mighty gaps which must otherwise have appeared between the regiments. Yet, if our line was spread so thin, at least the French artillery could do us little harm, for only a few men would be hurt by any shot wherever it fell. One or two salvoes burst among our left flank, and the bodies of men were thrown into the air as one might throw a rag. This caused many of the Highlanders to lie at full length in the long grass that they might not be seen by the French gunners. That was to little purpose, however, for it seemed to be chance rather than skill that claimed a hit.

'I would give something to have our own cannon grouped between the foot regiments,' said Captain Ogilvie.

'Be patient, sir,' said Colonel Fraser, 'our sailors are to bring two brass cannon and four other field pieces up the path. When they are here we shall not need to be galled like this without replying.'

Soon after eight o'clock the French line began to form before the walls of Quebec, and we saw their white and grey uniforms clearly enough. Their gunners now began to send grape and canister shot among us, which burst in all directions, yet we were still too thinly spread for them to damage us much. We might have seen more of the French but for the drizzle and the overcast sky which almost matched the colours of their uniforms. Our soldiers had been strictly ordered not to fire nor to advance until the order was given. The English regiments stood smartly to their lines but our Highlanders stood where they pleased, often grouping round the elders of their families or clans. Many thumbed their broadswords or sharpened the edges carefully, for these were more to them than their muskets. The pipers played and the men tested their swords. With such blades as these they might cut a man in two, through the waist or from head to groin. Indeed, they could take two or three heads from their bodies at a single stroke.

At a little after ten o'clock we saw the French line begin to move, their foot soldiers marching towards us, with muskets carried before them, in a line stretching across the entire plain. We heard their bugle calls and drums beating the attack. Our men stood to their weapons, the Highlanders looking to their officers and asking for the command to open fire or charge upon the enemy. Our men were galled by a number of Canadian sharpshooters on our flank who had lain concealed and now began an irregular firing which brought low some of our soldiers while the French advanced. We dared not notice them, for all our force must be spent against their main division. As one man fell, his place was taken by another from those few who made up our second line. The clansmen continued to ask for the order to attack, that they might avenge themselves upon the French and upon the more treacherous Canadians who had concealed themselves in the long grass to our left. Yet we dared not move, for there were hardly more black-kilted Highlanders than would form a single line of battle over so wide a front. Our comfort was that Montcalm's troops numbered no more than our own.

Far away to our right, it seemed that a score of French cavalry (which was all we could see) was gathering to attack the English regiments at the top of the cliff, where that path lay which was our only road to the beach and to our ships. All this was done to divert our attention from the main business but also because our sailors hauled up three field pieces by that route. Yet, if the French cavalry numbered so few, we need care little for them if we could once settle our score with their foot soldiers. Their line came on until it was a hundred yards, or rather more, from us. Our men still held their fire, standing like statues with their muskets primed, expecting when the order should come. We heard the note of the French drums change and saw the barrels of their muskets raised towards us. The crackling of their volley and the whip of their bullets past us was followed by a veil of smoke from their muskets, which for a moment hid their line from us. A dozen Highlanders, at least, fell close to me, the musket balls striking a man with a blow like a great fist, which might be heard at some yards' distance. Then it was only with the greatest strictness that we prevented our clansmen from charging in their fury upon the enemy line and doing execution with their broadswords. Though Fraser's Highlanders stood to their muskets, many a man had his kilt tucked between his thighs and his sword at the ready for the order to fall upon the French line.

For two miles across the corn and tall grass of the Plains of Abraham, the white and grey line of the French came on. The wind unfurled the great flags of their regiments, while their drums beat the rhythm of their march and the tattoo when they were to fire. Our commanders judged that they were still too far distant for us to fire upon them with any great effect, for beyond a hundred yards they made poor targets for our muskets. There was a fearful stillness in our ranks, the men knowing that they must endure a second volley from the French at closer range than the first. No man knew whether he would be alive or dead in a few minutes more.

As the enemy foot soldiers closed towards us with their drums beating harder, we were amazed to see their line halt and those same drums fall silent. Our eyes turned to where Brigadier Townshend and two other horsemen from General Wolfe's headquarters rode down the length of our line like souls possessed. Then I heard Captain Ogilvie shout, 'By God, they are got behind us!'

I did not see how this could be, and for a moment did not take my eyes off the French foot soldiers who now prepared to fire a second volley upon us from the front, for all that they were still too far off to do this with great accuracy. We had secured the roads from Quebec and not a single man could have passed to the rear without our leave. Yet I now heard horsemen, like a distant thunder, behind us and looking round I clearly saw the blue coats of the French cavalry spreading out across the entire western horizon.

'We are in their trap,' muttered Ogilvie, who strode over to me and unsheathed his sword. He cocked his hat and looked fiercely about him. 'Bougainville and his sons of whores were never in Montreal. They have been at Montcalm's call, waiting for this moment.'

Then the French muskets fired upon us again from the front, yet we should not have cared about that if their cavalry was not bearing down on our rear. Our line, over the extent of two miles, was often no more than one man deep, and we could not fight two enemies at once. Many of our soldiers began to fire upon the French without waiting for any further order, and some charged foolishly upon their line of infantry, only to be brought down by their muskets before they ever reached it. Such confusion fell upon us as must make it difficult to paint a complete picture of the rout of General Wolfe's army. The French foot soldiers we could have beaten, and would have done in a little while: yet our drummers had scarcely time to beat the retreat before our line broke in a dozen places under the weight of Bougainville's horses.

Each of our regiments strove to form a defensive square about its baggage and wounded. But the Highlanders were unused to such a tactic and tried to meet each horseman as he came, ducking beneath his sabre blow and stabbing the horse's belly with a dirk, that they might drag down the man and hack him in pieces. I saw clansmen run with the speed of wind by the horses, and with a mighty leap bring the riders from their saddles. Soon there were horses on the ground, tossing and pawing the air in their last spasms. Dismounted French cavalrymen, their helmets gone and their blue tunics spattered with blood of beast and man, cut and slashed with their sabres at the ring of kilted clansmen until they were borne down by our numbers and cut to death. Some ran here and there in the struggle, seeking in vain to cut a way out through our ranks.

We who were two miles from the cliff had least hope of retreat or safety, for the weight of the French force was turning upon us. Those English regiments who were nearest the cliff were soon driven pell-mell down it, where I afterwards heard there was great destruction. The sailors and marines who were still striving to draw our cannon up the muddy path were met suddenly by the general retreat going downwards, and such a struggle ensued as led to our men fighting one another. On the flat strand, where we had debarked before dawn, the boatmen were hard put to it to take off such numbers as swarmed down the pathway and the neighbouring cliffs.

The Royal Americans, who had been left to guard the path, showed much spirit in being the first down it.

The 43rd regiment and the 28th were close enough to this avenue of escape to make the best of their way towards it, but for Fraser's Highlanders and the 47th there was no passage to be hoped for. We were soon surrounded by five or six times our own number of the enemy force. The French had fired a small house which some of the 47th occupied, close to the road that ran from Quebec to St Foy, and as fast as our soldiers endeavoured to save themselves from the flames they were driven back into the inferno by the blades of the regiment of La Sarre, which formed a close cordon round the blazing ruin. So the poor wretches met their deaths in the flames, though they had long since thrown away their arms. I was afterwards told that the French commanders awarded their soldiers exemplary punishment for this piece of inhumanity.

Close beside me, Brigadier Townshend, unhorsed, his face blackened by the discharge of powder, and his tunic ripped where a sabre blow had almost cost him his right arm, endeavoured to rally some of the Highlanders and others of the left flank of our army. He held his sword drawn, and there was blood along several inches of its blade.

'It is a bad business, my lads,' he cried, 'but damme if it is any of my making!'

At that very instant, a mounted soldier of the French spurred towards him, whom the Brigadier met on foot with a loud ringing of swords. The rider reined in and came back again to where the Brigadier stood, aiming to cut him down. Yet two of our tall Highlanders had the Frenchman from his saddle and one, with a broadsword, killed him as he lay in a single stroke that took the head almost from the body, leaving it fastened only by the skin at the throat. Seeing that all must soon be lost, Captain Ogilvie, who had already received a bullet in his shoulder, assisted the Brigadier to mount the French horse and make the best of it towards General Wolfe and the main body of our force.

The weight of the enemy soon pressed upon us on every side and they might have killed us more quickly had they been given more space. Men and horses were packed in a crowd, among the snorting of the frightened beasts, the shouts and cries of men, the reek of burnt powder, beating of hooves, crash of muskets, and the ringing blows of swords. When our piper fell, his breast shattered by a musket ball, Sergeant Innes took the pipes himself and played on. The drummer, who still bore our standard, stood in the thickest of the fight, until he fell and bespangled the colours with his blood. Another clansman seized the fallen flag and wrapped it round his own body as he fought on. In the dense mass, where there was hardly room to use broadswords, the Highlanders gave a brave account of themselves with their dirks against the might of the French numbers.

Yet men, however brave they be, cannot prevail against

ten times their number. The survivors of our battle
endeavoured to withdraw, little by little, across the road,
towards the coppice and the blazing house, though there
was little enough sanctuary to be looked for there. As I
stood back from the thick of the fighting, I know not
from where but a musket ball hit me in the back of the
right ham, so that I fell on my side and could not, to save
my life, regain my feet. I suffered little immediate pain,
for though I saw by my hand there was some blood it
was not much and it was rather as if I had been bruised
so as to deprive me of feeling in that leg. For all that, I
could not stand nor hardly crawl. A French officer rode
hard at me but I threw myself over, so that the hooves of
his horse beat the ground some inches from me, while his
sword swung too short to perform me the favour he
intended. He rode on, no doubt seeking some worthier
prey. I pulled myself a little distance to where one of our
brass cannon stood idle, and I struggled to lie in the
shelter of it. For a little while I continued faint, and then
heard the sounds of battle grow more distant as the
French drove our survivors towards the coppice. Then of a
sudden, I know not how long afterwards, the firing ceased
on both sides.

Both armies had deserted their original place of battle,
which now presented the most horrid spectacle, being
left to the dead and the dying. Bodies of men and horses
were strewn across the grassy plain, the dead having
fallen so thick in several places that they lay not singly
but in a heap. Yet what was more terrible was the
appearance of the ghastly limbs and dismembered trunks,
where the swords of the French horsemen or of our
Highlanders had done their bloodiest business. The groans
and cries of men, cursing their fate and one another in
their last anguish, rose all around me.

I saw at a little distance that both the French and our
own men, who consisted principally of Fraser's High-

landers, were drawn up to face one another, though they engaged in no combat. I could not be certain but I believe it was Colonel Fraser himself who came forward to parley under a flag of truce. None could any longer doubt Montcalm to be the victor on the Plains of Abraham. Yet our men had stood to their colours valiantly and had cost the French horsemen dear enough.

How long the parley lasted I could not tell, but it was in the afternoon when I saw and heard the survivors of our regiments march in formation down the road towards St Foy at the command of their French conquerors. Then the sound of the drums died away and the field of battle was left entirely to the defeated and to the few curious French soldiers who surveyed the scene of their late victory. From the cliffs above the river I heard the bombardment between the French batteries and our fleet, who must soon be beaten back by the winter's ice. Was it to be conceived that our expedition should end in this manner?

Towards evening I was taken with a parching thirst and, though the blood no longer flowed, the pain of my wound increased so that I could not even crawl from the shelter of the brass cannon. What was a greater menace to the fallen, those Indian savages whom the French employed descended to turn the field of valour into a scene of the most barbarous inhumanity. Such naked villains, their knives held between their teeth and their eyes glittering, seemed devoid of even the most elementary compassion which such a prospect of suffering must inspire in the breast of any human creature. They robbed dead and dying alike. Then, no matter whether it was a living man or a corpse, they cut round the top of the crown to the skull bone, and raised up one side of the skin with their knife. Then they jerked off this scalp by the hair, and set up a triumphal whooping.

I was happy in finding a pouch of dry powder by the

person of a dead English soldier not many yards from me, and resolved that before I was despatched I would send to the devil as many of the savages as might be. I lay still as I could and, as the sun began to set, saw one of them crawling towards a wounded officer of the light infantry a little way off, who had fainted from his sufferings. Before I could use the musket, the savage had stabbed him again, though not mortally. In my rage, I made short work of this barbarity by taking aim and shooting the savage through the back of the head, so that the splinters of bone sprang from his brow. As soon as I had loaded the piece again and primed it, two more Indians came towards me. One of these I shot in the breast, laying him low, and then prepared to grapple with the other. Though I was held fast to the ground by the wound in my leg, life is sweet and never more so than when others would take it from us. I took the wrist of his right hand and strove to wrest the knife from him, but to little effect. We struggled to and fro, and I fear the only end of this grappling would have been his victory. Yet as we fought in this fashion there was a sound of firing and a shout of command, which caused the savage to jump from me and run off. I thought that our soldiers might have been given leave by the French to search for their wounded, but in the dusk I saw that these were horsemen, and I heard French spoken.

One dismounted and held a lantern over me, and then called one of his comrades. He too dismounted and crouched over me, while the lantern was held closer to my face. I begged them, in their own language, for aid to the fainting English officer to my left, and also (I am not ashamed to admit it) for relief of my own pain. I petitioned them eagerly to call off their savages from all our wounded men.

'There shall be no savagery here, monsieur,' said the man who first found me. 'I will give you my word on that as an officer of France.'

'And I, sir,' said the second man in English, 'will add to that the word of a Scotsman, although a Lowlander.'

By the light of the lantern, I now saw in this second man's features the chevalier in French uniform whom I had remarked on the shore at Montmorency while we were evacuating our men from that place, and who had looked at me as if he had recognised me. I recalled his face, the sharp nose and downward turn of the mouth, which might nonetheless betray a quick wit. He spoke with the accent of a Lowland Scot, though during long exile the French too had left its mark on the tone of his words.

'The army of France, sir,' he said, 'is neither so cowardly nor so barbarous as the placemen of King George would have you believe. Orders are already given that those who remain alive on the field of battle are to be saved instantly.'

I thanked him for his gallantry, and asked if I might have the honour of knowing whom I addressed.

'The Chevalier James de Johnstone, sir,' he replied, 'formerly aide-de-camp to Prince Charles Edward in his late attempt to recover the Kingdoms of Scotland and England from the Elector of Hanover, who now brazenly styles himself "George the Second". I am now aide-de-camp to Louis Joseph, Marquis de Montcalm, in the service of France.'

I attempted to introduce myself but was interrupted at once.

'You, sir, are the son of that ever-honoured Simon, Lord Lovat, who gave his life on the scaffold for his rightful sovereign, King James III, in 1747. Do not protest, sir, it is my business to know such things for believe me, sir, there is more in this day's work than the possession of Quebec or the barren lands of the Arctic.'

I had heard men speak of the Chevalier de Johnstone and his adventures after the butchery of Culloden, so that I expressed myself in terms of deference.

59

'Sir,' said the Chevalier proudly, 'the clansmen who fought today are the soldiers who fought for their Prince, Charles Edward, at Falkirk and Culloden. They shall not perish while it is in my power to save them.'

I would have questioned him further, for it seemed to me that he hinted at some action which was yet to regain the Crown of Great Britain for the exiled James III or his son, the Prince Charles Edward, and which would bring damnation to George II and the House of Hanover.

'Quebec, sir,' said I, 'hardly lies in the most direct passage from Rome or St Germain to Westminster or St James's.'

'Indeed not, sir,' said the Chevalier, 'but we shall talk more of this when you are recovered. Your servant, sir.'

I watched him walk away into the dusk, a man of tall, slender, but upright figure, with a common soldier leading his horse. While two French grenadiers assisted me towards the gates of the city, I saw that the Chevalier de Johnstone still moved among the fallen clan with his lantern, directing aid to be brought to the wounded and commanding decent burial for the dead.

20 September 1759. As many of our wounded as can be are tended by the nuns of the Ursuline Convent in their hospital. Being able to walk with a little assistance, I can now judge that those of our men taken by the French are, for the most part, Highlanders, with a few soldiers of the English 15th and 47th regiments, and must amount to 1,000 or more all told. Yet much of the French city is a sad spectacle. As we passed up the broad avenue, where stands the church of Notre-Dame de la Victoire, only the walls of the houses on either side remained. The roofs of the houses and the church, even to the beams, had been lifted cleanly off by our bombardment. All their doors and windows were gone. We saw only skeletons of handsome buildings and comfortable homes.

Inside the Church of the Jesuits all was desolation. The stone echoed to our footsteps and we saw where the paintings and rich ornaments had been taken down from their places. The decorated panels of the ceiling were destroyed, while the fallen wood and plaster was gathered into two great piles. I have noticed that when the roof of a building is broken in, which is always the first thing to be affected, they take down the exposed beams and store them in the roadway.

At a little distance from the Church of the Jesuits, where the road slopes downward to the lower town of Quebec, stands the Bishop's Palace, a graceful building in the French style built round three sides of a quadrangle with railings and an archway on its fourth side. The French officer who was our guide told me that this building had suffered little, though the houses on the road to the lower town were in a sad state. Between their ruined walls I could glimpse the river, and actually saw several of our own ships still riding at anchor. I supposed that the greater part of the army must have escaped, though weakened by defeat, and I wondered what terms were to be concluded for those of us who remained in Quebec as prisoners.

22 September 1759. At midnight last night, our men in the hospital of the Ursulines were woken by the most fearful bombardment, as our ships still anchored in the river opened their fire upon the city. Yet their captains must have known that many of our soldiers lay sick or dying within its walls.

The projectiles passed over our heads with the hissing of demons, and the crash of their impact was accompanied in some cases by the shuddering of the very ground beneath us. The French batteries soon replied. Our wounded men lay upon the floor of the great hall in every posture of suffering, so that the brightness of the

61

flames falling through the windows would have made one believe that this might be some antechamber of hell.

After half an hour, an unlucky broadside from the ships struck the roof of the Ursulines, bringing down tiles, plaster, and beams in a roaring like a great waterfall. Though the accident was at some distance from me, a thick cloud of dust and smoke rolled throughout the building, so that all who stayed must have been smothered by it. Our brave nuns ran with basins of water to damp out some small fire which had started, while Captain Ogilvie and I ordered the evacuation of all those men who might possibly be moved. With the aid of the good sisters, we carried out all we could in the next fifteen or twenty minutes, and left only the dead and the mortally sick in the hospital of the nunnery.

There was a chill in the open air enough to give a man his death of cold. From the terraced ground of the convent we strained our eyes to see whatever we could of the bombardment between the fleet and the city. Looking towards the place where the French gunners were engaged, it seemed as if they were not firing salvoes but loosing off bright serpents and other ornamental fireworks, which rose into the darkness with their tails glowing and spitting.

'See for yourself!' said Captain Ogilvie excitedly. 'The French are using red-hot shot! If our ships do not stand further back and keep their rigging clear, they are done for.'

Most of the wounded clansmen cared little enough what the French used, so long as their gunners put a speedy end to the English bombardment from which we suffered. For the first time they turned their voices against General Wolfe and the English commanders, cursing their masters of ordnance for sons of whores. General Wolfe's aversion to the Scottish nation was so well known that our men now believed he cared nothing for whether they or the French were hit by his cannonading. It was soon put about among the Highland officers that the General was already seeking to blame his defeat upon the cowardice of the clansmen, whom he accused of having fled in confusion at the sight of Bougainville's cavalry, throwing away their muskets as they ran. I wondered if the witty Brigadier, who had himself seen what passed and had witnessed how valiantly Fraser's outnumbered men stood their ground, would easily concur in this opinion.

It was an hour or two before the batteries ceased firing and I knew not what greater damage might have been done to the city or to the fleet. All night we watched the deep reflection of the fires in the sky and knew that they were not the flames of Quebec alone. When all was quiet, Captain Ogilvie and I climbed to a spot where we had some view of the river, while the citizens swarmed through the streets like a hive of bees, running to damp out the fresh fires which our guns had caused. From our vantage point we saw that the river was red with fire from two ships which burned from stem to stern, like set pieces in a display. I could not tell what vessels they were, for they were unrecognisable in the flames. Of the other ships, the English transports and the men of war, there was no sign. As we watched, the roar of an explosion made one of the ships heel over and the sparks shot up towards the sky. However, we had both fixed our thoughts upon those ships we could not see.

'They have gone,' said Ogilvie at last. 'It was impossible that they should stay. Why, man, the time is almost past when they might get safely through the ice at the river's mouth.'

'And for what purpose are the Highland troops left prisoner?'

'For no purpose,' said Captain Ogilvie, stamping his foot, 'except that they were never to land in Scotland again. As for being left prisoners, we must now throw ourselves upon the brotherhood of the French and make the best terms for ourselves and our men.'

And so we walked back in silence to the ruins of our place of refuge.

25 September 1759. It is generally known among our men that the English fleet has gone and that the only two ships which remain are those we saw burning. One of them has sunk in the middle of the channel, while the other is beached on the opposite bank and still gives off a smoke of smouldering timber.

Resentment runs high among the Scottish prisoners who have been left to their fate in this manner by those they now call the 'English bitches'. Can it be consistent with any form of military honour to disregard an army in this fashion? Wolfe is already far away and it is impossible that we should see his or any other English force before next summer. Indeed, there is little enough chance of seeing him then, for England has lost Quebec and has lost Canada as surely as if the General's expedition had never left Portsmouth.

29 September 1759. No fewer than fifteen officers of the Highlanders are said to have offered their services to the King of France, many of their men being likely to follow since they must otherwise be left to starve. A brigade of Irish exiles is already with the French army here, so our men will have company enough. I have heard it stated for a fact that two English officers of the 47th regiment have gone for mercenaries to the French army, but I cannot discover the truth of this. Come what will, our clansmen feel themselves basely deserted by their English ally and begin to mutter what they remember of the bloody field of Culloden and the butchery which followed.

Being recovered from my wound sufficiently to walk unaided, I received a summons to wait upon the Chevalier de Johnstone this afternoon at the Palace of the Intendant. I was taken there in a small carriage, one of the few I have seen in Quebec, and was led to an upper room where the Chevalier and Major Alexander Shaw, another Jacobite officer in the service of France, received me. The room had something of the size and style of a state apartment with long windows and handsome portraits. At the far end was a large table strewn with maps, some representing upper and lower Canada or New England. Yet the maps which seemed most prominent were those of the southern provinces of Virginia, Maryland, and the Carolinas. The Chevalier brought me to a chair placed close by this table.

'Sir,' said he, 'I am glad to see you well again. I have heard a great deal of your story, how you witnessed the bloody skirmish of Culloden as a schoolboy, how you were brought safely out to France and cared for there, and how you since returned to your own people as one of their commanders. Make no mistake, your rightful prince, Charles Edward, knows of you also, and holds you in great esteem. The past does you credit but it is now time we should talk of the future, for the tide of events moves faster than you suppose.'

I knew not what to say but only asked him if it was true that the English ships had sailed and that their siege was abandoned. He frowned at me and said, 'Sir, it was never possible that such a siege should have succeeded. Several weeks ago, a naval squadron of the French intercepted the very despatch from General Amherst to the Duke of Cumberland in which the whole of General Wolfe's plan of attack was laid down. The day before your landing, the Régiment de Guyenne took their positions above the Anse du Foulon. General Bougainville and his force have long been deployed between here and Montreal, so that General Wolfe might receive the attack on both halves. The Régiment de Guyenne might even have stopped your landing, but they were ordered otherwise.'

I congratulated him on his patience and ingenuity, at

which he smiled for the first time and said softly, 'To allow an enemy time to dispose himself in the most vulnerable formation has ever appeared to me the essential requisite of war.'

After some further compliments to myself, he added, 'When we last met, sir, after your sad battle, I gave you my word that the clans who fought with me at Culloden for their lawful sovereign, James III, should not perish while it was in my power to save them. I believe it is in my power, and I will order things in such a manner that they shall not starve. But make no mistake, Captain Fraser, the French in Canada cannot keep them. It is by remaining true to their real king that they shall be saved.'

I asked how this might be, and was incredulous at his reply.

'There are territories in the Americas, sir, which shall shortly declare for James III against the Hanoverian usurpation of George II. There lies the salvation of your clansmen, in being the army of King James and his son Prince Charles.'

'But how can such a thing happen while there is an English army in America?' I asked.

Major Shaw interposed, a pale man with freckles and a constant expression of anxiety upon his brow.

'An English army, Mr Fraser? The army of General Amherst?'

'Yes, sir, the army of General Amherst.'

'Why Captain,' said Major Shaw softly, 'General Amherst's army is lost. Much of it perished in a storm on Lake Champlain, and most of the rest in battle. The port of Boston must soon be besieged by the French troops, while the frontiers of Pennsylvania and Virginia are already held by the French and their Indians from the Ohio River. I have seen Virginia not four months ago, Captain Fraser, and even those who are not of our people say that they do not care whether King George, King James, or the devil

66

himself be on the throne, provided the war with France may be ended and the plantations left in peace.'

'And what of the French, sir?' I asked him.

Major Shaw spoke more quietly still, and more in earnest.

'It is on such terms, Captain, that there may be peace with France. France fears the power of Hanoverian England in America. For the moment, England's army is defeated, yet the northern provinces will remain loyal to Hanover. Then who knows when another English army may come? Before a general peace is concluded, therefore, the French hope to see Hanoverian power hemmed in by a restoration of the House of Stuart in the southern colonies.'

'Such a thing is not possible,' I said.

'No,' said the Chevalier, breaking in upon my words, 'in England it is not possible, nor in Scotland at present, as you and I well know, sir. In Massachusetts Bay or New York it is not possible. But I speak advisedly, sir, for I too have seen much of Virginia and Maryland. Two of the greatest men of Virginia, with all their plantations and militia, will cry "God save King James" with us. Five Virginian regiments shall be raised in a few days.'

'Virginians', said I, 'will not fight for King James. Frasers or Camerons will do so, Macdonalds or Stuarts, but not Virginians'.

'Why, sir, who are Virginians?' said the Chevalier pettishly. 'Have you forgot that one thousand of Virginia's soldiers are our clansmen who were transported to Virginia as felons after Culloden? Were they not kept as very slaves in that Province? When they fight, sir, they fight for their liberty as well as for King James. Add to the Virginian regiments two more regiments of Highlanders now in Quebec. Add to these a regiment or more of Irishmen, loyal to King James and now in the service of France. Add to these another regiment of English gentlemen in exile, still loyal to the old cause. Add Prince Charles's Life Guards and Fitzjames's Horse. Is nothing possible with an army the size of General Wolfe's? Is nothing possible when Charles Edward comes as his father's Regent to save Virginia from the French War?'

I only asked what part there was to be for our Highland soldiers after the war.

'Land, sir,' said the Chevalier. 'Land, their security, and the honour of that great Prince for whom the clans fought and died at Culloden. They have nothing else. General Wolfe does not want them. The Elector of Hanover does not want them. They might have been taken off in the ships but they were left here without the means of survival, and bombarded by the English fleet as a gesture of farewell. Every man knows that their Highland settlements are being taken from them and the clans dispersed. Such is the mercy of King George. They are already denounced as rebels and traitors by that usurper. They could lose little more, even if they were to suffer defeat in Virginia.'

'Except their lives, sir,' said I.

'What poltroon would value his life above the cause, sir?' said the Chevalier haughtily.

There was much more in this vein. Finally, I did not dispute any further with the Chevalier and Major Shaw but promised to consider the matter with great care. The Chevalier himself came with me to the courtyard and spoke more gently, though with great caution.

'Do not be deceived, Mr Fraser, we know the prize for which we throw. It is no less than to see the House of Stuart restored to an American kingdom greater than any domain of which the Elector of Hanover can boast.'

I kept all this in my mind and spoke to no one of it. As I walked by the river and meditated upon the Chevalier's words, the scheme which had at first seemed so remote from probability became more rational. If the army of

Virginia might be created and if the Chevalier spoke with the authority of the King of France and of James III, a peace might be made on such terms. With the defeat of General Wolfe and General Amherst it was in the power of France to impose terms in America. If the Province of Virginia, the greatest of all England's remaining American possessions, were to pass to the House of Stuart, France needed to fear little from those other English territories which lay from Boston down to Maryland. The Chevalier had spoken nothing of the health of King James but I deduced that it would not be the King himself who held power in Virginia, being too old and infirm by all reports, but his son the Bonnie Prince Charles, as his father's Regent.

10 October 1759. The clansmen assembled today before the walls of Quebec to honour their dead. The drums beat and the pipes played as the columns marched and counter-marched across the Plains of Abraham, forming into two great flanks. Some of the soldiers wore woollen stockings which the nuns of the convent had knitted them against the winter cold.

After all were in position, the lament of a single piper was borne across the silent grasslands towards the river valley, where so great a part of the battle had been fought. The rumour of the plot against Virginia (though I had spoken of it to none) had been current for several days and was now very widespread among our Highlanders. I heard that those officers and men who had offered their services to the French were now to be leaders in this expedition.

When the regiments were paraded, the Chevalier de Johnstone, whom many recalled from the campaign of 1745, spoke to them. He stood before them in the uniform of a Highland officer of King James. Though he spoke with all his power, his words hardly carried to some of the men but he stood nearest those who were already committed to his cause, and these gave the lead to the rest.

'You are all free men,' he cried, 'and none of you shall be compelled against his conscience. That I am to tell you from your lawful Prince by whose banner your clans fought and fell on the bloody field of Culloden. By his most gracious command, I come to offer you his protection for your freedom. Though you were sent to this place by a false king, see how he has betrayed you in his falseness! When your courage failed to carry the city of Quebec, what shelter was offered you by the generals of the Elector of Hanover, who calls himself King George? You might have been taken off, indeed you might, but your places were given to German mercenaries bought from the Hanoverian dominions, who are of more worth in the eyes of a false king than are free-born men.

'The Elector of Hanover consigns you to death, while James, your true King, offers you life in a new land. Our Sovereign does not send you to destroy but to protect, to prosper but not to plunder. To all of you he offers land in the Province of Virginia, where you are to be freeholders. What has the Hanoverian done? He has seized your lands in Scotland and scattered your clans. Yet you shall hold new lands under the warrant of the Royal House of Stuart. If any tyrant should then try to dispossess you, you will know how to meet him. I shall lead you myself, for I do not ask you to go before, my lads, but merely to follow me. I will compel no man to go but I will ask if there are any here who will follow me to the new land of Virginia?'

While he spoke, a clansman followed him, repeating all he said in the language of the people there, for fear a single man might be present who did not know the English tongue. Before the Chevalier demanded who would follow him, there were many of the Highlanders who knew well what was to be asked of them. These led the others, waving their hands and their swords in the air, as they shouted their allegiance. After their defeat by the French and their desertion by the English, they would have followed any man who promised them such salvation as this. The Chevalier spoke again.

'Are you content to hold the Province of Virginia for your lawful King, James III, and for his son, the Prince Charles Edward?'

Again there was a roaring of assent, though loud enough this time to shake the very vault of heaven. Many began to shake their neighbour's hand and almost to dance for happiness at all that had been promised them.

'Then God be with you all,' said the Chevalier, and turned smartly away towards the city.

Now that the moment had come upon us, what man of the Clan Fraser could have resisted such a call? The very name of Prince Charlie was enough to stir the hearts of the Highland soldiers more strongly than any figure of legend or romance. They had all, in their songs and their tales, dreamt for fourteen years past that their Bonnie Prince should one day come again to lead them in victorious battle against the bloody usurper.

I had so far doubted the certainty of success in any design against Virginia, for I thought that their allegiance might be to their songs and their tales rather than to the young Prince in reality. All such doubts were swept clear from any man's mind that heard how the regiments greeted the name of Charles Edward. Now we might add, to the loyalty they had pledged, the strength of the Irish Brigade, the fine spirit of the Jacobite Horse that the Duke of Berwick once led, and the possible assistance of some of the Virginia regiments themselves. I called to mind the Chevalier's question to me. What might we not accomplish with such an army, and with such spirit as our clansmen showed?

Presently, the Chevalier passed close by me. Seeing me

much occupied with my thoughts, which he took for unconquered doubts, he beckoned me to join him.

'You are uncertain of my wisdom, sir?' he asked. 'Is it not so?'

I protested that this was not the case, yet soon afterwards I happened to say that it was a great chance that must still be taken. Indeed it is.

'Come, sir, come,' said the Chevalier with a smile, 'the other chance is the worse. Your lands and the lands of your kinsmen in Scotland have been stolen from you. You and your men are to be proclaimed cowards and traitors in London by the ungrateful tyrant and his sycophants. Your womenfolk and children were butchered – aye, and worse than butchered, often enough – by the bastard Duke of Cumberland. Your own father, at 80 years old, was made a public spectacle. As sweet a gentleman as one might know, he was dragged to the block and beheaded by the mercy of good King George. His head was left to rot in the public view, the prey of birds, and we are to thank the noble tyrant that an old man's bowels were not ripped up while he was yet living. And, after so much, would you return to England and kiss the arse of the Hanoverian usurper? Come, sir, such things are not to be thought of!'

2

LETTERS OF 'H.W.' TO SIR HORACE MANN: 1759–1760

Copies of four letters from 'H.W.' to Sir Horace Mann, British envoy at Florence, are inserted at this point in the journal of Lovat Fraser. All four letters are written from Arlington Street, London, during the winter of 1759–1760, and appear to be some of those letters which Horace Walpole wrote to Mann, and which never reached their correct destination.[1] Their appearance among Lovat Fraser's papers is reason for suspecting that they were intercepted by spies of Prince Charles Edward, the 'Young Pretender', who was living at Albano, near Florence, during part of this time. The Jacobite leaders may have placed an unduly high value upon Horace Walpole's letters by virtue of his being the son of the former Prime Minister, Sir Robert Walpole.

To Sir Horace Mann

Arlington Street, 18 Dec. 1759

I have left my fairy castle at Strawberry Hill, and put my goldfish and my orange trees in the care of Pope's sullen ghost.

There is little to tell you, as yet, of what the House of Commons will do with General Wolfe. Upon the return of

[1] See *Letters of Horace Walpole to Sir Horace Mann* (London, 1833), III, 272.

our ill-fated expedition from Quebec, Brigadier George Townshend prevailed upon his brother and the Ministry to command an inquiry by the Commons into the conduct of the campaign. The Committee of the House has already heard much evidence, and must hear a good deal more before this parliamentary winter is over.

The loss of Canada, which I foretold you two months since,[1] is but part of that torrent of ill-tidings which sweeps down upon us. Now that the fashionable world is come to town, the talk is all of an invasion. Not a week ago, our regiments were under arms for eighteen hours together, expecting the French, who it is said will bring the Pretender's boy with them when they come. If ever that Bonnie Prince Charles would send our old King packing, he might do it now. Being whose son I am, I should have no choice but to follow the general post to Hanover. Do you picture me loyally breathing the damp air in my exile's garret at Herringhausen? Really, my dear sir, this is not pleasant!

The mob grinds its teeth and nails (being well paid to do so), and seems intent on enjoying a show of public vengeance, since it has been cheated of the spectacle of victory. We cannot revenge ourselves upon the French army, but it is the next best thing to seek satisfaction from our own generals.

George Townshend and the Ministry are most anxious for the impeachment of General Wolfe, lest otherwise they be impeached themselves. The ministerial pamphlet-writers pay Wolfe the compliment of saying they do believe a court-martial would serve his interest, for by his acquittal he might face his countrymen again with honour. And, if that should not answer, he might be shot, as Byng was, which proves a man's complete vindication! Was there ever such a pretty piece of chicanery?

The chatter of the season runs on. It is put about

[1] *Ibid.* III, 340

that the Duke of Kingston is shut up with the pox, and that the amorous Miss Chudleigh is his benefactress in the matter. Yet George Selwyn remarks that the Duke was never poxed in his life, but hearing the King was also enamoured of Miss Chudleigh, and being too loyal a subject to contest the business with his monarch, he put this tale about that he might have his mistress to himself. Was not this ingeniously done? Adieu! Yours ever, H.W.

To Sir Horace Mann

Arlington Street, 3 Feb. 1760

The devil of discord has made sport among us this winter as never before. Last Tuesday, the Commons' Committee arraigned General Wolfe upon sundry charges of cowardice, desertion of his post, negligence, and unsoldierly conduct of every kind which might more fittingly have been alleged against a picket guard than against a general officer. The world knows that he is neither a coward nor a deserter of his duty. Yet negligence is what any man may please to call it, and was sufficient to ensnare Admiral Byng. The other charges are brought only to destroy Wolfe's credit before ever his case can be heard. It is now decided that he was very wrong to leave the poor Highlanders in the hands of the French. They who accuse him thus can have little knowledge of the order given him that no Highland troops in arms were to be returned here or allowed to remain in England or Scotland once they had been enlisted. In carrying a thousand or more of the Pretender's loyal subjects to Canada and then leaving them there, Wolfe should earn the commendation of the Ministry rather than its blame!

Mr Yorke, for the Ministry, lets it be known that the Ministers themselves will take no part against General Wolfe but will leave him to the discretion of a Horse Guards' court-martial. Was there ever such a parade of washing one's hands since the time of Pontius Pilate? And would not *he* have made an admirable Attorney-General to the Duke of Newcastle?

The Duke, with Lord Mansfield's money and Charles Townshend's wits, thinks himself more secure in office every day, for all the defeats of our army. Sir William Pitt, who bid so fair to be the Duke's rival a year or two since, has found other employment. He lately kissed hands on his appointment to Lisbon, where he hopes to find that the gentle climate of the country may undo some of the ravages of its wine. He is fast approaching that point when, as George Selwyn remarked, a man's own constitution is more to him than that of any government.

The widow of Sir George Lee assured me last night that the French army, under General Bougainville, have sacked Boston and that this time the report will be proved true. Really, if it is so, I cannot see how she should come so early by the news, though her husband might have held the Exchequer had he but outlived his monarch. As the stories go, I shall not be surprised if we lose the Borough of Southwark, or even Cheapside, to the French by Easter. Adieu! Yours ever, H.W.

To Sir Horace Mann

Arlington Street, 21 March 1760

I was at the Horse Guards today for the court-martial which sat with so much ceremony and so little compunction upon General Wolfe. Admission to the chamber by Whitehall was as hard to come by as tickets for the Venetian ambassador's masquerade, nor was the company greatly different from such an assembly. The court of general officers who sat in judgment upon Wolfe had between them just so much knowledge of the law as would disgrace a country attorney.

Lord Loudoun and General Robert Napier, sometime military secretary to the Duke of Cumberland, were most assiduous in questioning the witnesses, of whom George Townshend was the first in importance. It was Townshend's opinion that Wolfe, in neglecting the advice of all his brigadiers, had undertaken a most rash and unwarranted assault upon the heights of Montmorency and, afterwards, against the city of Quebec. A contrary plan might have succeeded by landing a force higher up the river and taking the town from that side.

During this evidence, General Wolfe sat at a table a little apart with his attorney, Mr Serjeant Davy, by him. He seemed content, for the most part, to let the witnesses have their way with him. Then George Townshend began to divert the court with a burlesque account of how Wolfe had disposed his men upon the plain before Quebec, as if for the convenience of the French commanders, and then on seeing the first horsemen of Bougainville had cowardly broken off the action.

'Pray, sir,' says Wolfe with the colour in his cheeks, 'how can you say that you know such a thing? Was you not with the Highlanders and the 47th regiment of foot, two miles off?'

'Indeed, sir,' says Townshend, 'and did I not form those men into a defence, seize a horse from the French, and ride to you, urging you to stand fast that we might give battle on both sides, and so carry the day?'

'As to what you *did*, sir,' says Wolfe, 'you alone must be the judge. As to what you *said*, why you know as well as I do that I lacked the benefit of your opinion until after the battle had cooled and 3,000 of our army, including yourself, sir, had safely retired.'

'And so might 2,000 more have retired in safety,' answers Townshend with a fierce gesture, 'who are now left to their deaths or to be prisoners of the French. And you know, sir, that I urged resistance upon you before hardly a man of our army had left the field of battle.'

There was much more of this sort, which Lord Loudoun,

as President of the Court, deplored from time to time as not pertinent to the cause. Brigadier Monckton, who had seen something of the battle, said little against Wolfe, but what was more damning he said not a word in his behalf either. Admiral Saunders swore that the fleet must have withdrawn in any case, but stopped to hint that the haste need not have been so precipitate as Wolfe made it, and that he in no way counselled the General to take the action which he did.

A little way into the afternoon, the mobility assembled in Whitehall and on the Horse Guards' Parade, calling for sentence and execution. A while later, when it was dark, the torches which they carried lit the windows of the judgment chamber from the outside. Three or four of their leaders were found to be footmen or servants of George Townshend, who encouraged the others in throwing their caps in the air for the King, the Commons, and Brigadier Townshend.

After dinner, of which General Wolfe ate little, the court with much deliberation passed its sentence of execution against the prisoner. Lord Loudoun spoke as one who would have rejoiced to find some other way, though at the same time taking the greatest care not to find one. It is said that nothing is yet decided, for the judges may now find fault with the proceedings, or else His Majesty may exercise mercy. But it was not so with Admiral Byng. However, when General Wolfe is no longer the butt of popular resentment, it is hoped by all moderate men that he may be permitted to retire to the country with a small allowance. Good night. Yours ever, H.W.

To Sir Horace Mann

Arlington Street, 30 April 1760
Wednesday last saw the most melancholy of scenes, and the close of General Wolfe's career. After the solicitations of his family and friends, both the court and the Ministry

were busy with seeking some means to arrest the judgment against him, without ever finding that they had left themselves the means of doing so. He has too many enemies, poor man. It is said that the Duke of Cumberland is still in such a rage at the loss of Canada that he vows to his father, the old King, to lead an army himself to America and recover our lost valour.

When the judges found no means to meddle with the sentence passed upon General Wolfe, Lord Loudoun himself thought to mitigate royal anger by interceding with the King at a levée. He gave it as his opinion to the King that Wolfe had acted the part of a madman, rather than a traitor, and therefore merited charity rather than severity.

'Mad, is he?' replied the King. 'Then pray God he may bite no more of my generals!'

You may imagine that, when even Lord Loudoun was treated thus, it was soon found that all other avenues to royal clemency were closed.

The time appointed for General Wolfe's execution was at noon. They brought in the death warrant to him on the last night, as he sat at dinner. He rose early in the morning and took his customary draught of physic, as if he were to live many a year more and must care for his constitution. After praying, as was his habit, he ate a good meal and swore that he had slept the last night as soundly as a child with a good conscience. He bore the pomp of a tedious procession from the Tower to Whitehall with equanimity, and the mob which had earlier shouted for his blood stood silent for him as he passed.

Over the Horse Guards' Parade, where he was to meet his death, every window was crowded with figures of fashion, like so many boxes at the theatre. People there made a trade of letting out spy glasses at a halfpenny a look. In Whitehall the mob was so great that the coach bearing him could go no further, and he was escorted thence on foot by officers of the Dragoons with drawn sabres and crape sashes. All this time his courage bore him up, and made men wonder how the imputation of cowardice could ever have been laid against him. He seemed a small and delicate figure, his face fine-boned and handsome, among such armed pomp as surrounded him. Yet he walked as firmly there as before his men in battle.

His coffin was borne before him and set upon the Horse Guards' Parade with a cushion upon it, at some distance from the archway and in the view of all the crowd. There was a little sawdust scattered near and a wooden screen erected behind. Twelve soldiers, their muskets primed and at the ready, faced him as he knelt upon the cushion. Four of them were down on one knee and four more crouched to fire over the heads of these. The four who stood furthest back were not to fire unless the first two ranks did not despatch him. Two of the muskets were loaded only with powder, that the murder of General Wolfe might not be charged against any individual man.

Neither the sight of the muskets nor the prospect of his own coffin caused General Wolfe to falter. Among the officers who stood hard by the execution party was his old adversary George Townshend. Yet Wolfe never so much as glanced at him while the sharp beats of the drums which had preceded him changed to a more rapid drumming. (They say this was done to prevent his making a last speech to the people.)

They blindfolded him with a white handkerchief as he knelt upon the cushion, not that he feared their muskets but rather because the soldiers might fear to shoot if they saw his eyes upon them. In the noise of the drumming, the officer commanding the firing party cried, 'Cock your firelocks! Present!'

General Wolfe held a handkerchief in his hand, which he was to let drop as a signal. He prayed a moment longer with the barrels of their muskets levelled at him. Then he allowed the handkerchief to flutter down. The eight shots were fired raggedly but he fell at once and must have been dead before the third rank could fire.

How it happened, no one knows, but by an unlucky chance one of the eight shots hit the wooden board and glanced back, wounding George Townshend close to the seat of majesty. How others may view this none can tell, though George Townshend himself replies gruffly to all inquiries as to where the fragment struck him, 'Why, sir, not a dozen paces from the Horse Guards.' Is not this exquisite? I am informed by George Selwyn that Monsieur Voltaire, on hearing of the accident, observed that it was small wonder the English had lost Canada with such marksmanship, for of the eight bullets fired only one had found its proper lodging. Adieu! Yours ever, H.W.

3

REGENT OF THE AMERICAS

The entries in Lovat Fraser's journal, which ended in October 1759, begin again in May 1760, during his voyage from New York to Hampton, Virginia, in company with the Chevalier de Johnstone, Lieutenant Louis de Johnstone, Simon Fraser, Captain James Ogilvie, Major Shaw and one other, unnamed, Jacobite officer. The party had made a secret journey down the Hudson valley to New York in the early months of 1760, and had joined a ship there in the guise of merchants and planters returning to Virginia.

18 May 1760. Last night the weather grew squally and our ship rolled as badly as ever I saw. Gabriel, whom the Chevalier de Johnstone gave me as servant in Quebec, was very sick and no more inclined to play the lover with one or two maids on board.

This morning I ate cake and chocolate for breakfast, and then summoned Gabriel to shave me. He assured me that there had been much disorder in the infernal regions of the ship during the storm. Some of the crew slept but others were retching, groaning, blasting their legs and thighs, or damning their livers, lights, and lungs. The high seas obliged the sailors to batten down the hatches, so there was no escape for Gabriel from this scene of profanity.

When I ventured on deck at noon, the sky behind us was dark and changing, but the day became warm though a little cloudy. Our vessel is an ordinary enough merchantman, but for our own party of seven. We sighted a sail this afternoon with the French colours, but she neither harmed nor even approached us. I walked upon the deck after dinner and saw another ship, but she made from us. The Chevalier kept me company, talking much of the Province of Virginia, its foundation and its great families. Much of his hope seems to rest on Colonel William Byrd III of Westover, grandson of a Stuart courtier and a great landowner in the Province, though an inveterate gamester. There is hope, too, in Fitzhugh of Marmion, and in young Robert Wormeley Carter, who would join us if only to spite his Whig father. The Chevalier said nothing of how Prince Charles Edward might be brought to Virginia under the guns of the English ships.

Our own vessel, of no more than 200 tons burden, brings us as seven of an innocent party of travellers between New York and Hampton. Our Highland regiments are marching somewhere between Quebec and the Ohio, while General O'Sullivan's Irish must find a suitable crossing of the Potomac. Captain Ogilvie and I would have gone with our men but were chosen to be of the party that was to go by sea and, landing first, prepare our friends in Virginia for the arrival of our regiments.

One of our own party is the Chevalier's son, Lieutenant Louis de Johnstone, a tall, fair-complexioned youth whose manner assumes a languor which his eagerness for battle contradicts. Like his father, Lieutenant Louis (as the Chevalier's son is commonly called) has known little of life except as Fortune's soldier. He shares also his father's quickness to resent an insult and to call his man out to offer satisfaction upon the field of honour. This will not do for an innocent trader in Virginia!

21 May 1760. Our sailors found ground this morning at twenty fathoms. Captain Ogilvie and I both saw land to our north for half an hour, though we lost it afterwards. The weather being squally again, the sailors stowed the main topsail a little after dinner and close-reefed the mainsail, so that we might scud under the breeze. The Chevalier assured me that the land we had seen to our north was Cape Charles, such a name being a favourable omen, and that we were now in the mouth of that great reach of water which they call Chesapeake Bay and which forms almost the entire coast of the Province of Virginia.

22 May 1760. At dawn this morning the sea lay calm and our sailors found white sand and shells at twelve fathoms. By early light, we made out land to the south, which the Chevalier now swore was Cape Henry. In a little while, the depth was no more than five fathoms, so that our captain hoisted a flag for a pilot boat to take us in to Hampton. Soon the pilot brought us to anchor in the James River, just off the town, which consists of well-built homes along the shore and several exceedingly handsome houses upon the higher ground. Next to the grandest house of all rose a tall flagstaff, from which the British flag flew. A brig and a sloop of the Royal Navy were anchored in the river near us. Hampton is well built and the inhabitants comfortable, yet I could not help remarking to the Chevalier that it was small by comparison with ports in Europe.

'Indeed, sir,' said he with satisfaction, 'so it is. A sergeant and a dozen common soldiers might take Hampton for us and hold it until the crack of doom. You once thought our little army too feeble, Mr Fraser, yet with no more than four regiments we shall outnumber all the people of Williamsburg, Hampton, and Norfolk put together.'

23 May 1760. The Chevalier, Captain Ogilvie, and I

came ashore this morning with three other members of our party. As we left the ship, a pinch-faced gentleman with the air of a spy about him came aboard. He expressed much interest in one of our passengers who had died on the voyage between New York and Hampton and had aroused our suspicions strongly. With a great parade of sanctimoniousness, the new arrival inquired the date of his friend's tragic death.

'Why, damn my blood,' says the Captain bluffly, 'he's dead ten days ago.'

The solemn-faced gentleman, whom I now felt to be in league with the dead man to spy upon us, went on to suppose that his 'friend' had been buried at sea.

'Buried?' says the Captain with surprise. 'Bless you, no. There was not ballast enough for that. We have pulled out his guts that they might not rot him and stowed him in a rope-locker, where he lies even now.'

The rest of this conversation was lost to me as our wherry pulled away from the side of the ship towards the shore of Hampton. Yet we watched the solemn gentleman, who a moment before had been so anxious to pay his respects to his late friend, casting many urgent glances at us as we were rowed across the stream.

Our landing was a jetty piled high with casks or hogsheads of tobacco, which waited a ship to London or Bristol. We were met by Major Alexander Shaw, who had gone ashore an hour or two before us. The Major had procured horses so that we might ride the forty miles to Williamsburg, the capital city of the Province, before any news of our coming could precede us. This was well advised, for the Chevalier seemed well known to several of the Virginians, who addressed him as 'Colonel' Johnstone and welcomed him back from his 'journey to New England'.

Williamsburg, the principal city of Virginia, is a pleasant and well-appointed town. It is more than an

English market-town, though nowhere as great as the cities of England and France. In its area and spacious quality it has something of the air of Bath or Tunbridge. Though not great in size, its buildings were finer than I had expected. The main street runs for a mile and at one end is an elegant structure by Sir Christopher Wren, the College of William and Mary. At the far end of the town is the Capitol or Parliament Building, built like many others in a pleasing brick. It has two wings with handsome bays and these two wings are connected by a gallery and arcades. Along the length of the main street, or close to it, is the great building of the Governor's Palace with its formal gardens, as well as coffee shops, taverns, theatre, and many elegant houses. The houses are like those built in England during the years of Queen Anne, with steps leading up from the street to the doors.

The inhabitants and their negro slaves number less than two thousand, yet when the time comes for parliament, the courts, and the fashionable rout of Virginia to attend, there is three times that number. Then the taverns, theatre and race-course are much in demand. There is a fine church in Bruton parish, which serves as a Chapel Royal to the Governor's Palace. That Palace itself is unmistakable with its cupola, iron gates, gardens, orchard, and canals. It is a residence which the finest gentleman in Europe would look upon with envy. The oval track of the race-course lies a little way out of the town. When the races are held there in season, greater wagers are made than even at the card-tables of the Virginian gentlemen.

24 May 1760. The plain reason why men in Virginia call the Chevalier 'Colonel' Johnstone is that he is owner of an estate on the bank of the James River (though not one of the great Tidewater plantations) and that he is therefore a member of their House of Commons, which they call the House of Burgesses. His return here is timely, for Williamsburg buzzes with news that a military governor is to take the place of Governor Fauquier in the Palace, and that he will be the Earl of Loudoun. Now that the French have driven the English from Canada and much of New England, they prepare an attack in strength across the Ohio, which threatens the destruction of Virginia. In face of this, it is Lord Loudoun who must make bricks without straw to save the remaining American provinces for the Elector of Hanover.

The House of Burgesses met today, where I was a witness by the Chevalier's invitation. We drove together to the Capitol and were set down just under the cupola that bears the arms of Queen Anne.

'Believe me, sir,' said the Chevalier, 'our time is not idly spent, for the Elector of Hanover and the French will both strike at us soon and we must anticipate them both.'

I asked him what that might mean.

'Why, sir, what remains of the English army is fighting to save itself in New England and along the Hudson. Every man knows that our neighbours in Pennsylvania have disbanded their militia and will fight the French no more. Here in Virginia, the Burgesses respectfully tell "King" George of England that they have 300 men under arms, and cannot raise one more to fight French or Indians.'

I looked closely at him and asked the consequence of this.

'The consequence, sir? The consequence is that Virginia cannot defend herself and must soon be destroyed unless she makes a separate peace with France. Yet Colonel Byrd has Governor Fauquier's ear, and from his information I may tell you now what all the Burgesses shall hear today. The Elector of Hanover and his Ministers, after their defeat at Quebec, have sworn and determined that Virginia shall provide men to defend herself, and shall be made to pay the whole cost of war. Orders are now to be given for the raising of four new regiments. Virginia's ships are to be requisitioned by the English navy, and taxes imposed by the Parliament in London upon the Virginians, that they may pay for the war. It is not so in the northern colonies, for they have stood against the French – so says King George and his Ministers. But Virginia has been disloyal to Hanoverian England and must be treated without ceremony.'

In the chamber of the House of Burgesses the assembled representatives listened to the new measures as they were announced by the Speaker on the Governor's behalf. It was warm in the building, with an abundance of the small flies and mosquitoes which I have already noticed make a plague here. The Burgesses listened very restlessly to the judgment passed upon them.

'Four regiments of foot soldiers to be raised in addition to those already under arms, the said regiments to be raised and disposed of by the Earl of Loudoun or his commanders. . . . All vessels of more than thirty tons burden to be entered in a naval register for service under His Majesty's command. Trade between the Province of Virginia and other territories to be subject to the provision of vessels by other means. . . . In order to the supplying and victualling of the army and fleet, a duty to be levied upon tobacco before it is shipped from Virginia and a duty upon goods bound for Virginia to be levied before they are shipped from Great Britain. . . .'

At this point there broke such a storm as I had not heard since the French fired upon our boats at Louisberg. A dozen gentlemen rose and shouted above the tumult but the general uproar lasted some little time with several wigs askew and every face shining with the heat of the day and the indignation of the moment. From time to time the Speaker, a plausible and fluent gentleman, continued to deliver himself of his pronouncements.

'Goods bound to Virginia from all other His Majesty's dominions, excepting the American colonies, and from all other foreign parts, to be dutiable on their first arriving in Great Britain.'

This aroused greater roaring than the first, a stout gentleman close by me shouting the word 'robbery!' till his lungs might burst. Soon the debate broke out and then it was apparent how great a quandary the gentlemen of Virginia faced. A tall, fine-featured man, whom I later knew as Colonel William Byrd III, spoke bravely for making peace with France.

'If there be peace with France,' he said, 'these measures will be of no consequence. That there may be peace between Virginians and Frenchmen every man knows. That there must one day be peace, no man denies. That these present measures will succeed in beggaring us while failing to defend us is an open truth. Four or five regiments of militia will not defeat the French army or save the Virginian plantations, but they will enable King George to fight a new campaign in Hanover. . . .'

Here he was interrupted by groans and hisses from the Hanoverian faction.

Colonel Landon Carter of Sabine Hall, who had the face and manner of a careful farmer, seemed to be the champion in arms of Hanover.

'I take no man's part who does not wish damnation to the French and to all the King's enemies,' he cried. 'For my part, I much regret that the proposed measures are necessary. Yet I have no doubt that they are necessary when the French are almost at our doors.'

After this he could hardly proceed without interruption from republicans and Jacobites alike, who saluted him with insults. Through the din, he talked much of the knavery of the French and the beastly cunning of traitors in the midst of honest Virginians.

After long and loud debate, the Chevalier de Johnstone rose. He spoke softly but rapidly, as was his habit, so that all grew silent to hear his words.

'The streets of Williamsburg are filling with those who fly from the French or the Indians on our frontiers. There is no army to defend us and we shall certainly be destroyed before Lord Loudoun can raise a single man for his new militia. Where then is our safety? The English army will fight no more wars in America and is already retiring upon the ports of Boston and New York. We may thus be left to the mercy of the French and their Indians. Yet there is another army in America, an army of Englishmen, of Irish, and of Scotsmen. Where it is, I do not know, but that it is numerous enough for our defence I have no doubt.'

Here the Chevalier paused, and his listeners sat in perfect silence.

'Yet', said he, 'it might be better to see our homes burned, our plantations ruined, and our families murdered before embracing such an ally. That army, gentlemen, is indeed an army of our countrymen, yet they are countrymen who for fifty years have maintained their allegiance to the House of Stuart.'

Here there were cries of 'treason!' and 'rebels!'

'Very well,' said the Chevalier, and he inclined his head a little, 'it is our privilege to reject the protection of soldiers loyal to the Stuart kings of England. But no gentleman can tell me how we are to be saved by the House of Hanover. The Ohio has fallen and the Pennsylvanians throw themselves upon the mercy of the French. Boston is in flames and New York may soon be in ruins. I have come from these places, and I tell you what I have seen. Are you so loyal to the House of Hanover that you will become subjects of the King of France rather than accept the protection of King James? Are you determined to be first robbed by the excisemen of Hanover and then murdered by the soldiers of France? Can you not see that both are equally your enemies?'

There was more noise at this. When all had had their

say, the House stood adjourned and its members drew into small factions in the corridors and adjoining rooms. I stood with the Chevalier, Colonel Byrd, and Fitzhugh of Marmion in the shadow of the arcade, when Colonel Landon Carter and his party came our way.

'Sir,' said Colonel Carter to the Chevalier, 'it seems you would make us all slaves to the rule of a Stuart tyrant and the Popish religion. You would have the Pretender as King of Virginia, since no one will have him king anywhere else!'

Here he laughed with a derisive anger.

'I said nothing as to a king, sir,' said the Chevalier smoothly. 'I spoke of a protector, a defender. King George cannot protect us, sir, and all your words will not defend us. The French seek only to digest New England before they devour us. Would you deny Virginia a defender, sir?'

Colonel Carter shook his sleeve angrily and his lusty voice carried across the lawns.

'Do not talk to me of protection, sir!' he cried. 'I tell you that if there were not so many damned Scots knaves in Virginia, we should never have heard such treason spoken as has been uttered today!'

The Chevalier's colour deepened and he put his hand to his belt, where the pommel of his sword might have been.

'Is it your intention that I should resent that comment, sir?'

'Resent a fart!' swore Colonel Carter, and strode off with his companions.

A little while later we were joined by his scapegrace son, Robert Wormeley Carter, and by Mr John Randolph, a clever young attorney of Tory inclinations whose father, Sir John, had been a great man in Virginia. Mr Randolph spoke warmly to the Chevalier, congratulating him on having spoken in the House as a man of sense. The

Chevalier was much taken with this and arrangements were made for another meeting at which some understanding might be arrived at. Mr Randolph and several of his acquaintance seem anxious to discover what their reward might be for supporting the claim of King James or his son. No such reward tempts young Mr Carter, who is for King James because his father is for King George.

At night our little group gathered at the Raleigh Tavern to discuss business. It seems that Mr Randolph would declare for King James if only the King would then make him comfortable in the office of Attorney-General. The Chevalier could promise nothing but swore to use his influence. Mr Randolph was skittish and would not be coaxed or wheedled, and then finally was, having forfeited the House of Hanover's favour and seeing nothing for it but to embrace the Stuart cause. Our conference was ended by a great shouting at the far end of the street and the sight of torches burning brightly by the Capitol.

It was some little while before we could safely reach the place and the perpetrators of the act had disappeared before our arrival, leaving a crowd of two or three score to look on. Before the entrance of the Capitol a makeshift gallows had been erected and there hung what at first we took for three bodies. Yet on coming closer our fears were somewhat quieted for they were only effigies that hung there. The rag and straw King of England kept company with the Pope and Prince Charles Edward.

22 May 1760. By whose hand they were printed I do not know, yet Williamsburg is alive with copies of a declaration of Prince Charles Edward, made some years since, of his allegiance to the Church of England. I find also a pamphlet entitled *What if the French Should Come?* which bears the style of Colonel Landon Carter and urges loyalty to George II and Lord Loudoun, his newly designated Governor, for fear of what must happen to Williamsburg and its people in the event of a French conquest. In all this it is hard to find what the citizens of the pleasant town think, for the mob will generally cheer him who pays them best.

I went in company with the Chevalier and Colonel Byrd, a man of vast parade and delicate humour, to see the races. The Colonel seems to be the greatest man in Virginia, as his father and his grandfather were in their time. His lands include the estate of Westover and the new settlement of Richmond on the James River. That such a man should favour our cause is great fortune indeed.

We rode out to the race-path, which lies in a circle a mile or so beyond the town. There was a purse of a hundred guineas to be won today. It appears a time of considerable festivity, for there was a great crowd pressing round the course and a great deal of entertainment. I saw acrobats, tightrope dancers, and fire-eaters or salamanders performing, to whom some of the crowd threw small gifts. All fear of the French seemed to be forgotten.

Among a great deal of genteel company, we met young Mr Carter, who offered a wager for the bay mare against the grey horse. I agreed to accommodate him.

'And what would you consider to be a just wager, Captain Fraser, sir?'

Before I could reply, the Chevalier interrupted us.

'Two guineas a side and a gallon of rum is a gentleman's wager here, Mr Carter.'

I thought Mr Carter seemed a little disappointed, but he said, 'Is that your wish, Mr Fraser?'

'Oh, by all means,' said I.

'And you, Colonel Byrd, sir,' asked Mr Carter, 'will you wager me two guineas?'

Colonel Byrd stroked his nose for a moment and then gave a powerful laugh.

'I will do better for you, Mr Carter. One hundred guineas against your bay mare.'

'And a gallon of rum?' asked Mr Carter facetiously.

'Oh, indeed, and a gallon of rum as well, sir,' said Colonel Byrd, greatly amused at this.

'And you Colonel Johnstone? What will you wager?' inquired young Mr Carter.

The Chevalier, who seemed impatient for something more than horse races and wagers, turned and pointed towards the cupola of the Governor's Palace.

'I will wager you, sir, that when this race is next run, Prince Charles Edward shall sit in that house as his father's Regent.'

'Ah,' said Robert Carter, 'and how much will you wager?'

'My life, Mr Carter,' said the Chevalier softly, 'and I shall ask no man to be my creditor.'

For all their urging, he would wager nothing on either horse. When the race was run, it was gained easily by the bay mare, so that Robert Carter won both his wagers. I paid him his two guineas and remained his debtor for the gallon of rum.

At night we attended the playhouse to see the comedy of the *Mock Doctor*. It is remarkable how, in all the boxes, the ladies sit with their black servants standing behind their chairs to attend upon them. As for the theatre and the performance, it was for all the world as though one were in Drury Lane or the Haymarket, rather than in a land of savage tribes and undiscovered territory.

I sat with the Chevalier and Colonel Byrd when, during the second act, there began an altercation in the next box between Colonel Landon Carter and his son, who had won both wagers at the races.

'Do you take such pleasure in torturing your father, sir?' cried the Colonel. 'Damn it, but your behaviour is past all bearing! Though I have tried every way, nothing will please you but you must keep the company of the most pernicious gamesters and spendthrifts. Yet I, sir, as well as I can, must keep my buckle and thong together.'

What reply Robert Carter made I could not distinguish, but it was such as to provoke a louder outburst of parental anger.

'Gaming, sir, huskanaws a man to every other duty. Yes, you may sniff at the Pretender's tail, sir, for a man who will stake his fortune is not long in staking his liberty as well. As for your loyalty, it is a base sacrifice to use such a word, for no gamester ever knew its meaning. Tell me no more, sir, for I have heard enough.'

The sound of a door slammed to informed us that the outraged father's call upon his son was over. We heard soon afterwards that Colonel Landon Carter and his party had left Williamsburg and were riding hard towards Sabine Hall, where his followers were to gather. When the play was finished, we passed from the theatre to the coffee house and there listened to the talk of the day. Then it was that the Chevalier showed us a *Morning Chronicle* of two months since, which had not long come from London. It warned its readers that 'the Pretender, in the character of a private gentleman', was busy in instigating the people of America to cast off their loyalty to the House of Hanover.

'It is time, sir,' said the Chevalier to Colonel Byrd, 'that we should leave Williamsburg and attend to more serious matters, for the event cannot be much longer delayed.'

'With all my heart,' said Colonel Byrd with a great flourish and bowing. 'Your servant, Colonel Johnstone, sir.'

We took a walk as far as the Capitol building, it being a warm night and the air of our little rooms oppressive. It was then that we observed a singular omen, for the three effigies which hung from their gallows had undergone a change. We now looked upon the burlesque figures of the Hanoverian King of England, the King of France, and Colonel Landon Carter.

95

23 May 1760. News comes from Charlestown this morning that the affairs of Carolina are in great confusion. The new taxes and impositions were announced there in the absence of the Governor. These measures provoked such an outcry that it seems certain of the gentlemen of Carolina have seized the government for themselves and refuse to yield it again to the representative of George II. The truth of this no man can tell, but it may yet serve us for an example.

The coming of this information delayed us somewhat, and it was almost noon when the Chevalier, Colonel Byrd, Captain Ogilvie, Major Shaw, and I, attended by Gabriel and the servants, rode out of Williamsburg on the way to the great estate of Westover. Our horses trotted briskly, as if they knew the way well enough through long habit. We left the town by a level, sandy road which ran between clusters of umbrella pines. Marsh grass grew plentifully on the low ground and there was an abundance of redbud and dogwood. Presently, the pine woods were interspersed with wide plantations and gentlemen's houses. Thickets of plum and cherry were all in full blossom, for it is warmer here already than the height of summer in England.

My attention was taken by the plantation fields, some growing Indian corn, some cotton, and most of all tobacco. In the tobacco fields were as many as ten or twelve negroes at a time, for the most part men though some of the younger women also. They hoe the sandy soil into small round heaps, the size of a molehill, of which there are some four thousand in an acre. Then they make a small hole with their fingers and put in a plant like a cabbage, which is the tobacco.

'Why,' said Colonel Byrd, 'a good pair of slaves may plant two or three acres in a day. Your servant, Captain Fraser, sir.'

And he spurred forward to carry the same information

to Major Shaw and Captain Ogilvie who rode a little ahead of us.

For all the great houses that look so English, the land here is more like Italy than England, as the fruit that grows so abundantly bears witness. There are crops of pumpkins and melons, while the strawberries grow in profusion. Finding that I rode alone with the Chevalier for a while, we talked of the news from Carolina. I said that the time was never better for King James III and his son to take their own again.

'Never better, sir,' said the Chevalier, who looked directly ahead of his horse and never turned his face to me.

'It only needs a single ship to carry the King or the Prince from La Rochelle to Williamsburg,' said I, 'for I believe every honest man would be for them once they were here.'

'I believe so, sir,' said the Chevalier.

We rode on for some minutes more without speaking until I remarked that a great chance must be taken in the Prince's voyage.

'A great chance indeed, sir,' said the Chevalier.

'The English fleet still holds the seas,' said I, 'and they may easily seize or destroy any vessel.'

'They may indeed, sir.'

We rode on in silence again through the trees of a small pine forest, where the cool green darkness seemed unaffected by the prickling heat of noon. I was puzzled by the Chevalier's indifference and I could not help recalling what his enemies used to say of him, that he was no man's ally but sought only his own advantage through others. If the government of Virginia, or a great part of it, were to pass into his keeping, and if the Prince for whom he held it were then destroyed, the Chevalier must become a man of consequence.

It was almost evening when we came within sight of Westover. We approached the house through a park in which it lies and discovered a fine brick building with a handsome white door that would not disgrace any gentleman's country seat or a house of the *bon ton* in any part of the world. I had not known what to expect but did not imagine so noble a house as this. These lands are only one of Colonel Byrd's estates, though they lie as far as one can see in three directions and are bounded by the James River on the fourth.

Within the house were fine leather chairs, polished tables, pier glasses, portraits by the first masters of Europe and a great library such as any gentleman in Edinburgh or London would regard with pride. That such a degree of civilisation should exist in the middle of a wild and savage territory seemed wonderful indeed. The elegant gardens are laid out on the English model, with such refinement that one might walk there every day and never tire of them.

We ate some hashed beef, also a little dish of strawberries with milk, brought us by one of the Colonel's servants. These are not negroes but, in this case, a domestic called Annie, for whose red hair and green eyes the Colonel appeared to feel some great attachment. He then entertained us with a bowl of punch and some chestnuts, while we talked of the army that might be raised.

'The Highland regiment is on the Ohio and might reach us in a few weeks,' said the Chevalier. 'The Irish regiment under General O'Sullivan has entered Maryland and must soon approach the Potomac.'

'I cannot think,' said Captain Ogilvie facetiously, 'that General O'Sullivan will shed a tear, let alone a drop of blood, for his Prince. There was little love between them after Culloden.'

'Make no mistake, sir,' said the Chevalier sharply, 'General O'Sullivan is the Prince's man. We are all the Prince's men now, for if once we falter, there is a noose round all our necks.'

'Have no fear, sir,' said Ogilvie raising his glass. 'Once they have made a noose to fit General O'Sullivan's neck, there will be no rope left for the rest of us!'

Colonel Byrd gave a shout of laughter, lifted his glass, and cried, 'Uncommonly well said, sir! Here's a toast to you, Captain!'

'Colonel,' said the Chevalier, when the toast was drunk, 'our dispositions are made. We must now wait on yours. A thousand Highlanders and a hundred English soldiers formerly at Quebec are on the Ohio. They are released by the French on condition of their taking no further part in Canada or New England. Eight or nine hundred Irish foot-soldiers, who have never renounced their loyalty to the House of Stuart, have won their release from French service and will soon approach the Potomac to our north. So much we have done. More than that, the Prince shall be accompanied by two hundred English exiles, gentlemen who have shared his exile. These make up the formations of his Life Guards and Fitzjames's Horse. When these are provided with horses, our two thousand foot soldiers will be escorted by two hundred cavalry. The rest, sir, depends on Virginia.'

Colonel Byrd put down his glass and looked at each of us.

'I speak not only for myself but for my friends, young Mr Carter and Fitzhugh of Marmion. The second Virginia Regiment is mustered under my command, as you shall see tomorrow. They are my militia and they will go where I go. Two more companies of my men are raised in Richmond and Henrico County against Virginia's enemies. Six hundred warriors of the Cherokee tribe are under my allegiance and pledged to fight for my cause. The companies of Carter and Fitzhugh may make another regiment. The greatest chance, however, is with a battalion of Royal Americans who have lately come from Carolina without their Colonel Bouquet, who has resigned. They are not twenty miles from us and are temporarily under my vigilance. Major Shaw shall have the command of them.'

'Your servant, sir,' said the Major, inclining his head a little.

'Therefore,' said Colonel Byrd, 'we may promise a thousand of our men under arms, and six hundred Cherokee who will harry the enemy in every possible manner. We have good hopes of three or four hundred more of our militia and three hundred regular troops from the Royal Americans. Leave aside the Indian braves, we have a thousand men promised and five or six hundred more to hope for. With your own force, we might field at least three and probably four thousand men.'

'For all that,' said the Chevalier, 'it is less than I had hoped.'

'Only win the first battle, sir,' said Colonel Byrd, 'and all Virginia will be with you.'

'It is a motley army to win a battle with,' said Captain Ogilvie with some bitterness.

'Then you had better look to General O'Sullivan, Captain,' said the Chevalier with some spirit. 'It is no mere chance that he leads the Irish brigade. We saw some of his merit, sir, even at Culloden. Yet we have seen much more of it since in the service of France. There is no better quartermaster in all the armies of Europe. If General O'Sullivan cannot bring together and victual our regiments, then it cannot be done by any man. Indeed, sir, the French generals say of him that he understands the art of irregular warfare better than any man in Europe, while his knowledge of regular warfare equals the best of their commanders. Believe me, sir, we have given more thought to this campaign than ever we did to Prestonpans or Culloden.'

'Then let us drink the health of General O'Sullivan!' cried Colonel Byrd. 'Oblige me, Fraser, by pushing another glass Colonel Johnstone's way.'

'And damnation to the Elector of Hanover,' said the Chevalier boldly.

With that, we pushed back our chairs and gave all our attention to Colonel Byrd's rum punch, since the Chevalier swore he would not for the world begin gaming so late at night.

'Your toast, then, Ogilvie,' called Colonel Byrd.

'I shall be drunk, I tell you,' protested the Captain.

'This one bumper, dear Ogilvie,' said I.

Ogilvie rose noisily to his feet and said bravely, 'Success to the vessel that bears him now.'

We stood and emptied our glasses to this, though the Chevalier laughed more loudly than I had ever heard before.

'Hey to the midnight! Hark-away! Hark-away!' sang Colonel Byrd and filled the glasses again to the brim.

28 May 1760. It was decided that General O'Sullivan's Irish should march from the north, through Maryland, for there the people are Catholics and likely to welcome him. The Highlanders, by coming from the west into Virginia, will pass through lands settled by their own countrymen and may be favourably received also. Yet the latest news from Robert Carter in Williamsburg is that it is the French who are coming, in perfidious disregard of their understanding with King James. They carry all before them and it is said that the town of Fredericksburg must soon fall to them, if indeed it has not done so already. Our task must be to deny them the road from that town to Williamsburg.

Today was appointed for the mustering of the Virginia soldiers under Colonel Byrd's command. All told, there are some two regiments of militia encamped by the James River, though they seem little enough to turn back the French army. Three hundred Royal Americans, all who could be found, are marching to join us here under the command of Major Shaw.

About eleven o'clock we rode from the Maycox estate, which is now the Chevalier's land, crossed the river, and came to a great field: that is the review ground, where the Virginian soldiers were drawn up. One regiment was mounted and the other on foot. The wives and families of the men, all in their finest summer clothes, watched with great pleasure as their menfolk went through the evolutions of cavalry movements or formed lines and columns on foot. All this among the chattering and strolling of women in their bonnets and their rustling dresses, pink, white, and blue. Colonel Byrd had provided dark blue, and white spatterdashes, for the men, which gives some appearance of a regular army. Yet the disorder of the movements was such as would have disgraced the leavings of a recruiting sergeant.

After an hour or so of this parading, in which I endeavoured to command a party of foot soldiers, all thoughts of war were set aside while men and women alike crowded into another field by the tents. This had been turned into a sort of cookhouse, where roast pork and water melons were laid out on trestles and where the whole occasion seemed more like a country marketplace than any preparation of an army for war. As soon as the Royal Americans joined us, we were to be marched to Fredericksburg to meet the French. Yet I could not believe that such an army as this would ever take the field against the French.

The two regiments which an hour before had marched and countermarched, the columns of cavalry raising a constant screen of dust as they wheeled to right or left, were now sprawled in the shade of the trees, eating roast pork and yams, or drinking their fill of rum and the rough Virginian wine. I looked at them in astonishment and thought of the title of Colonel Landon Carter's treatise, 'What if the French Should Come?'

The day still being warm, this dinner was followed by

sleep, our entire army with its wives and women dozing in a meadow, while its deadliest enemy approached closer at every minute. With the Chevalier and Colonel Byrd, I rode back the little distance to Westover, where the Colonel proposed a game at billiards to some of his guests before the military review was resumed later in the afternoon. The Colonel was very proud of his billiard table and told me, in confidence, that when his father had quarrelled with his wife or any of the women of the house he would make friends again in the billiard room and end by giving them a vigorous 'flourish' upon the fine table.[1]

The upper rooms of the house were curtained against the heat of the day, and the shutters closed. To these rooms the ladies of the party retired (some attended by their maids) to protect the fairness of their skins in the cool darkness. Those goddesses who followed the European fashion for stays and tight lacing were also enabled to escape from their imprisonment for an hour, while still being able to exchange scandal in the cool bedrooms.

Somewhere after three o'clock, the Chevalier and I sought Colonel Byrd again. At last we made our way back to the billiard room. As we approached it, the door opened and there came out a most pretty young 'Miss Pert', who had married a sergeant of the militia not three months since. There followed Colonel Byrd, the very pattern of dignity down to his ruffles and buckles. Yet I could not help noticing that there was no one else in the room and that the back of the damsel's white dress bore ample traces of the green nap of the billiard table. I inquired courteously of the Colonel if he had enjoyed a good game.

'Very fair, Mr Fraser, sir,' he said solemnly. 'Very fair, sir.'

---

[1] See *The Secret Diary of William Byrd of Westover 1709–1712* ed. Louis B. Wright and Marion Tinling (Richmond, Va., 1941), pp. 210–211.

We rode out to watch the men wrestle, cudgel, shoot, and run, for the swords and guns which were offered by Colonel Byrd as prizes. Each company formed a hollow square in which the wrestlers or cudgel-players fought. What these men lacked in formation, they made up for in power and agility. Afterwards there was shooting at a mark. Never have I seen such close work. Indeed the centre of a mark was hit so often that it was soon shot to pieces. This may give some hope of what they can do to the French, if the chance should come.

By nightfall, the drinking which had begun at noon was resumed in earnest, while the Chevalier and I took supper with Colonel Byrd and some of the Captains of Militia. We walked in the garden as the sun set and the lights of the camp fires shone through the trees. The sun had gone down and the light had dwindled to a mere gloaming, when we heard the sound of horsemen and saw three riders coming at a trot towards the house. The Chevalier and Colonel Byrd went at once to meet them, while I directed our two Captains of Militia another way and then followed the Chevalier at a little distance. The three riders had dismounted, though it was impossible in the darkness to make out their features. One of them stood a little in front of the other two and it was to this first man that the Chevalier had gone forward alone. Yet what was most striking was that the Chevalier was kneeling before the stranger.

29 May 1760. I was not presented to the Prince Charles Edward last night, for none in the house except the Chevalier and Colonel Byrd knew of his arrival. This morning the Chevalier told me what all the world must soon know, that when we talked of the dangers of the Prince crossing from France the Chevalier knew that His Royal Highness was already in Virginia in the character of a private gentlemen (as the London papers foretold) and that he had been so for some time.

This afternoon I was brought by Colonel Byrd and Lord Elibank (who with the young Lord Caryll had accompanied the Prince) to the library at Westover. There, at the Prince's command, I was presented. Charles Edward sat at the far end of the room but rose as I came in and walked forward in an easy and familiar manner, so that I could hardly kneel before I was obliged to stand again. All that men spoke of the dignity of his bearing and fineness of features is true. The tall forehead, dark eyes, clear skin, and handsomeness of profile distinguish him so nobly as to make all disguise impossible. This must increase the peril to him in our present undertaking. His voice, too, has something of the Scots in it but is also tempered by the softness of French or Italian, which makes him easily recognised.

If he seemed hardly older than at Culloden, this was not his appearance but his easy manner. He smiled often and frowned seldom. There was a quickness of humour in him and an eagerness for the new adventure, which had the mark of a man in his first youth. He led me aside and was kind enough to compliment me upon the conduct of my kinsmen at the time of Culloden and upon my own support for his present cause. I expressed my admiration for the intrepidity of his own behaviour, first in the Highlands and now on the frontiers of the New World.

'Why, Captain Fraser,' said he, 'I will tell you something in confidence which I would not tell everyone. I believe I would rather live in the Highlands or on the Ohio River with my followers than in any court of Europe. For all the dangers, I think I was never happier than in Scotland with a price of £30,000 on my head. What do you suppose, by the way, became of that money when the Elector of Hanover could find no one to reward with it?'

'Having begged it from his masters, sir, I am sure he has done the justice of returning it to his mistresses,' said I.

'There you have it!' said the Prince. 'Tell me, though, this Virginian land goes straight to a man's heart, does it not? My friend in Switzerland, Monsieur Rousseau, would make a new religion of nature. Yet if he is to worship at the true temple, he must come with me to the Ohio or the Allegheny mountains. But it is easy enough, Mr Fraser – is it not? – to be a prince and play at shepherds and shepherdesses. Yet how sad to be a shepherd that longs to play the prince.'

He seemed melancholy for a moment, so that I said, to divert him, 'Have you already been as far as the Ohio, sir?'

'We have seen something of that way,' said His Highness, 'for that is where our clansmen must come if they would interpose between us and the French army. It is said in England, Mr Fraser, that I am the creature of the French court. God knows how any man who has known it so well as I, expected so much and received so little, could ever be its creature.'

Then we took another turn towards our companions and the Prince said, 'We must ride to Fredericksburg tomorrow, Mr Fraser, to do what we can against General Bougainville. I hope you will ride with us.'

'I think I can answer for Mr Fraser, sir,' said the Chevalier. 'He is of our party and will accompany us.'

'Your servant, sir,' said His Highness, 'but in my party every man must answer for himself.' Then he laughed at the Chevalier and clapped a hand on his shoulder so that his friend should not feel put down.

There was never a prince in whom it seemed so natural to please, or who appeared at such ease among his companions. By his appearance and manner he seems set fair to win the hearts of all honest Virginians, particularly those of the gentle sex.

30 May 1760. Colonel Byrd will remain with the Virginia regiments at Westover to prevent any direct French advance upon Williamsburg. The Prince, the

Chevalier, Mr Ogilvie and I (who are both promoted Colonels by the Prince's commission) are to ride a hundred miles across country to Fredericksburg on the Rappahannock River, where we may meet with the French and attempt a parley, since we cannot offer battle. Young Lord Caryll accompanies us, while Lord Elibank remains in attendance upon Major Shaw and the Royal Americans. Their three hundred men are to follow us as soon as may be, so that we may secure the road between Fredericksburg and Westover.

Last night, in discussing our plans, the Prince gave us his estimate of the French.

'If General Bougainville wishes to take all Virginia,' said he, 'they must seize Williamsburg and reach the sea at Hampton. They may advance directly by the James River, where we will leave the army of Virginia to deny them the way. Yet they may choose to seize Fredericksburg instead and take the northern route by the Rappahannock River. We must scout well, gentlemen, for if they are on the Rappahannock our soldiers must turn north, to meet them there.'

At first light, our little party with two guides and a single troop of Virginia Cavalry (and that at less than full strength, being only thirty men) rode out of Westover towards the Rappahannock River. The Prince, Colonel Ogilvie, and I rode ahead of the troops, for there were still no more than a dozen men in Virginia who knew that Charles Edward was anything but a private gentleman. He sat upon his horse with his wig as neatly tied and powdered, his cuffs as spotless, as if it had been a military review at St Germain. The Chevalier rode behind us, commanding the main body of horsemen. Major Shaw and the Royal Americans, marching on foot, were to start later and could not be expected to draw level with us until the following day.

Between the rivers, the country grew wilder. The road

was good enough in most parts even for carriages, however, and before nightfall we had reached and crossed the hills that lie to the north of King William County, putting the greater part of our journey behind us. By the advice of the Chevalier and our guides, the Prince agreed that we should presently halt for the night, since we might miss the French by continuing our march in the dark.

As the light was fading, I found something amiss with my horse, making him seem a little lame, and I fell behind the others, promising to make up the distance as soon as I could. After riding a little way on my own, I found that the path forked and looking carefully at the ground, which however was quite dry, I concluded that their direction lay by the left fork. I followed this in the darkness for an hour, without a sign of them, and resolved to go no further until daybreak. Then I saw a fire about two or three hundred yards ahead of me and I approached it cautiously, knowing it could hardly be our army and fearing that it might be the French picket line. To my surprise, I found only three Indian women and a boy, who were as much amazed as I was.

Since neither of us understood the language of the other, I could put no questions to them. I marked the direction of my path on the ground, made a small channel in the earth and poured it full of water, and then lit a fire beside it. I lay down by the side of the fire and prepared to pass the night. I feared nothing from the Indian women, though I would have given a great deal to know what they had seen, in the way of soldiers, passing that spot.

While I rested, the youngest girl, a copper-skinned maiden whose blossoming charms were not altogether veiled by her costume, approached me. She unsaddled my horse, unstrapped the belt, hobbled him, and turned him out. Then she spread my blankets before the fire and made signs for me to sit down. The oldest woman, whose beauty had already reached the fall of the leaf, made me a little hash of dried venison and bear's oil, which eats very well, though without either bread or salt.

After this supper they made signs that I should go to sleep. I lay under my blanket and heard them whispering together. This made me a little uneasy for I did not know what mischief they might intend. There were sad tales of the fate of our men who had been taken by the Indians and given to the women for their amusement. The barbarities inflicted by these amazons, with splinters, knife, and hot iron, upon their poor members were such as to make one feel faint at the mere recital of the deeds.

At last the two eldest women and the boy lay down beyond the fire, at some little distance from me. The youngest girl, she who had taken so much pains with my horse, came and sat down near me. I could not help thinking she must have some amorous design upon me. In about half an hour she began to creep nearer and pulled at my blanket. I saw what she wanted and lifted it up, so that she might slide in naked beside me. She had taken off her Indian costume and the exact shape of her body showed admirably clear as she moved against the light of the fire. She was young, handsome, and healthy with fine regular features and beautiful eyes. Unlike many of her sisters, she had not painted her body in any way.

The invitations which she made by postures and caresses were artful enough to rouse love to a most extraordinary degree and to maintain our joys at their zenith until the conclusion of the affair. In all things she appeared vigorous and determined, remaining as passionate afterwards as she had been before. She seemed to sleep little, only watching for a sign of wakefulness before goading me into the repetition of our willing toil. I considered how wise it was of the French King to offer a dowry to all his subjects in Canada who would take an Indian girl for a wife. No man could have asked for a better partner than mine and, truly, we may accomplish by love what we could not win in battle. As for the souls of the poor Indians, how sweet is this way of converting unbelievers.

That Indian ladies should offer their caresses in this manner, as a good and hospitable wife among our own people might offer her guest food and drink, must appear very extraordinary to those who never witnessed such a custom. Yet among the Prince's followers how many have owed their very deliverance to the arms of an obliging young mistress? Not to speak of His Highness in person, the Chevalier himself makes frequent reference to the charming Peggy, who hid him under the eyes of the ministerial spies when he fled to London from the field of Culloden.

It is not in the nature of a soldier's life that he should enjoy the softer companionship of the fair sex as though he were by his own hearth. Such drabs as most of the soldiers' women are cannot but disgrace their whole species. We are more fortunate in our sweet Indian maids, whose simple and unfeigned pleasures must delight a man's heart. What endearments they cry in our ears we cannot tell, when they speak no language but their own. Yet their caresses and soft embraces make all other endearments seem ill-bestowed.

That the Chevalier should have a wife and a fine son is by good fortune, for most of those who fled the defeat of our army in the '45 were hardly allowed to rest anywhere long enough to hear the marriage banns. Our *amours* were brief and our departures sudden. In all that time I was never with any mistress more than three weeks together, my longest dalliance being with Miss Betsy on our voyage from New York to Hampton.

We two lived every day and night securely in our cabin, she having the finest skin, the darkest eyes, and the most tumbling raven curls that could be imagined. While the light of the sconce trembled on the wooden walls, she stood in the pure costume of Eve, anointed from nape to ankle with oil of jasmin. As in a May game, she would run, stooping and stretching in the candlelight, to gather dried petals of rose that were scattered upon the floor, the flame revealing her changing postures. Then, as we played and rolled like two puppy-dogs, she would cry, 'My heart, my soul, my sweetest rogue!' She was quick to grow warm and beautiful in the deed of kind, yet she had not the simple complaisance and innocent art of my young Indian squaw.

31 May 1760. At first light, my bedfellow went into the woods and caught her horse and mine. She saddled them, put my blanket on the saddle and prepared everything with a great deal of apparent good nature, positively refusing my assistance. The old woman got me some dried venison for breakfast. I made them understand that I was bound for Fredericksburg, which name they seemed to know, and before taking my leave I returned thanks to them as well as I knew how by signs. My bedfellow insisted on being my guide and conducting me through the woods, where there was no sign of a path. After half an hour we came within sight of the camp which our troop of cavalry had made. She talked to me all the way in Indian, which I attempted to repeat, thereby causing her a great deal of amusement. I was loath to part from her and she, moreover, looked forlorn at the prospect of separation. Yet I could not take her among so many soldiers, for there is only one end to Indian women there. Through one of our guides, I made her understand that I would come this way again on our return from Fredericksburg and would resume our acquaintance. When the Chevalier heard this, he nodded wisely and remarked, 'Why, sir, you have done the very thing every sensible man should do. For if you do not take a squaw in this country, you will be importuned by every Indian woman you meet, most of whom will be neither so young nor so handsome as this. Yet I promise you they are a more handsome people than the English.'

I wondered if the Prince, whose success among the fair sex was so universal, had by now conquered the heart of some Indian maid.

As we rode on, I could not help reflecting that it was one year ago to the day that General Wolfe had made his attempt at Louisberg, where we had been beaten back by the fire of the French. I wondered whether we should suffer the same fate at Fredericksburg. In the middle of the day we saw the Rappahannock River lying in sunlight below us. It is wider than I thought and one might sail a good-sized vessel up towards the town. Fredericksburg itself appears larger than I expected, having become used to such small Virginian settlements, for its buildings are well scattered.

Our little army approached but there was no sign of either the French nor the townspeople. Several dogs barked in the distance but an awful stillness hung over the houses. Our thirty troopers followed us, two by two, as we rode closer. Then a man's voice called from the dead town but what his words were or in what language he spoke, it was impossible to tell. The Chevalier halted our little troop of cavalry and approached the Prince.

'There can be no going on towards the town yet, sir,' he said abruptly, perplexing the Prince as to which of them held the command.

'Do you say so?' said His Highness.

'I do, sir, for there may be one man or there may be an army lying in ambush among those houses. I advise a flag of truce, sir. Let us go forward under that.'

'No flag ever protected a man from an ambush, Colonel Johnstone,' said the Prince a little peevishly, 'yet I see you will have it so. Then you and I shall go forward together.'

The Chevalier shook his head.

'That cannot be, sir. You must stay here. If there is an ambush laid, your loss would be the end of all our hopes.'

'I see you are determined to command, Colonel Johnstone,' said the Prince, turning the matter into a jest, 'and I must obey you. You shall take Colonel Fraser with you, while Colonel Ogilvie and Caryll remain with me here.'

The Chevalier chose a trooper to bear the makeshift flag of truce. Then the three of us put spurs to our horses and crossed the open plain towards the town, at a canter. I recalled how close the French had let us come at Louisberg before their sharpshooters began to play upon us, and I wondered if they were waiting their time now. For all that, we rode past the first buildings without being prevented in any way.

The principal street of the town is about half a mile in length with some little distance between the houses, which are sometimes wood and sometimes brick with blue wooden slates. The street was barricaded at certain points but we rode almost as far as St George's Church, before we reined in close to the council chamber, the gallows, and the pillory. It was as if the town had been destroyed by the plague, for we saw the bodies of two men lying beside a building and another not far from the church. Yet as we dismounted we were met by two men, who belonged to no army, coming from the council chamber. These were two of the citizens of Fredericksburg, one of them a tall, dour-looking man with dark eyes. The Chevalier watched this man closely as he walked towards us, while his companion kept a brace of pistols pointed at our breasts. Then to my astonishment the Chevalier said, 'Why, Dr Mercer, is this any way to greet a clansman who was your comrade-in-arms at Culloden?'

The melancholy man looked in astonishment at us both.

'The Chevalier James de Johnstone, sir,' said the Chevalier, bowing slightly, 'now, as then, aide-de-camp to Prince Charles Edward. Your servant, sir.'

'You have come in the service of the French. Be damned to you!' said the man with the pistols, whose name proved to be John Cameron.

'We have come to fight the French, sir, if that should be necessary,' said the Chevalier. 'May I present, Dr Mercer, Colonel Lovat Fraser, son of the ever-honoured Simon, Lord Lovat.'

There was a pause, then Hugh Mercer, who like so many of our people had been transported here after Culloden, came forward and embraced us both warmly. John Cameron lowered his pistols and they told us a dismal tale. The French army, under General Bougainville, had marched from the Ohio and camped close to Fredericksburg. When a detachment of French cavalry had approached the town, Mercer and some of the citizens had taken muskets and fired upon them, killing two or three. In revenge, the French had ridden upon the town, like the horsemen of the Apocalypse, burning several buildings and killing almost fifty of the inhabitants.

Last night, Hugh Mercer, who had been an officer as well as a surgeon at Culloden, took the command. It was resolved that the men of the town should escort their womenfolk and children to the estate of Belvidere, seven or eight miles down the river, for the French had sworn to return and take the town with their entire army. Then the people of Fredericksburg might look for no mercy from the dragoons of France. Yet there had been no escape, for as soon as the column of women and children was prepared a party of French cavalry had been seen crossing the road which runs from Fredericksburg to Belvidere.

At once, the Chevalier instructed me to remain with Hugh Mercer while he rode back to the Prince. Mercer and John Cameron took me inside the market house, where a throng of women and children pressed around me, seeking news of the French. The pick of their militia, fifty husbands, sons, and fathers with their muskets, stood by the doors and windows, prepared for what must be the final attack. These men looked sad and without hope, for there had been little means of defence against the French marauders last night. The women were dispirited and some wept to see their homes, their few possessions and their lives forfeit to the French. I was surprised to find how many families there had been driven from the Highlands after Culloden and who well know the fate that befalls the conquered. Some cursed the French and others cursed the English government which had determined to take their bread from them, as they said, and had then left them to the mercy of an enemy.

I swore to these that I and my thirty companions would not desert them, for we had been of the same party at Culloden and would now conquer or perish with them. Then came the sound of a single horseman in the street, which was Colonel Ogilvie. We spoke privately and he told me that the Prince was resolved what should be done. His Highness, the Chevalier, and Lord Caryll would take ten troopers each and scout that night for the French. As soon as their army was found, news would be brought to us and a safe road out of Fredericksburg might be chosen for its womenfolk and their children.

1 June 1760. We passed a wretched night, expecting at any moment to hear the hooves of the French cavalry driving towards us. Our townsmen stood to arms the entire time, occupying as many houses as they might. Some hours before dawn those who slept were woken by several musket shots from close to the Rising Sun Tavern near the river. Colonel Ogilvie and I investigated this at once. There we found a man and all his family weltering in their blood, their house burning and an order of the day scattered far and wide in the name of General Bougainville. The people of Fredericksburg, says the General, have violated the code of war by taking up the sword as civilians, and must therefore die by the sword as an example to the other towns of Virginia that they may not resist the French. The dead man was a close neighbour of Hugh Mercer and it may be that the French cavalry believed that it was Mercer and his family whom they were butchering.

A little while after dawn, a trooper from the Lord Caryll's party came riding like a madcap into the town with news that the French, some 3,000 strong, were camped last night no more than ten miles west of Fredericksburg and that they make preparations to march upon the town today. Our womenfolk and children must be despatched to Belvidere and thence to Williamsburg with all possible speed. We made arrangements at once for as many as possible to go by the wagons, while others went by boats from the wharves, and those who could go no other way would walk. Yet even before these plans could be realised a message from the Chevalier's troop informed us that the Régiment de Guyenne (which we remembered from Quebec) had got round us and was across the road to Belvidere, no more than five miles from Fredericksburg. Their guns commanded the river itself, so that all evacuation was now impossible.

Here was weeping and wailing from some of the women, and despair in the hearts of the men. The French army enclosed us with 3,000 men, while the army of Virginia was with Colonel Byrd at Westover, a hundred miles from us. Our consolation was that both the Prince and the Chevalier might live to fight another day, though we had no word of Charles Edward and his ten soldiers since yesterday. In the market house, where we guarded the women and children, the heat of the day, the great crowd, and the noise and stench added to the misery. Colonel Ogilvie and I had as much as we could do to keep the swarms of flies off us.

'I did not think', said Ogilvie, 'that we should fight the French again, for it was they who allowed us to come to Virginia.'

'It is not for that we may fight them,' said I. 'The French now find the game is altered, since their victory over the English is greater than they supposed. Now they would take Virginia first and then install Charles Edward as their pensioner. But he would secure Virginia with its frontiers intact, and then damnation to the French and Hanover alike.'

About noon, Colonel Ogilvie and I rode out to a small bluff which overlooked the town and from which we might see the first sign of the French. Ogilvie swept the land with his spy glass, saying, 'I should give something to have our three hundred Royal Americans with us now, or even our thirty troopers.'

'As to that,' said I, 'we may continue to hope. If we can warn the people of the first sign of the French approach, and if they fight valiantly enough we may yet delay the issue until nightfall. Then there may be some means of escape.' We chose to speak in this manner to give heart both to ourselves and to the citizens of Fredericksburg.

Our position was concealed by a plum thicket, which also afforded us a little shade from the heat of noon. We were on our mettle, however, and in little more than an hour saw a light-coloured curtain of dust drifting upon the horizon towards the west, where we heard the French camp lay.

'Those are their cavalry,' said Ogilvie, 'and they may reach us in half an hour if they choose. Will you ride into the town and raise the alarm while I stay here?'

'By all means,' I said, and putting spurs to my horse I made the best of it into Fredericksburg. It was easy to imagine what my reception would be there. Men feared so greatly for their families that they would have thrown away their muskets and asked pardon from General Bougainville that instant, if such a thing had been possible. I went to the market house and there met John Cameron, whose face was as long as any other. Hugh

Mercer had taken a small party of men to the Kenmore estate on the edge of the town, where the French might most easily invade us.

The dust of the approaching column grew so tall that we soon saw it from the town itself. Every street was now deserted and the silence of death settled over the buildings once more. There was no sound in the market house among the refugees, except for the wailing of a single child, terrified at it knew not what.

I wondered if Ogilvie was still safe on his bluff, for I had expected him soon. Already we could hear the first strokes of the drums and the music of their army. John Cameron looked closely at me.

'Do you hear?' he asked.

'I hear them,' said I, 'though I take little enough pleasure in their music.'

'But do you hear?' he said intently, and listened again.

I tried to distinguish what other sound there might be, apart from the music. Yet it was the music which John Cameron listened to, for he began to sing to it as it drew closer.

> 'Oh, it's hame, hame, hame,
>   And it's hame I wadna be,
> Till the Lord call King James
>   To his ain country. . . .'

'Sons of whores!' said one near by, 'for the French to take our songs from us!'

'French be damned!' said another. 'Those are the pipes!'

And so they were. For a moment there was bewilderment among the people but soon the voices were clearer and the words unmistakable.

> 'Bid the wind blow frae France
>   And the Firth keep the faem,
> And Lochgarry and Lochiel
>   Bring Prince Charlie hame. . . .'

After that there was a fury of excitement, especially among our own people. Men and women who a moment before had expected nothing but a bullet or a knife now felt the promise of safety. Yet I alone could guess why the pipes of the Highland regiment should be playing the forbidden music of the 'Jacobite' cause. I went outside and was no sooner in the street than I saw Colonel Ogilvie, riding as if the devil was at his tail with a hot spit.

'They are coming from the west,' he cried, 'the Highland Regiment and two squadrons of cavalry.'

'Cavalry?' said Cameron with disbelief. Colonel Ogilvie dismounted and turned to him.

'Fitzjames's Horse and the Life Guards of Prince Charles Edward. I may tell you now what everyone will know in half an hour, and what our friend Dr Mercer has known since yesterday. Fredericksburg is not to be saved by the upstart Elector of Hanover but by Prince Charles Edward, who has been in Virginia some time and whose army is now gathering to protect the Province from the forces of France.'

After a moment's hesitation, this news spread with the speed of fire. The faces of many of our own people showed a double joy, while those who had been born in Virginia and had never expected to see a nobleman of any kind, much less a prince, were overcome by curiosity and anticipation at seeing the grandson of King James II. Men and women now ran out of their houses and swept along the street towards the edge of the town, where the Highlanders approached. At the head of the little army rode the Life Guards, no more than a hundred of them but each one in a scarlet tunic, the sun flashing on his helmet and scabbard, forged in Virginia itself.

We did not then know what we afterwards discovered, that while the Chevalier and Lord Caryll searched out the French the Prince and his ten troopers had ridden hard to the west to find the Highlanders with their little escort of cavalry, who were then just this side of the mountains that lie between here and Winchester. The French had ordered things so that the clansmen should not arrive in Virginia until long after General Bougainville had done his business. Yet with the Prince at their head, Fraser's men marched all yesterday, the greater part of last night, and today to reach Fredericksburg by skirting the French army. The 'Jacobite' cavalry showed little sign of its forced journey but the poor Highlanders must have felt the lack of food and rest very severely.

With the Prince at their head on a dappled grey horse, his wig tied and powdered, his Highland dress as fine as it ever was, the column passed between the excited mob on either side of the road. Women ran out from the houses with bowls of milk, though they had little enough, for the foot soldiers to drink. Charles Edward soon dismounted and went forward among the crowd, pausing to greet 'my own people' as he called them, to comfort them and assure them of their safety.

At the market house, the throng was so great that he stood on a small cart for them to see him. There was a great cheering, for they would have cheered the devil himself if he had only rescued them from the French. When there was a pause, His Highness said bravely:

'Virginia may yet be the friend of France, but while I live I swear she shall be no man's vassal, either Frenchman or Hanoverian.'

At this there were more hearty hurrahs for 'Prince Charlie and his brave boys'. The Highlanders marched on through the applauding crowd. Their main force, under Colonel Simon Fraser, took up their positions of battle with Hugh Mercer (now once more a Stuart Captain by the Prince's commission) on the southern edge of the town. Here the French might best be met. The extreme feeling for the Prince and his men, beyond all rationality, may be judged by the speed with which the white cockade, worn at first only by his soldiers, was improvised by the citizens and appeared on all sides. His Life Guards were hard put to it to rescue him from the eager adulation, so that he might superintend our battle preparations. Life was never sweeter to men and women than when it had been so nearly lost to the French.

The events of this memorable day moved swiftly, for a little past two in the afternoon came the Chevalier and his ten horsemen from Belvidere with news that the Régiment de Guyenne had decamped from their position and were marching to the south to join the main body of the French army which was grouping to attack the town of Fredericksburg.

I was fortunate enough to be with the Prince and his party when this news was brought. His Highness gave orders at once.

'Colonel Johnstone, we must prevent this battle, for this is neither the place nor the contest that we seek. Yet, if it must be, I would fight rather than yield the town to the French. You and I shall parley with General Bougainville. Colonel Fraser will accompany us. We shall take no others.'

I was honoured by His Highness's choice, though I felt that it was the chance of being present just then rather than my own merits which made me one of the Prince's counsellors.

The heat of the afternoon in this climate makes one think of Spain or the Kingdom of Naples rather than England. The horizon to our south, beyond which lay the might of the French, wavered in the intense light, and the red clay appeared parched. We rode out beyond the lines of the Highland regiment and the Prince's troop of Life Guards into the stillness and the heat. The land and the fields seemed abandoned by all human creatures, where all that broke the silence was the beat of our horses' hooves.

In a while we saw the massive outline of the French,

their regiments drawn up exactly, stretching to left and right in a most formidable array. I could not doubt that their army was two or three times the size of our little force. The colours of their regiments flew bravely in the sunlight above the white and grey uniforms. As we rode closer, a bugle sounded and two of their horsemen came out to meet us. The Chevalier then demanded our safe-conduct to General Bougainville in the name of the Prince, as Regent for his father, James III. This was quickly granted and we were led through the French lines (where men turned to regard us very curiously) to where General Bougainville's tent had just been pitched.

The General is a man somewhat advanced in years and coarsened by the campaigns of Canada and the Ohio. He rose to greet us with great deference and a wealth of compliments exchanged with the Prince and the Chevalier.

'We come in peace, monsieur,' said the Prince at last, 'for I promise you that Virginia is no enemy to France.'

General Bougainville was pleased to hear it and wished only that our troops would stand a little out of the way, so that he might march to the sea and take Williamsburg for the Prince.

'Virginia is no man's enemy, sir,' said the Prince sternly, 'but nor will she be any man's vassal.'

There was much more argument of this sort, until the General swore positively that he must march to the sea.

'And be shot for your pains, as General Wolfe was?' asked the Prince. 'If you would march to the sea, you must fight us first. If you fight us here, you will surely be destroyed and your position on the Ohio will be lost. All the Elector of Hanover's force will be turned against France in New England and by next spring you will be clapped up in Quebec again without hope of rescue.'

General Bougainville smiled and shook his head.

'You may smile, sir,' said the Prince, 'yet I offer you more than you can ever gain in battle. Consider, sir, there is an army before Fredericksburg, there is another behind you where General O'Sullivan will deny you supplies from your own people. Even should you defeat both, there is the army of Virginia between you and the sea. Yet you have it in your power to win Virginia for France more securely than by any battle. Would you, then, unite against you the very people who might be your friends?'

As His Highness was arguing earnestly with the General, one of Bougainville's aides-de-camp entered the tent, where our negotiators sat on either side of a plain trestle table. The General begged us to excuse him for a moment and then withdrew.

'It is a great chance, sir,' said the Chevalier doubtfully to the Prince.

'So it is,' said His Highness, 'but while we talk here our little army at Fredericksburg may grow. The longer we talk, the more time there will be for our friends to join us.'

After a few minutes longer, General Bougainville returned and his face seemed a little sad.

'What is it you propose?' he asked.

For all this sudden change, the Prince remained prepared to pursue his purpose.

'Peace,' said His Highness, 'between the territories of France and the territories of Virginia. You, sir, shall withdraw your army to the Ohio and retain your own lands, we shall retain ours. If the Elector of Hanover chooses to fight you still, you may face him in New England with your entire army and we shall be your friends. The representatives of Monsieur Vaudreuil, as Governor of New France, and those of our own people shall meet and conclude a treaty of peace for our frontiers. Virginia and those provinces who become allied to her will then fight you no more and will be no hirelings of the Elector of Hanover. In short, sir, France may become more secure in America than she ever anticipated.'

General Bougainville seemed not to consider the

proposal for long before civilly promising to convey it to Monsieur Vaudreuil. In the meantime, he undertook to march his troops back to the Ohio River. I was dumbfounded at this last concession, never imagining the General would give ground, and could not conceive why he should have yielded to the Prince. Indeed, I wondered if he and the Prince had perhaps been in league over the whole matter for some little while.

We parted from the French officers with a great exchange of compliments and rode back towards our own men. On our arrival we found a greater state of excitement than ever, for while we had been parleying with the French Lord Elibank, Major Shaw and the three hundred foot soldiers of the Royal Americans had crossed the final hill and marched bravely down into Fredericksburg. Yet, what was more, Lord Caryll's troop rode into the town later in the day and brought news of General O'Sullivan's Irish brigade, which crossed the Potomac at Harper's Ferry yesterday and are to camp tonight in Prince William County, half a day's march from Fredericksburg.

We guessed then what it was that had been told General Bougainville during our parley and which had made him so suddenly apt for peace. Surprised to find our little army before Fredericksburg, which he had thought an undefended prize, he was then perturbed to hear of a second army from the Potomac closing on his left. (For he must have had news of General O'Sullivan as soon as we.) Then, even while we parleyed, his scouts could not help but see the regiment of Royal Americans marching on his right, and must have concluded this to be the vanguard of a third force. Believing himself menaced on three sides, the General was obliged to fight or turn back. Being so far from his own people, and having the greater part of the French army at stake, he declined the wager of battle.

It is considered by the Prince that we should remain in

Fredericksburg until the arrival of General O'Sullivan and that the day after tomorrow our Royal army should set out for Williamsburg, where we must determine to win all or nothing. Lord Elibank has brought two omens, neither of them favourable. The first is that news reached Westover, after our departure, of Lord Loudoun and a retinue of English officers having landed in Williamsburg to govern Virginia 'as it deserves'. Our second omen is the first prisoner of the campaign, who met the Royal Americans as he rode from Fredericksburg. Thinking them the Elector of Hanover's men, he announced himself to Major Shaw as being on his way to Williamsburg to rouse the town and the militia against a 'Jacobite rabble' which had invested Fredericksburg.

The wretch was summarily escorted back to Fredericksburg and lodged in the town gaol as a spy. When he was brought before a summary court-martial in the market house, where the Chevalier, Colonel Ogilvie and I sat, we knew him for the solemn-faced gentleman who came aboard our vessel as we left her at Hampton. He is Lemuel Bradstreet, a New England trader. The Chevalier was severe enough in demanding what the man had to say for himself, which was little indeed. Then the Chevalier instructed a sergeant and two private soldiers of the Royal Americans to make serviceable the gallows in the market place.

The wretched man began to tremble and turned pale, being repeatedly assured by the Chevalier that he should not be kept waiting long. Meanwhile, the Prince observed the gallows work going ahead and came to inquire what might be the reason for it. He was shown Bradstreet, who crouched in a corner, canting and praying. His Highness encouraged the man to stand up.

'So, sir,' said he, 'you are my enemy?'

The wretch shook his head, swallowing but unable to speak.

'Then,' said His Highness severely, 'you shall see how I treat an enemy.'

And here he put a little gold upon the table, at which Lemuel's eyes grew brighter, for all his fear.

'Take it, sir,' said the Prince, 'and go to London with it, or to Boston, and tell the Elector of Hanover's men of the barbarities you have received at my hands. Or take it, sir, and remain here to serve me. Yet serve me faithfully, or else you may fall into peril again.'

So the poltroon went on his knees to the Prince (though first snatching up the coins) and blubbered his allegiance until he was raised to his feet and led away to be given his supper. The Prince left us, and the Chevalier turned to me with a frown.

'Mark my words, sir,' said he angrily, 'no good ever came of pampering up a snivelling rebel!'

It was arranged that the Prince should lie tonight at Kenmore, the handsome red-brick plantation house of Fielding Lewis, which stands in an estate of eight hundred acres on the verge of Fredericksburg. The richly moulded ceilings and the great crystal chandeliers might have been the envy of any gentleman in Scotland or England.

Our party was most hospitably received by the mistress of the house, one Elizabeth Washington. As we sat at table, she talked to the Prince of the late war and the part played in it by her own brother, George, who had been commander of the soldiers of the Province, and had come off with distinction from the ill-fated expedition of General Braddock some years since. His Highness, who had already learnt of these things through Colonel Byrd's close friendship with Colonel Washington, only expressed a polite wish that he might one day hear of these exploits at first hand from the gallant gentleman.

The remainder of the evening passed pleasantly enough with toasts, country dancing, and the songs of the good old cause. The Prince danced every dance with a skill and grace that drew admiration from the ladies. When the songs were sung, His Highness gave us 'This is not my ain house', to the delight of all. It is generally agreed by those who know him best that his conduct exhibits a gaiety and confidence that was not found in him when his victorious army was marching from Edinburgh to Derby fifteen years ago.

3 June 1760. Having allowed a day to pass for the arrival of General O'Sullivan and his Irish soldiers, we prepared to march at dawn today for Williamsburg. Three hundred of the Highlanders under Colonel Simon Fraser are left to guard Fredericksburg and Lord Elibank is left by the Prince as Governor of the town. Captain Hugh Mercer busies himself in raising a local militia loyal to the Stuart cause. We left with lighter hearts, for yesterday morning our scouts brought us news that the whole of the French army had decamped at first light and were marching westwards towards the Ohio and their own territories.

Our force, more than 2,000 strong, took the road for Williamsburg with General O'Sullivan and all his vanity as part of the Prince's entourage. The General is an excellent soldier but with more fineness than the polish of a gentleman requires. He is, I believe, a little put out that the Chevalier de Johnstone is also named a General of the Prince's army. We had hardly begun our march when the Chevalier reproached him lightly with allowing his Irishmen to lag behind a little. General O'Sullivan first protested at a slur upon the honour of his corps, then threatened to retire to bed. He was so nice in all his conduct that the Chevalier turned about, muttering, 'Whip-stitch, sir, your nose in my britch!'

None of this becomes a pair of general officers.

The army set forth with the Prince's party and the hundred Life Guards leading it and making a brave display. Fitzjames's Horse, a hundred strong, rode next, followed by a company of English gentlemen exiles on foot. These were followed by the Highlanders with their pipes and songs, the three hundred Royal Americans, and General O'Sullivan's men, who for all their Irish names often spoke with the accent of France. The remainder of the horses were spared for the dozen small field pieces, two brass cannon, and the baggage wagons, which formed the rearguard of the army.

The Highlanders had been most severely admonished and told that they were not passing through conquered territory, so that any offence against the people or property of Virginia would be answered by summary punishment. Yet there was scarcely need for this, since the news of our coming sped before us and the people greeted us as their saviours from the French. At every settlement along the way the inhabitants turned out to admire the Prince and his brave men, applauding our army as it passed. Many were our own people, brought here as prisoners after the '45, so that there were several joyful reunions between them and certain of the Highlanders. Indeed, when the Chevalier and I rode back to the rear, as we prepared to camp for the night, we were astonished to find that our army had collected one or two hundred followers, who were destined to march with us into Williamsburg.

4 June 1760. As we drew close to the more populous banks of the James River, our progress appeared more like a triumphal procession than an army on the march. The people heard of the departure of the French, the promised end of the war, and the determination of the Prince that they should neither be oppressed nor taxed by the representatives of the Elector of Hanover. Many were so happy to have their lives and their lands secure that they would have cheered for the devil himself at the head of an army of his fiends. So much the greater was the admiration for the figure of the Prince on horseback, and for the gentle words which he spoke to them all as he passed.

Colonel Byrd had arranged our reception at Westover, where we camped at night to prepare for the march to Williamsburg. We found ourselves welcomed universally there as the liberators of Virginia. The Virginia militia, assured of their safety and that they might soon return to their homes and peaceful employments, cheered us to the echo. At night, Colonel Byrd provided a truly royal banquet under the stars, with roast pork, venison, every sort of fruit in season, and the wines of both France and Virginia. Afterwards we looked on while the Prince and the Colonel carved upon the trunk of a fine old oak the names 'Charles P.R.' and 'William Byrd III' adding underneath the date '4th of June 1760'.

6 June 1760. Today our march upon Williamsburg reached its conclusion. Though we were prepared for a battle rather than a royal entry into the town, our followers would not be turned back. Some gathered at the rear of our column, others ran along beside us, whooping and hollowing, while a few capered in front of us like tumblers at a carnival.

Before we reached the bridge into the town, where it crosses College Creek, the first of the inhabitants had come forth to stare at us. They appeared undecided as they silently watched our soldiers march past. There was a stillness over the whole town when the vanguard of the Prince's column approached the stately building of William and Mary College, which lies at one end of the principal street and marks the beginning of the town. At the Prince's command, our regiments halted and he rode forward with the Chevalier and me on either side of him.

A most extraordinary sight met our eyes. Down the great length of the street were two or three thousand men and women, packed on either side and standing silently. At a little distance, three horsemen of the English army rode towards us from the carriageway which leads off to the Governor's Palace. As our two parties drew closer, the Chevalier swore that it was Lord Loudoun and two of his officers, for he had seen his lordship at the time of Culloden. Both sides rode steadily forward and I became apprehensive that the Prince was now hemmed in by the silent crowd on both sides and might be destroyed by them or by Loudoun's officers before any rescue could be attempted. Yet His Royal Highness rode with the same charm and grace as if he had been at a levée. When no more than twenty or thirty paces separated the two parties, the Prince raised his hand and there was a general halt. Lord Loudoun began to unfold a scroll of paper.

'I pray you, sir,' said Prince Charles Edward, 'let us have none of these proclamations.'

Lord Loudoun appeared a soldier rather advanced in years but who had never lacked a good dinner and a bottle of wine.

'Sir,' said Lord Loudoun in a great voice, 'you and your followers are proclaimed rebels, and any man who aids you must pay the price of treason. This is given in the name of His Majesty King George.'

'Indeed, sir?' said the Prince coolly, 'then when I proclaim myself Elector of Hanover and seek to take Hanover from him by force of arms, let me be punished. When he, as Elector of Hanover, steals the Crown of England and Scotland from my father, James III, then it is your King George and his followers who are traitors, sir, not I and my soldiers.'

There was some interest in the crowd at this. Lord Loudoun looked again at his roll of paper and continued.

'For all your treason, sir, His Majesty the King is inclined to be merciful. You are to leave his dominions, sir, and take yourself wheresoever you will, first signing a declaration that you will never return. That, sir, is your safe-conduct.'

'And my soldiers?' asked the Prince.

'They must look to the King's mercy at a different time,' said Lord Loudoun gruffly.

His Highness looked hard at Lord Loudoun and said, 'Be so good as to convey my own offer to the Elector of Hanover. He is to quit my father's dominions at once, a safe-conduct being guaranteed him back to Hanover. There my father shall allow him ten thousand pounds a year to supply the needs of his pinchbeck monarchy.'

There was some amusement among the crowd at this reply but the Prince was in an angry frame of mind.

'Moreover,' said he, 'you may tell the Elector of Hanover that, should he refuse mercy, he shall taste justice at Tyburn, for the oppression he has inflicted upon my subjects in Scotland, in England, and now in Virginia with his cruel taxes and evil politics.'

'Very well, sir,' said Lord Loudoun in full voice, 'you have refused mercy. The English fleet might destroy you now if the order were given and, shortly, the might of English arms shall sweep you and your rabble from the Province of Virginia.'

With that, his lordship and his aides turned about and rode off down the street. I was a little troubled at the ease with which the Prince had named Englishmen, Scotsmen, and Virginians as his own subjects, as if rejecting the royal prerogative of his father, King James III. Yet some of the crowd's murmuring was now on his behalf, for he had shown how easily he rejected the offer of a safe-conduct which would have bought his own passage while leaving his followers to their destruction.

Charles Edward had come among the great crowd in a manner which showed that he trusted them as his friends. Seeing that he thought them his friends, a number of them determined to be such. They made way for him to stand at the top of some steps leading up to the door of a house, so that as many as possible might see him and hear his words. The Prince raised his hand.

'Your war is over,' he said. 'The French army, which was to have attacked Williamsburg in a few days, is sent packing to its own territory. My soldiers shall make sure that it never returns to plague Virginia again. Those of you who have fled here may return to your homes without fear of attack. Moreover, the gold which the Elector of Hanover would have taken from you to fight his war is returned to you, for the war is ended. Those ships, which he would have stolen from you, are yours again. The men, whom his soldiers would have taken from you and made to fight his Hanoverian war, are to be returned to their families.'

There was a murmuring at this, and then the Prince continued.

'To every man is given the liberty to live and speak as he chooses under the rule of law. To every man is guaranteed the freedom to practise whatsoever religion he may choose. To every man who wishes it there shall be given land in the territory now freed from the French, together with freedom of trade, that he may prosper there. Fate has forced me to learn that a prince must often live as an ordinary man. I am now determined to try the experiment whether ordinary men, in the new world of the Americas, may not all live like princes. I boast no less than this, but I can do nothing without your assistance. Will you not join me in this attempt?'

There was no resisting the charm and youthful vigour of his appeal, the person of a prince who would have made beggars' rags seem regal. For a moment his words hung heavily in the warm air. Then there was a stirring in the crowd and a score of voices shouted 'Aye!' Once these had done so, their neighbours judged it time to be shouting as well, and soon the muttering and roaring ran like fire among the whole crowd till it reached those who had been too far away to hear his words and had no idea what they were cheering for.

For all that, he was less enthusiastically received here than at Fredericksburg. Our troops were kept prudently camped outside the town and entered only in small parties. At night, Lord Loudoun quit the Governor's residence and made for Hampton, where he has gone on board a British sloop anchored in the James River. It is from here that he proposes to invade us when the time comes.

9 June 1760. The general mood of the town is a little improved, for they see that our soldiers come as their friends. The Prince has moved much among the people, all of whom are taken with his easy and generous manner, as well as the striking handsomeness of his person. Lord Loudoun having quit the Governor's Palace, His Royal Highness has taken up his residence there.

Much has been talked of the Prince's religion, yet he won many hearts on the morning after his entry into the town by attending the church of Bruton Parish, where a solemn *Te Deum* was sung for deliverance from the French. The next day, which was yesterday, also saw him rewarded with the people's favour for his martial valour. In the forenoon, two British sloops appeared in the James River, close to College Creek, and opened a bombardment, both upon our camp and upon several houses from that distance. At great risk to his own safety, the Prince ordered the assembling of our field pieces close by the shore, himself supervising the two brass cannon. He commanded much of the action and his long experience in Europe earned him the laurels when one of our salvoes hit the leading sloop (in which Lord Loudoun was) so hard that she began to go down by the stern. Lord Loudoun and his men were hastily taken to the other vessel and carried downstream. However, detachments of our army have been sent post to Hampton and to Norfolk, so it seems unlikely that his lordship will be able to put into any port of consequence in Virginia.

15 June 1760. Two vessels belonging to Virginia merchants both report that Lord Loudoun's sloop has cleared Cape Henry and so put out to sea. It is impossible he should go south, for there is extreme disorder in the Province of Carolina. Therefore, all conclude him to have sailed for New York, and so it may be that we have seen the last of the government of King George II.

The Prince's success in defending the town from bombardment has increased his popularity with the crowd. Last evening he attended the playhouse, where the play of *Lucius Junius Brutus* was performed in his honour, and he is much spoken to by the citizens, who find him amiable enough. The rump of the House of Burgesses is still closeted in the Capitol debating what should be done now that Lord Loudoun has gone and 2,000 of the Prince's troops are encamped by the James River. A few, who are consummate republicans, will never accept the Prince, yet many others are inclined to support whoever brings them peace and makes fewest demands upon their purses. They say that the House of Stuart could hardly be worse than the House of Hanover. It is expected that there will be a compromise, whereby the Prince or his father will be taken for Virginia's protectors, without saying if they be kings or not.

One may judge the general mood from what I heard in Williamsburg tonight. Passing by an open window I heard some who were Scots and some who were not trying out the newly arrived ballads. I could not help smiling at the strangeness of the words borne on the warm night air of Virginia and sung by some of those who had never seen Scotland nor, indeed, any part of Europe.

> 'Let the rivers stop and stand
>   Like walls on either side,
> Till our Highland lad pass through
>   With Jehovah for his Guide!

Dry up the River Forth
 As Thou didst the Red Sea,
When Israel came hame
 To his ain countrie.'

The Chevalier and General O'Sullivan may have brought Prince Charlie home, as the song says, and in a month or two the Ministry in London will hear of what has occurred. I would give a great deal to know what will happen then.

4

THE FRENCH PEACE

The next set of entries in Lovat Fraser's journal occurs after an interval of several weeks and describes the events leading up to negotiations with the French emissaries at Fredericksburg, in July and August 1760. The so-called 'French Peace', by which Virginia sought her own treaty with France, in defiance of Hanoverian England, seemed to put the Province still more certainly under the protection of Prince Charles Edward.

The army of George II in America was still fully occupied in fighting the French for possession of New England and the Hudson valley. It had no troops to spare for dealing with the 'treason' which was spreading through the southern provinces. Any action against Virginia had to be delayed until reinforcements should be sent from England. Since these reinforcements could no longer arrive in time for the summer campaigning season of 1760, Charles Edward seemed secure from external attack until the following spring. However, an opportunity was offered in the meantime to the agents of George II to exploit internal opposition to the Prince. This opposition began to show itself openly with the arrival of an unexpected visitor, who seemed to many Virginians to be the embodiment of all that was most suspect in the Royal House of Stuart.

8 July 1760. During the forenoon an express rode exhausted into Williamsburg from the north, bearing news that Lord Loudoun is landed in New York. There he bristles and threatens the traitors of Virginia, not that he hopes to terrify them but rather that the Ministry in London may see how little it was his fault that Charles Edward came to town as he did. His lordship swears that he will do such things that he does not know what they shall be, yet they will be the terror of the world.

'To say the truth,' remarked Colonel Ogilvie upon hearing this, 'Lord Loudoun is the very figure of St George upon the signboards. Always on horseback, but never rides on.'

'But yet', said I, 'it is not time for him to raise an army and march south upon us. He would find the winter come before so much could be done, and that would be no time for campaigning.'

'Your servant, sir!' said Ogilvie. 'And if he should delay still longer, he would come in the summer, and a great heat must follow. So that is no time to be campaigning either. In short, sir, there is no weather that is Lord Loudoun's weather.'

We were standing with the Chevalier, Lord Elibank, and Major Shaw of the Royal Americans in the shade of the Capitol's colonnade. It happened that these witnesses seized upon this last saying of Ogilvie's and it was decreed the fashion, for the future, that the hottest and most befleaed weeks of July should be named 'Lord Loudoun's weather'.

We were still in conversation as to what might be necessary to deny Lord Loudoun's army the passage of the Potomac and a road to Virginia, when Colonel Byrd and Lord Caryll reined in their horses, and dismounted. They were hot with the news that a Spanish merchantman had come to anchor in the York River and was even then discharging a cargo of weapons at Yorktown landing.

'Sir,' said the Chevalier sharply, 'I cannot conceive whose work this is, though it must be of our friends. Yet we must see to it that it does not benefit our enemies. I am for Yorktown at once, to take command of those weapons in the Prince's name, and bring them safely to the magazine here in Williamsburg. Mr Ogilvie, sir! And Mr Fraser! Will you keep me company there?'

We were ready enough to do that and not ten minutes later we rode out on fresh horses the dozen miles to Yorktown. A troop of the Prince's Life Guards came with us as escort for the precious cargo.

'There is a mystery, sir,' said the Chevalier to me as we rode, 'for how can a ship of Spain come so early as this? Neither in Spain nor in England do men yet know that the Prince is here. How do these gifts come so soon to us, and who is it that bears them?'

Neither Ogilvie nor I was wise enough to answer the riddle entire.

'Perhaps', said I, 'the ship comes from the Spanish New World, where they may know of the Prince by this time, as they do in New York.'

'Yes, sir,' said the Chevalier, 'but how did they know to have a ship ready in New Spain? Our plan for Virginia was known only to ourselves and to the close advisers of King James in Rome.'

When we reached Yorktown and rode down the bluff to the landing, we saw that Colonel Byrd had alarmed us more than was necessary. The ship, a large merchantman, the *Santa Caterina*, was indeed made fast but had not as yet begun to discharge her cargo. Our escort of Life Guards was told off to oversee the unloading of muskets and powder, and arrangements were made for the removal of the weapons by wagon to Williamsburg.

Captain Macinnes of the Life Guards received the Chevalier's orders to do all that was necessary. While they were talking, I was watching the ship and the Spanish seamen who came from it. Then I observed a gentleman with two servants, a man not yet of middle years, in a fine suit of black clothes. His wig was carefully powdered and tied, his profile one of great distinction, and the carriage of his head rather high. He came ashore and stood for a moment, looking about him. Then he walked towards the Life Guards with the slow, dignified pace of one accustomed to be received as a great lord. I felt that I should have known his face, and yet I did not. I was still more confused at seeing the same gentleman's coach swung across from the ship to the landing. It was a most handsome coach whose sides were like polished ebony. Upon the panel of the door was painted a design of the royal arms of Great Britain and France. Yet above the arms, where one might have looked for a crown, there was what appeared to be a cardinal's hat.

In a moment the Chevalier turned, and saw the same prospect. I could swear that he almost bit his tongue not to say something worse than he did. He spoke half to himself, yet loud enough for me to hear.

'Why is *he* come?' And then, '*Timeo Danaos et dona ferentes*. I fear the Greeks, Mr Fraser, even when they bring us gifts.'

I was still no wiser. Then the Chevalier went quickly over to the stranger and knelt to him, even going so far as to kiss his hand or one of the rings upon it. They exchanged some words and afterwards the Chevalier attended him towards the fine carriage, which had been made ready. As they passed not far from me, it seems that the Chevalier thought it proper that I should be presented to the stranger.

'Sir,' said he to his companion, 'Colonel Fraser has been of the Prince's party since Quebec and was lately with us at the affair of Fredericksburg.'

The black-suited stranger stopped and murmured something to the Chevalier about wishing to be better acquainted with me. The Chevalier stepped forward to me and said solemnly, 'Approach, sir, that I may present you to His Royal Highness, Henry Benedict, Prince of Great Britain, Duke of York, Cardinal and Vice-Chancellor of the Holy Roman Church, Cardinal-Bishop of Tusculum, Ostia, and Velletri.'

I knelt as he had done, wondering how to account for this sudden arrival of the Cardinal Duke of York, that Prince Henry who is the younger brother of Prince Charles Edward, and therefore next in line of succession to the throne.

'The service you have performed to me and my brother, sir,' said the Cardinal Prince, 'shall not be overlooked. You may be very well assured, sir, that these recent events are a great satisfaction and contentment to My Father and Myself.'

He spoke as one to whom English was a native tongue but who had never been accustomed to speak it except according to the accent of France or Italy.

'You will both', said he, turning to the Chevalier, 'give me the pleasure of accompanying me in my coach, so that you may inform me of my dear brother's latest success. I have had so much anxiety for him, while I waited with the ship at Trinidad. We sailed from Cadiz three months since, but could do nothing until a port in Virginia was open to us.'

As we rode with the Cardinal Prince in his well-appointed carriage, I complimented him a little awkwardly upon bringing us so useful a cargo at such a time as this.

'I bring more, sir,' said he, looking thoughtfully from the window at the groves and plantations, 'for I bear also the blessing of King James to his son. I am the messenger who shall go between them and unite them in heart. But I own, sir, that running before the Elector of Hanover's fleet with a cargo of powder and *fusils* is a greater care than being Bishop of Tusculum, Ostia, and Velletri.'

And here he burst out a-laughing, like a schoolboy who has contrived something behind his tutor's back. Though he is more thoughtful and generally more silent than Charles Edward, there is an amiability about him which hardly matches the stern title of a Cardinal Prince.

11 July 1760. The arrival of the Cardinal Prince, however well intentioned he may be, has done little good to our cause. Prince Henry and Prince Charles fell upon one another's necks in the Palace at Williamsburg and embraced as true brothers, yet the Chevalier swears that they never can be reconciled in their characters. The Prince is a soldier by disposition, and proud as Lucifer: the Cardinal is subtle and would do by diplomacy many of those things which his brother believes must needs be accomplished by the power of arms. Soon or late, says the Chevalier, the differences between them must appear.

Yet the worst is that those Virginians who shouted for Bonnie Prince Charles did not intend that their generosity of spirit should extend to being ruled over by a Prince of the Church. Among ourselves, we hardly know what is to be done. Colonel Byrd and Lord Elibank counsel patience, but the Chevalier is in such a mood as never I saw.

'Is all to be lost for this, sir?' he demands angrily. 'Have we come so far only to be turned back because the Duke of York will play Mercury the Messenger between Williamsburg and Rome? I tell you, sir, this is past all bearing!'

Even as we spoke, the children in the gardens of some houses were noisily playing the game, not unlike Blind Man's Buff, which they call here 'Break the Pope's Neck'. It is to be imagined the variations that are drawn from this theme. I was with Colonel Byrd at the race-path yesterday where, after the final wager, there appeared an old, lame horse, which someone had turned out on to the track. This poor, thin beast had a broken saddle upon its back, and a pillion behind it. It ambled round the path, where all might see it and might read the paper which was set upon its head.

'Let nobody stop me – I am the equipage of Prince Charles Edward, and I go to fetch him gold and whores from his masters, the Pope of Rome and the King of France.'

There was some murmuring in the crowd at this, but some laughter also. It was not discovered to whom the poor beast belonged that was made the innocent bearer of such calumnies.

Yet, what was more extreme, the very town itself seemed filled with lampoons and pasquinades. It is said that the players lately conceived a desire to present us *Othello* with the noble Moor in the costume of Prince Charles Edward, the wicked Iago in a black suit corresponding to the Cardinal's, and Desdemona as the very personification of ill-fated Virginia. Upon the expectation of a riot in the playhouse, this was not done, and perhaps it never was intended. So much is spoken of and so little proves true. But with my own eyes I saw the notice that was discovered this morning upon the gate of the Palace, having been fastened there by dark.

'Lost or strayed out of this house, the wits and sense of a self-elected man of honour who came a journey to call himself a Prince. Whoever shall bring word to the church-wardens of Bruton Parish that he and his brother, the Preaching Friar, have taken ship again for Rome, shall receive four shillings and sixpence reward.

'N.B. This Reward will not be increased, nobody judging him to deserve a Crown.'

It is much to be regretted that all this comes at a time when we are to return to Fredericksburg, there to conclude a peace with the emissaries of King Louis of France, which the Prince himself promised when General Bougainville undertook to draw his army back again to the Ohio River.

'Sir,' said the Chevalier, 'the Prince must be in his

Palace at Williamsburg, for the city is not otherwise so secure as we had hoped. I shall remain here with Lord Elibank, Lord Caryll, and the greatest part of our army. It is for you and Colonel Byrd, with a sufficient party of soldiers, to be our embassy to General Bougainville at Fredericksburg. When you have made terms or conditions, inform me. Only then shall the Prince come there to be a signatory, for though he must secure Williamsburg, the people of Virginia must also see that he brings them peace, and the world must see that his name seals our treaty with the French.'

'And the Cardinal Prince, sir?'

'While he remains,' said the Chevalier, 'I shall not stir from his side. Why, sir, he talks already of going out to greet his father's subjects! He is an honest man, sir, but no politician.'

We walked a little in the garden of the Palace, and presently the Chevalier said, 'Confer an obligation upon me, sir. My son, Lieutenant Louis de Johnstone, is at Fort Cumberland, hardly more than a day's ride from Winchester. I should be obliged to you if he might be withdrawn from there so that he may be present at the treaty. He is young, sir, and apt to consider that war is won by the profession of arms alone. I would have him see what more may be done by negotiation. Also, sir, the peace may be more easily preserved if Lieutenant Louis be withdrawn a little.'

28 July 1760. A week since I rode from Williamsburg before dawn with a troop of Virginia horse and a baggage train. Colonel Byrd, who is to be the Prince's plenipotentiary at Fredericksburg, was already on the road, as indeed was Lord Caryll who, for all the Chevalier's arguments, had left the city the day before me. We crossed the Pamunkey River near Eltham and bivouacked the first night by King William Court House, close to the banks of the Mattapony. From there it was but a day's journey to Fredericksburg.

It was expected that the French plenipotentiaries from the Ohio would shortly be in the town and Colonel Byrd had expressed some anxiety to me that they should pass safely by our forward position at Fort Cumberland, two days' hard riding from where we then were. It was at the fort that the Chevalier's son, Lieutenant Louis, commanded a small force. To redeem my pledge to the Chevalier, I offered to Colonel Byrd to ride with a small party, secure the passage of the French emissaries, and bring back Lieutenant Louis, agreeably to his father's wishes.

Next day, with an ensign and twelve Virginia troopers, I took the road to Winchester, passing through country which was then new to me. It seemed that for two days we moved through a great forest, hills carpeted with trees rising more steeply on either side of us as we drew closer to the lower slopes of the Blue Ridge Mountains. Beyond the little town of Winchester, the track grew more tangled and we moved with greater difficulty upon our way. It was not an hour after daybreak when we saw a single horseman riding hard towards us from the way we were going. He and his charger were in such a lather as if they had galloped through the night since dusk.

'Sir,' said he, his breath almost gone, 'we must retire upon Winchester at once. There is an army of savages in the hills before whom all the settlers are fleeing. Some have loaded their possessions into carts, and many more are on foot with whatever they can carry. They make for Winchester, which must now defend itself against the cruelties of the savage tribes.'

Even as we spoke together, the first of the carts began to pass us on that difficult trail, piled high with household treasures. Those who rode or walked beside it wept at the loss of their homes but thanked God that they had, at the least, escaped with their lives.

I inquired of the horseman how many savages there might be, and at what distance from us. He only shook his head and said helplessly, 'It is never possible to discover their numbers, sir, for they conceal themselves too well. But they are close enough. Not half an hour ago, I heard the shrieking of the poor wretches who had fallen into their hands. The torments they put them to make death itself a blessing. Sir, we have heard the horrid screams all night, and have seen at a little distance the smoke of the cabins they have burnt.'

'But have you seen the savages, sir?'

'Yes, sir. Not ten minutes since, there were two of them swarming through the verge beside the trail not a mile from this place. I did not wait, sir, for my express to Winchester stays for nothing and for no man.'

With that he pulled his horse's head round and galloped off in a cloud of dust, while more carts and straggling fugitives pressed past us. They wept, pushed, and even jostled one another off the rough track in their terror, crying that they would all be taken, themselves horribly murdered and their women made whores of by the Indians.

Our party of fourteen pressed cautiously in the direction of the general rout. We had gone only a little way when we heard the whooping of the savages at a distance, and then saw that smoke was rising in a great cloud from a settlement, where one of the buildings was on fire. I judged that we must take them from all sides, while they were glutted with their horrid triumph and no way prepared to fight. Beyond the building that was smouldering there lay a broad opening, like a meadow, with trees in a curtain all about its edge. I ordered that our men should take their places silently behind this screen of foliage and then open fire upon them when the command was given, taking good aim.

The troopers moved to their places. Yet what was my

surprise, when I came to view the prospect, to discover that all this whooping and all the fear proceeded from six persons! Three of these were indeed Indians, though of the gentler sex. Their companions, however, were troopers of the Virginia light cavalry, drunk as draymen and yelling defiance to all the world. With their squaws, who had diverted them the greater part of the night, they had consumed a good portion of rum. By dawn they were so fuddled with this that one had prolonged their celebration by knocking open the lamps in the outbuilding and drinking some of the spirit which they contained. It was during this theft that a pipe had touched a broken lamp and the blaze had gone up through the roof. One man was roaring about the field in his shirt, while the Indian damsels were in a state of perfect nature. Such was the savage warfare which had sent the whole country fleeing towards Winchester.

Drink had done such things for the three troopers that it required our combined strength to subdue them and to put them under guard for Winchester. Indeed, one drew his sword (though standing only in his shirt) and bid us all come at him. The young squaws we covered decently and sent about their business, though they would have kept their lovers company to the gaol house. As for those savages who had been seen in the underbrush by our first informant, they proved to be only a negro and a mulatto slave sent by their master in search of his straying cattle.

The morning's business showed clearly enough the state of terror which prevails in these parts after four years of frontier war. Men of the greatest valour are unnerved and jump before their own shadows. Whatever may be thought in Williamsburg, the people here will kneel to any prince who can deliver them from such fears as these.

It was not until the following day that our party came within sight of Fort Cumberland, near the river which is called Wills Creek. Being our last forward position of any significance in Virginia, it seemed little enough of a fort but rather a rude stockade. The walls are of pine trunks driven upright into the earth and sharpened at their upper ends, some twenty feet above the ground. These wooden ramparts appear to extend for quite a hundred yards on every side. Within the fortress a wooden platform runs below the tops of the four walls, where soldiers may fire through the loopholes. A few timber buildings and some tents are all the cover provided within the stockade for the little force of soldiers encamped there. There is no well to supply these defenders with water, but they must crawl down a trench from one end of the enclosure to the river. And what if their savage enemy should not be so obliging as to stand aside for them? I cannot learn what should induce people to think of making a fort or a deposit for provisions here. It covers no country, nor has it any certain communications behind it, either by land or water.

The wooden gate was opened to our party and we entered the enclosure of the fort. I asked for Lieutenant Louis and was brought to a cabin, where he sat in a chair with one of his legs supported over the corner of a table, while his servant rubbed at the boot with a cloth. Upon my entrance he waved the man away and stood up, greeting me warmly.

'Sir,' said I at length, 'I bring your father's blessing and his wish that you should return to Fredericksburg to be present at the French treaty.'

'By-and-by,' said Lieutenant Louis. 'Tomorrow shall do for that. Today I have a little more fire to eat.'

I felt some alarm, and spoke hastily to him.

'You do not propose to call your men to arms, sir, while the embassy of the French King is even now preparing to talk of peace? The combat is over, sir. The war is done!'

'Done, sir?' said Lieutenant Louis. 'War is never done in these parts! This is not Williamsburg, nor Fredericksburg neither. Step a mile outside Fort Cumberland and call to the savages that the war is done. If you get no worse than an arrow in your breech for your pains, you may count yourself lucky!'

I referred to the Chevalier's wishes again, adding, 'I speak not only as he is your father, sir, but as he is aide-de-camp to Prince Charles Edward!'

'Stuff!' said Lieutenant Louis. 'You might as well talk of aide-de-camp to your grandmother. There is a party of savages not two miles from here whom I must first see clear of the Prince's domain. I dare swear that they know nothing of aides-de-camp, and will not be so obliging as to wait quietly for my father to come and explain the matter to them. If you doubt the peril which they must otherwise keep our settlers in, you may see for yourself.'

With that, he buckled on his sword and gave an order to the sergeant of militia who stood close by the door. We were then alone. It was a situation of the greatest nicety. I might have used my newly conferred seniority to order Lieutenant Louis's obedience. Yet he acted upon the instructions of a commander more senior than I. Moreover, it was well said that neither the Chevalier nor I could know the circumstances of the war around Fort Cumberland so well as he.

Tired though I was, I set out with Lieutenant Louis and his party of twenty or thirty militia a little before dawn the next day. We had also a dozen Cherokee, being of a tribe that was loyal to us. As we made our way through the thickest of the forest, towards the old territory of Half King, two of our Indian scouts returned to inform us that they had found the trail of wheels and horses at a mile distant across our front.

Lieutenant Louis halted his men and despatched more scouts, who returned presently with the news that a hostile camp had been set up not two miles from us.

'We must parley,' said I.

'Not yet, sir, by my advice,' said Lieutenant Louis, 'for this may be the bait that is set to trap us. Let our men move securely into position around them first, and then let us parley by all means. For otherwise the enemy and his savage warriors may take us as we pass through to them.'

It did not seem to me then that I should countermand those instructions which the young officer had been given. Our men moved as silently as they might through the underbrush until we came close to a broad clearing with a rocky bower behind it. A score of French soldiers sat in the clearing, eating and drinking. Lieutenant Louis gave a silent motion to his men to occupy a half circle where they would be hidden by the trees. Yet to complete the circle our soldiers must appear upon open ground, where they would be in full view of the French.

Lieutenant Louis himself assumed the command of this section. He stepped forward from the shelter of the trees, a clear target for the French guards, drawing his men across the opening, so that the entire French party was within our circle and we might parley in safety. Yet, as soon as their party saw our men, they began to run back to the rocky bower, where they had left their muskets, and there was a scene of such confusion as is beyond description. Our own men, not choosing to wait until the French sharpshooters were prepared, opened fire, each one upon his own authority. Soon there was a general fusillade on either side, which could not easily be stopped for all that I endeavoured to prevent it. It was not intended that we should give battle at so delicate a time as this, yet I saw two Frenchmen fall and their musket balls came close enough to us.

Their soldiers, at a command from their officers, went to take cover among the rocks. But as they did so they found that our Cherokee were advancing upon them from that side, their scalping knives ready. At this, all resistance ceased, the French soldiers running back towards us, throwing away their muskets and lifting their hands in the air, anxious only to surrender to us that they might not be taken by the savage warriors.

As I had feared, these Frenchmen came in peace, not war, being part of that deputation to the treaty at Fredericksburg. They sent an officer under flag of truce to parley with us, who confirmed this. Our men were at once ordered to ground their arms. When this was done, and a safe-conduct promised, their commander, a Colonel who accompanied part of the baggage of General Bougainville to Fredericksburg, stepped into the clearing with his aide-de-camp. Lieutenant Louis greeted them heartily, saying, 'Welcome, messieurs, to Fort Cumberland!'

As we rode back to the fort together, I could not help expressing my strong displeasure to him at the turn which events had taken, and the ease with which his men had been allowed to open fire upon those who came only to negotiate a peace between ourselves and France. I hinted strongly to him that such men as he were going the way to prolong a ruinous war. He seemed to resent this little enough, only saying, 'But set aside the treaty, sir, and did you ever see a more charming piece of work than that just now? May I be poxed by all the bawds in Hanover if ever I saw men taken more neatly than these messieurs this morning!'

He was so content with himself that all further talk upon the topic appeared profitless. Yet his satisfaction with the morning's work allowed him to be persuaded to leave with our party of French and Virginians for Fredericksburg the next day. Lieutenant Louis knows only one trade and may be greatly put out if Virginia should ever find itself entirely at peace.

8 August 1760. All the world, it seems, has come to Fredericksburg. We lack only the Prince and the Chevalier, who are to remain in Williamsburg until such time as the treaty may require His Highness's signature. In the courthouse of the town are gathered the plenipotentiaries of either side, those of King Louis of France being spoken for by General Louis Antoine de Bougainville, whose horsemen scattered the Hanoverian army before Quebec, and who two months since faced the Prince in arms not ten miles from this very town of Fredericksburg.

The Sieur de Bougainville, whose ministers were drawn up opposite to our own across a long table, spoke much in confidence to a French officer who sat beside him. Who that officer might be I could not at first tell. His colour appeared too dark for a Frenchman, yet not so much as an Indian. He was somewhat advanced in years, and his hair silvered. In height, he overtopped any there, and in his sprightly manner looked ready to outrun us all. At night I asked Colonel Byrd, who led our negotiation, to name the stranger.

'Why, sir,' said the Colonel with a laugh, 'have you never heard of Philippe Joincare, the Sieur de Chabert? That is he. He has the manners of a courtier and the reputation of a lion. His father, sir, was a French officer and his mother a Seneca squaw. He is as much at home with the Indians as with the French. Though he has long been an officer in the service of King Louis XV, yet he is also regarded as a great chief by the six nations of the Indians. His name stands so high among their tribes that he is worth ten regiments of soldiers to his French master.'

It was at Kenmore House, where we and some of the French officers were hospitably received during the treaty by Mr Fielding Lewis, that I saw Captain Joincare again. He spoke long and amiably with a younger man in a fine coat and ruffles, whose height was more than a match for the Sieur de Chabert himself. The dark hair, black brows, and tall forehead of this other man formed a profile as striking as that of his French companion. I soon learnt that he was Colonel Washington, who had preceded Colonel Byrd as senior field officer among the forces of Virginia. Two years since he resigned his command, after several years of honourable warfare against this very Joincare, choosing instead to marry the Widow Custis and retire to his estates at Mount Vernon. The same Colonel's sister was the wife of Mr Lewis of Kenmore House.

They who had once been enemies now met as guests. Yet when Colonel Byrd saw Colonel Washington, he crossed to him at once and greeted him as a brother. They had long been friends, and were later comrades-in-arms, so that the deepest amity endures between them. I was present afterwards when they drank a bowl together and talked much of the prosperity of Westover, and Mount Vernon, and the goodness of the Widow Custis. Yet Colonel Byrd would also ask pleasantly, from time to time, after one Sally Cary and how she did. This seemed to throw Colonel Washington into a little confusion, who braved it out at first but then yielded to laughter as though admitting some secret to Colonel Byrd. This I take to be a reference to some ancient *amour* of Colonel Washington's which is known only to a few acquaintances of his.

Colonel Byrd then began an attempt to persuade Colonel Washington to quit the dalliance of husbandry for the field of arms, saying finally, 'Why, sir, even if there should be a French peace, you may be sure that it will be broken one time or another. It would be a boon to us to add your weight to ours in Fortune's scale.'

Colonel Washington shook his head and spoke in his slow and flat manner.

'The scale of Fortune, in America, sir, is turning no man knows whither. Yet I am now, sir, I believe, fixed at Mount Vernon with an agreeable consort for life, and hope to find more happiness in retirement than I ever experienced amidst a wide and bustling world.'

'Let Fortune be the judge of that, sir,' said Colonel Byrd, amiably, 'for she confers her commission upon a man whether he will or no. And you may think yourself secure and retired at Mount Vernon, but if Fortune chooses you shall be with a regiment on the Ohio for all that.'

They talked pleasantly enough, but never spoke, to my knowledge, of the Prince or of what had brought us to Fredericksburg. At first I supposed this was a sign that Colonel Washington was for the House of Hanover and the Whig settlement, so that to speak of such matters might have been to breach friendship. Yet, as the hour grew late, I rather wondered if it was because Colonel Washington was in some way waiting upon events and had not yet paid his loyalties to any side. I went so far as to test him a little upon this, at which he replied very shortly.

'Sir, I never had any other motive or loyalty than the pleasing hopes of serving my country. If I have gained any credit, or if I am entitled to the least countenance or esteem, it must be from serving my country with a free and voluntary will.'

'And your King, sir?' said I.

'I spoke, sir, of my country,' said Colonel Washington with some heat. 'And I may tell you, sir, that I came here as it might be in me a friendly act at the time of the negotiation, and not as I expected to be called upon to expose my character to public censure.'

Even before I had spoken my last question, I could see that Colonel Byrd was growing impatient of my discourse. When we had left Colonel Washington and were returning to our lodging in Mr Lewis's coach, Colonel Byrd burst out at me in the most unaccountable manner.

'Sir, this cross-questioning of yours is ill-chosen!' he exclaimed. 'Virginia contains men of great virtue like Colonel Washington, honest and brave. They are not your courtiers, sir. They have barely heard of Prince Charles

Edward and his actions here, yet you must needs be holding up an oath of allegiance already, and bidding them swear it! They care nothing for the Prince, as the Prince, but only as he is an honest man or not. If he is an honest man, why they will come round in time and be his ministers. If he is not, then they will bid the headsman sharpen his axe again. The issue is in His Royal Highness's own hands.'

I was put out at this, and attempted some reply.

'He is not a Prince because he is honest, sir. He is Prince because his father is King James, and his father is King by divine right. There are many honest men in the world, sir, but God forbid they should all hold that as their title to a crown. Charles Edward is Prince, sir, by divine right.'

'Hark, Mr Fraser,' said Colonel Byrd softly. 'The great planters of Virginia will not give a hogturd for such nice distinctions as that. If he is an honest man, well and good. If not, the only divine right that will be granted him is that of departing by the next vessel for France, Rome, England, or wheresoever he may choose to go. This is Virginia, sir, not Europe, and I speak of things as they are, not as I would have them be.'

'Charles Edward', said I, 'is Prince by divine right, for nothing else can make him so.'

'Fiddle-faddle,' said Colonel Byrd, and would talk no more upon the matter.

15 August 1760. For several days the course of our negotiation remained in doubt. The Marquis de Vaudreuil, Governor of Canada for His Most Christian Majesty of France, would impose harsh terms upon Virginia. General Bougainville swore at first that France must positively hold the Ohio River and all that lies beyond it. Yet they have no true settlement there but mere trading posts the length of the Ohio and the Mississippi. For our part, Colonel Byrd insisted that the Ohio could be no frontier. France might have Canada and Louisiana, as well as free navigation the length of the Mississippi, and a passage between New Orleans and her Canadian kingdom. But for Virginia to allow her own western lands to terminate upon the Ohio was to deny that great Charter by which the first King James granted her a continuing territory to the shore of the Pacific Ocean.

The length of a hot day, with the roof of the courthouse hot from the sun and the air stifling within, the plenipotentiaries faced one another across their table with a sprawl of maps, deeds, and papers between them. They sought some wonder of geometry, by which the French line should run from north to south, and our line from east to west, but one should never interrupt the other. When all such attempts had failed, as they must have done from the start, Colonel Byrd addressed himself again to General Bougainville.

'Sir, Virginia's frontiers stand upon the western as well as the eastern ocean. That, sir, is the grant of King James I, more than a century ago, and we could not shift from that even if we would.'

'Why, monsieur,' said one of the French wittily, 'have you not shifted kings since then?'

'No, sir,' said Colonel Byrd, 'we have not changed our King, though the Hanoverians may wish it. Our King, sir, is James III, the great-grandson of that first James.'

But all this was to no purpose. That same evening, in company with Colonel Byrd and Mr Robert Wormeley Carter, I was again with Colonel Washington, whom all on the Virginian side sought out for his wisdom and his knowledge of the wild lands of the Ohio.

'Sir,' said Colonel Byrd to him, 'there must be a peace with France. Yet this matter of the Ohio River sticks and sticks.'

'You have chosen the wrong time,' said Colonel Wash-

155

ington, 'for France is not defeated, nor is Virginia. And I tell you what all history teaches us, that until one side or the other be so beaten as to have no stomach for war peace will be difficult to treat of and still more difficult to preserve.'

'They would have our frontier upon the Ohio, sir,' said I, 'while we would have no limit there, nor on the Mississippi. What would you have us do?'

'Make peace, sir,' said Colonel Washington at once, 'for they will never settle the Ohio. They will settle Canada and Louisiana, but the Ohio and the Mississippi are no more than roads to them. If our people settle the wilderness as far as the Ohio, neither French trading posts nor any other obstacle will prevent them crossing. If they do not reach so far, then it is no great matter for the present. I may tell you, sir, that the fault of the late war has been to advance our forts too far and our armies too quickly into the wilderness. Had we gone no further than Fort Cumberland, we might have held that with security and given protection to the settlements against both French and Indians. But what folly was it, sir, to send an army like General Braddock's into the wildest reaches of the Monongahela River, as though he had been making a campaign in Flanders or Hanover! And how dearly did it cost us!'

'Then you would have us draw back, sir?' said I.

'What I would have, sir,' said Colonel Washington, 'is Virginia strong on this side of the Ohio, and not weak on both sides. This is no time for war, sir. I have returned to my own estates because unless men make peace and return to care for their land the Province will run to ruin. The profession of arms is sometimes every man's greatest duty, but it is not so now, and ought not to be made so by refusing a peace.'

I could not doubt that these were wise sentiments, though I believed that we might yet bring the French to more favourable terms than they had offered us. It was not to be forgotten that all their interest lay in seeing Prince Charles Edward secure in Virginia, so that the Province might not be part of the Elector of Hanover's empire. After our discussion, Colonel Byrd privately asked me for my opinion.

'Why, sir,' said I, 'Colonel Washington is right. I have been at Fort Cumberland not two weeks since, and I may tell you that the troop captains there are talking of going into winter quarters and ending their campaign season so early as the beginning of August! There is such a weariness, sir, that this thing cannot hold much longer.'

Upon the following day, when the plenipotentiaries met, there seemed a disposition to yield somewhat on both sides. I assured Colonel Byrd that the French must really want peace before the Elector of Hanover should bring fresh troops to attack them in the north, and that we must play this as a strong card. So I believe it happened, for after many days of going to market and haggling, the agreement came marvellously swift.

In short, it was concluded that all lands east of the Ohio River were to be guaranteed to Virginia. The trading posts and the free navigation of the Ohio and the Mississippi Rivers were to be guaranteed to the King of France. Nothing was said of the wilderness to the west of the rivers, for that was not of immediate concern. It therefore appeared that nothing had been decided as to the grant of James I, which would lay the claim of Virginia across the entire continent to the Pacific Ocean. The marvel of geometry had been sought but not found, and what the genius of Euclid could not resolve may yet be tried by the force of battle. As to Louisiana and Canada, Virginia guaranteed these whole and entire to France, which was hardly generous in us since France holds them already so tightly that it must be a prodigious power can ever take them from her.

23 August 1760. Despatches bearing the terms were sent at once to Williamsburg, where the Prince, the Chevalier, and Sir John Randolph deliberated much upon them. Yet, since this was no time to think of going to war again with the French, it was determined to ratify the treaty. Upon the Chevalier's advice, Lord Elibank and a thousand soldiers were left close to Williamsburg while the Prince rode to the treaty. Yet the absence of the Prince from the city during those few days was held so dark a secret that the royal standard of the Stuarts was kept flying above the Palace during all that time. It might have flown, indeed, for the Cardinal Duke of York who remained there, and who was so closely guarded by the Chevalier, and then by Sir John Randolph, that he found himself little better than a state prisoner.

The Prince and his party reached Fredericksburg two days since. He was received with much ceremony and a good deal of affection by the people who remember him as their deliverer from the French not three months ago. I was shown a noble piece of pottery made lately in the town to celebrate the peace and the Prince's coming. The nobility lies rather in the sentiment than in the craft, for it is a simple salt-glaze jug. Upon it there stands the rude representation of a lion that wears a crown, its tail frisking up, and the year 1760 between its feet. Beneath all this is inscribed in a simple style, 'Good success to the Prince of Virginia'.

Whatsoever simplicity there may have been in such greetings to the Prince by the common people, the treaty itself made a brave show. It was concluded between 'the Most Serene and Most Potent Prince, James the Third, by the Grace of God, of Great Britain, France, and the Americas, King, Defender of the Faith,' and 'the Most Serene and Most Potent Prince, Lewis the Fifteenth, by the Grace of God, Most Christian King.'

The treaty was signed in the courthouse of Fredericksburg with a great deal of ceremony, as though it were all happening at the court of Versailles with courtiers standing in perfect silence as the quills scrawled against the parchment. It was signed on the one side by Charles, Prince Regent, for his father, and on the other by Louis Antoine de Bougainville for His Most Christian Majesty of France. When all was done, I remarked to the Chevalier that France had now made her peace with the Stuarts but not with the Hanoverians. Having signed one treaty with 'His Britannic Majesty James the Third', how would they do when they came to treat with the Elector of Hanover, who styles himself 'His Britannic Majesty George the Second'?

'Sir,' said the Chevalier, 'they will style him a Britannic Majesty too. Why, sir, they do not care how many Britannic Majesties there might be, the more the better, so long as they do not have to fight them all at once. And, sir, remember that both our King and the Elector of Hanover are pleased to style themselves the Kings of France. Why, sir, a nation that can swallow the imposition of two other kings beside its own Louis XV will not jib at making peace with two kings of another country.'[1]

He was in excellent spirits, swearing that the success of the French peace would do more for the Prince than ever the presence of his brother, the Cardinal Duke of York, would do against him.

At night there was a banquet at Kenmore House, where the light of every candelabrum and torch seemed to shine upon fine linen or sparkle upon silver and glass. The Chevalier showed only a moment's impatience then. It happened that he saw his son, Lieutenant Louis de Johnstone, acting the most outrageous fop in his dress and talking in his bravest manner to several Virginian damsels at the same time. He is of an age when young men are prone to play the blade, but his father (with whom I was)

---

[1] In the Peace of Paris, 1763, George III was still referred to as King of both Great Britain and France.

met him soon enough and growled loud enough for several to hear, 'Sir! Do not affect singularity! It is no part of a gentleman!'

The Prince was much himself, dancing with one or other of the ladies every dance, and killing all other passions but those which aimed at him. He spoke in French with the Sieur de Chabert, Philippe Joincare. While in company with Colonel Byrd, he spoke also with Colonel Washington, whom he knew by reputation as having been senior field officer of the Province until his retirement two years since.

As they spoke together, the Colonel's face remained without much expression and he seemed at pains to show that whatever charm the Prince might have was without effect upon him. Yet, after they had been together some while, Colonel Washington was at least sufficiently assured that he might speak freely in the presence of this Prince, even to declaring his resentment of the Stuarts.

I had drawn back a little to speak to Lord Caryll, as a matter of courtesy, and when I again picked up the thread of the talk between the Prince and Colonel Washington, there was a good deal of frankness passing between them.

'Come, sir,' the Prince was saying, 'you cannot believe that after all my travels I am yet so sensitive that I cannot bear to hear an adverse opinion. Knowing your estimate of the world and its affairs, I do not expect that you should approve me. Why, am I not a Stuart? And might I not come knocking at Mount Vernon any day to tax you for Ship Money, or summon you before Star Chamber? Is not that at the heart of it?'

'And so it may be,' said Colonel Washington earnestly, 'but that is not to the true purpose. It matters nothing whether I like you or not. Put you and King George in the same room and, why, you may be much the more agreeable companion of the two. But that is neither here nor there. I will go further, sir, there are men in Virginia who believe that King George's Ministers betrayed us in this late war, for they took our taxes and gave us no means of defence in exchange that we might drive off the French or the Indians. There are even men in this Province who swear that we should have done better by ourselves. For then we might have let England go to the devil and made our peace with France long before this time. Yet now we have that peace. If England cannot protect us, sir, it may be that we shall look to a protector of our own. But are you the one, sir?'

The two men stood face to face in perfect stillness, the light of the candelabra falling upon their powdered wigs. Colonel Washington's face was a little flushed with the intensity of his discourse. The Prince regarded him in a courteous but level fashion.

'Am I not the one, sir?' he asked.

'Consider who you are, sir,' said Colonel Washington softly. 'You must succeed your father, wherever he may rule. There is no other in your house who stands before you. But we must have a settlement in Virginia and in all America. There must be government and order, not mobs waving their hats at whoever may come wearing a crown. Now, if you take the Elector of Hanover from us, what will you give us in his place? Yourself? I say, consider who you are. When your reign is done, who will continue in your place? Your brother, the Cardinal? It cannot be. But, even were he to succeed you, he can have no heirs. And there is an end of your line. So you would leave us then to send to Europe for a prince of God-knows-where. Or else, after some few years, must we go back to the House of Hanover and cry repentance? No, sir. When that time came we should shift for ourselves, but we may as well do that now as later.'

The Prince listened to all this with the greatest attention and then asked, 'Would you like me better, Colonel

Washington, if I had a fine wife and two or three prattlers in leading-reins?'

'It signifies nothing,' said the Colonel, 'whether I like you or not. I tell you, though, that you would then show the way for your own House. I am not a Stuart, sir, and never was. But the men of Virginia will be damned before they will fight the French and King George merely that the House of Stuart shall be restored for a pleasant interlude of some few years.'

The Prince nodded, as though he were of the same mind as the Colonel in this matter.

'No man in his senses would fight for that, sir,' he said thoughtfully, 'and no prince ought to demand it of him. You have spoken your mind, sir, and I am your debtor for what you have told me. I seek no flatterers, and I trust that those men who are about me will always speak as you have done.'

It may have been that this royal thanks was not entirely welcome to the Colonel, for he drew himself up tall and rather stiff, as if he were on sentry-go. Then the two men drew a little apart, with hardly any formality of farewell, and the Prince was with the Chevalier again.

'Colonel Washington is not of our party, sir,' said the Chevalier.

'Who talks of parties?' remarked the Prince. 'I do not suppose such men as he are of our party or any other party. What does that signify? The fewer parties in Virginia at the present, the more secure shall our peace become.'

With that, His Highness took his leave of the company, in a more thoughtful mood than was his custom. The next morning, escorted by his Life Guards and the Virginia Cavalry, he and our expedition made all haste for Williamsburg again. Upon our arrival we found great satisfaction among the people at what had been achieved through the French peace. None but fanatic politicians would raise their voices against the Prince in that respect. Yet those voices may grow louder, or the Elector of Hanover may soon enter the game. It behoves Charles Edward to fix himself in the hearts of the people before such events can overtake us.

5

THE COURT OF WILLIAMSBURG

*Between August 1760 and February 1761, Lovat Fraser appar-
ently made no entries in his journal. However, immediately following his account of the French Peace at Fredericksburg, a dozen
pages of manuscript in another hand are bound into the volume
containing the journal. These pages represent the only surviving
section of one of the 'lost' intimate histories of the 18th century:
John, Lord Hervey's* Memoirs of the Court of Charles III.
*Hervey, the Whig courtier of George II, and the 'Sporus' of Pope's
satire, is best known to posterity for his revelations of court life
and politics in his* Memoirs of the Reign of George II, *not
published until 1848. Born in 1696, he was taken dangerously
ill in 1743 and his life was despaired of. It was even rumoured
that he had died, at the comparatively early age of 47, and his
disappearance from public life lent some credence to this story at the
time.*

*Although Hervey lived for another twenty years, the remainder
of his time was spent in a vain search for health. He tried every
medical fad of the day, from living on a diet of asses' milk to
taking voyages to sub-tropical 'resorts'.*

*Hervey spent the early summer of 1760 in England, and was in
London when the Duke of Newcastle was dismissed from office.
Newcastle had avoided this downfall for several months but he was,*

ultimately, made to share some of the disgrace for the failure at
Quebec, and was sacrificed by the King to placate Parliament.

In June, Hervey was persuaded to try the fashionable cure of a
Jamaican voyage, but after two months on the island he abandoned
this and set out for England again in October. Returning in the
same convoy of vessels were the Member of Parliament for
Aylesbury, John Wilkes, who had an interest in certain sugar
plantations, and Samuel Johnson, who was not to meet Boswell
until three years later but was already known for his Dictionary
of the English Language.

Hervey describes the great Atlantic storm of November 1760 and
the circumstances which brought him and his companions to the
shores of Virginia, where he was obliged to spend the next few
months. Before this time, he was no admirer of the Stuart cause
and his comments on Prince Charles Edward make a sharp and
distinctive criticism by comparison with Lovat Fraser's over-
reverential attitude towards his leader. Yet, even though Hervey
was never to be won over to the Stuart cause, it is clear that by the
end of his stay in Williamsburg the renowned personal charm of
Bonnie Prince Charlie had begun to have its effect upon him.

Throughout all his memoirs, Lord Hervey refers to himself in
the third person, in order to avoid what he calls 'the disagreeable
egoisms with which almost all memoir writers so tiresomely
abound'.

1760

The beginning of October, those invalids who had sought
the recovery of health in the West Indian islands were so
plagued by looseness and infirmities that they began to
think only with what haste they might return to the most
noxious winter that England could offer them. Of those
who came out the previous summer, there took ship Mr
Wilkes, the Member for Aylesbury, Mr Johnson, the
dictionary-writer, and Lord Hervey.

The Monday following, the vessels all being a little way
from the Carolinas, the wind changed at night to north-

west, and blew a most prodigious storm. They who before had believed that no security existed save in England now considered with what haste they might find safety upon the American shore. There being no further prospect that one ship could aid another, the frigate of the convoy fired a gun, as a signal for every vessel to take care of itself. Accordingly, each tacked about and they were, for the most part, obliged to cut all their masts and scramble into several harbours of Virginia.

Being thus thrown, without masts and extremely shattered, upon the coast near Hampton, the travellers were entirely cast away. Lord Hervey dined this disagreeable day at a tavern or ordinary. The affair of the Pretender's son at Williamsburg then made a great noise throughout all the Province. Mr Wilkes, from a curiosity, and Mr Johnson, from a tenderness towards the House of Stuart, were for setting off to that city, *au grand galop*, to see how he did. Lord Hervey, having been always steady to his party and constant to his friends, was uncertain how he might be received by the Jacobite faction. Yet being strongly taken with the prospect of witnessing the pauper courtiers paying adoration to this new idol, and knocking heads together to whisper compliments and petitions as their Prince passed by, Lord Hervey at length agreed to make one of the party. By being the first to bring to Williamsburg the news of the Duke of Newcastle's disgrace, he was in hopes that he might in a manner be credited with having brought about that catastrophe.

All Virginia, it seemed, had removed to Williamsburg. The very streets, that until a few months since used to be no more than pleasant thoroughfares for hay-wains, were now thronged from morning to night like the 'Change at noon. Men of fashion, and women of none, filled the very stairways and antechambers of the Governor's Palace, where the Prince had made his residence, shouldering one another as if at St Bartholomew's Fair. In the midst of all this jostling, Charles Edward found himself set up at auction, each man bidding for his favour at the expense of the others, and many taking as much satisfaction in their neighbour's disappointment as in their own success. These petitioners of a Prince, who himself had nothing that was his own to give them, did not seem to feel the ridicule or the contemptibleness of their situation but were as well satisfied to be bowing and grinning in an antechamber at Williamsburg as if they had been admitted to the royal levée at St James's or Versailles.

The Prince's character was amiable and gained one's good wishes. His demeanour, while it seemed engaging to those who did not truly examine it, appeared condescending to those who did. His manner had a show of good humour, from his natural and habitual amiability, yet his cajoling of everybody carried this general benevolence so far that he condescended rather below the level of a Prince.

Those who had the ear of the Prince lost no opportunity to irritate and blow him up against his brother, the Cardinal Duke of York. It was whispered that a match must be made for the Prince in Europe, and that the Cardinal Duke must play Cupid. By this it was intended to gratify the Province by ridding Virginia of His Eminence, and to flatter the Cardinal himself by bringing him as close to a woman as he might ever honestly come. Yet had he not made his departure so soon, an open rupture must have been the consequence of his American visit.

The Cardinal Duke was one of those unfortunate people, who are to be met with at every court, whom it is the fashion to abuse and ungenteel to be seen with, because they have little to expect and nothing to give. Upon the very day of his departure for Europe, it was known by the whole Court whom his brother, the Prince, would take for a wife.

'Why,' said Mr Wilkes to Lord Hervey, 'all the world

knows that it is to be Flora Macdonald, who rowed him over the sea to Skye when he escaped by a hair's breadth from the English army after Culloden.'

At this Lord Hervey burst out laughing, and remarked that it was all got up out of a romantic tale and would never be found true. For it was one thing to be obliged to a young woman for taking an oar at such a time, but quite another to embark with her upon a lifetime's voyage.

At the beginning of December and the assembling of the House of Burgesses (as their House of Commons is called), the revolutions of the Court favourites were the talk of the whole town. Colonel William Byrd and Sir John Randolph had outfaced all other contenders for the Prince's favour. Great was the fall of Colonel Landon Carter, the Whig leader, who not a year since would have made all Virginia take its directions from him. Now he turned the Capitol or Parliament building into a desert. His presence in its chambers, that used to draw admirers whenever he appeared, soon emptied every room he stood in. Those office-seekers who a little while ago were so assiduously clearing the way for his triumphal progress, now scrambled over one another's backs to get out of it, that they might not share his disgrace. He was a plodding, heavy fellow, with great application but few talents.

At the playhouse, the piece which excited most admiration that month of December was the tragedy of *Irene*, for it was performed in the presence of its author, Mr Samuel Johnson. He sat in a box with Mr Wilkes, whose politics did not prevent Mr Johnson from conceiving a great affection for him, and Lord Hervey was of the same party that evening. It was suggested to Mr Johnson that he might visit the players in their green room, but he would not, fearing as he said that the fair skins and naked legs of the actresses might excite his amorous propensities.

This eminent author combined a great bulk and a conspicuous mode of dress. His wig that set upon his large head (one eye of which was quite blind) was shrivelled and unpowdered. The brown suit of clothes was rusty, and offered strong evidence that he could hardly see to guide some of his supper further than his waistcoat. He was not, he said, fond of clean linen. Beyond this, his shirt-neck and the knees of his breeches were loose, his black worsted stockings ill drawn up, and his shoes generally unbuckled. His hands seemed always busy in front of him, as if he caught at flies or midges, and all his movements appeared erratic or convulsive in their nature. He was commonly taken, by those who did not know him, for a poor Bedlamite pitied and protected by some more fortunate man.

His tragedy of *Irene* was received with much applause, and Mr Johnson was afterwards the centre of all conversation in the Apollo Room of the tavern. He was indeed a less shocking and less ridiculous figure in such trappings than one would have expected. It was said that he talked well, but his talk consisted most of answering smartly. When Major Shaw, who had been some while at Fort Cumberland with his Royal Americans, spoke of the wild landscapes and savage tribes, Mr Johnson exclaimed, 'Why, what a wretch must he be, who is content with such conversation as can be had among savages!'

'Sir,' said the Major, 'it is worth any man's journey to see the dances of the Iroquois. You can really have no notion, sir, of how they come like apparitions from the dark, leaping into the firelight, beating on the deerskins stretched over their water-pots. They paint their faces with great art, in the most fearsome manner, as they do when they go to war to make themselves terrible to their enemies.'

'Yes, sir,' said Mr Johnson, 'and so may one dog look terribly at another cur, to drive it off from some bone of contention.'

'But, sir,' said the poor Major, 'if you have not seen

them yourself, you must be quite ignorant of how far above barbarous arts their best dancers are.'

'There is no dispute, sir,' said Mr Johnson, 'that one dog may dance far better than another. Yet no man of sense would occupy himself with such sad stuff.'

This peremptory answer drew out Colonel Landon Carter to try a fall or two.

'You say you are a man of sense, sir,' said the Colonel, 'and you must therefore oblige us with your opinion on a matter of greater consequence. Consider Charles Edward Stuart, the Pretender, for that is what he is. He has no property, no wife, and no heir. It is true we hear that he ruined a young woman, Miss Walkinshaw, and got a bastard by her. But, sir, if men of sense in Virginia must have a king, are they to choose this itinerant whore-monger?'

'Sir,' said Mr Johnson severely, 'observe the word "whoremonger". A whoremonger is a persistent dealer in whores, as an ironmonger is a dealer in iron. But as you don't call a man an ironmonger for buying and selling a penknife, so you don't call a man a whoremonger for getting one wench with child.'

This was enough to convince Colonel Carter that he had conjectured well.

'Sir,' he cried, 'you are nothing but a damned Jacobite! Burn me if you are not!'

'It is not in your power, sir,' said Mr Johnson, 'to say whether any man shall be damned or not. But, as I am a Jacobite, I thank you for the compliment. A Jacobite, sir, believes in the divine right of kings. He that believes in the divine right of kings believes in a Divinity. A Jacobite believes in the divine right of bishops. He that believes in the divine right of bishops believes in the divine authority of the Christian religion. Therefore, sir, a Jacobite is neither an Atheist nor a Deist. That cannot be said of a Whig, for Whiggism is a negation of all principle!'

At this, both parties broke into so great an uproar that neither heard more than a single syllable of the other. Lord Hervey, who heard all this conversation, was close by when Mr Wilkes said to Colonel Carter, 'I wonder you don't behave like a true Whig, sir, and settle the matter by a parliamentary election between King George and King James. If you do, who knows but I may canvass your vote for King James.'

'Vote for the Pretender, sir!' cried the Colonel. 'I would vote for the devil himself first!'

'Ah,' said Mr Wilkes, 'but what if your friend should not be standing?'

Mr Wilkes afterwards told Lord Hervey that this was one of several rods he always kept steeping for such as Colonel Carter, and that it was not until he saw and heard such men that he knew how greatly the Prince Charles Edward was to be preferred.

The 18th of December, Mr Wilkes, Mr Johnson, and Lord Hervey were, with other guests, at dinner at the Palace in Williamsburg. The Prince told Lord Hervey that he always looked upon him as one of the ablest men in England, and asked him if the people in London did not grow every day more discontented under the Hanoverian Ministry. He inquired also of Lord Hervey how the country had received the news of the Duke of Newcastle's disgrace.

'The disgrace of the Duke of Newcastle', said Lord Hervey, 'was a singular one. For it is often the case that the country, from political considerations, approves of a man's dismissal, though none rejoices at his personal misfortune. Yet, with regard to the Duke, it was rather the reverse. In a political light, nobody thought that his fall was of any consequence, for his successor Charles Townshend is no better than he. Yet, from personal dislike, all rejoiced that he met with such mortification.'

The Prince laughed extremely, and seemed as pleased

with this little stroke of satire upon the Hanoverian Ministry as he would have been with any flattery to himself.

At dinner, the Prince talked much to Mr Johnson, who had never resigned his allegiance to the House of Stuart, and who now swore that the battle of the Prince's army at Culloden had been 'a brave attempt'. He repeated this phrase several times, as though well satisfied with it. Mr Richardson was then talked of, the Prince admiring the tale of *Clarissa Harlowe* and vowing that no man had ever written such a history as that. Afterwards he asked Mr Johnson how he liked the new world, at which Mr Johnson seemed perplexed and said, 'Why, sir, I thought formerly that there was little to be observed in America but natural curiosities. I find it like an agreeable country place, though on the edge of a wilderness.'

The Prince said that no land ought to be more envied for its unexplored beauties, which Mr Johnson thought a wilderness. Then, thinking of his acquaintance Monsieur Rousseau, the philosopher of such wild places, His Highness remarked, 'Why, Mr Johnson, would not the forests of Virginia make an excellent home for Rousseau and his natural philosophy?'

It is certain that Mr Johnson mistook the drift of the Prince's question, unhappily supposing from it that His Highness shared his own disgust for the deistical views of the French sophister.

'Indeed, sir!' he cried, 'I would sooner sign a sentence for his transportation, than that of any felon who has gone from the Old Bailey these many years! Yes, I should like to have him set to work in the plantations!'

This unlucky turn to the conversation cut short a *tête-à-tête* which had otherwise promised to continue long into the night. However, another bowl was crowned, the Prince and Mr Wilkes now growing close as tavern neighbours. Lord Hervey observed that, in their cups, they soon allowed their passions and inclinations entirely to get the better of their reason and understanding. In a little while, the Prince's banquet resembled nothing so much as the fireside of a carmen's stage. His Highness and Mr Wilkes spent a pleasing hour discussing the frailties of womankind, the Prince inducing Mr Wilkes to furnish the party with the grosser passages of his burlesque *Essay on Woman*, which he was composing as a riposte to Mr Pope's famous *Essay on Man*.

Long after this, Lord Hervey, who had engaged the Chevalier de Johnstone in conversation upon the subject of Quebec, was able at the same time and at some distance to hear Mr Wilkes warning the Prince that the possession of a crown must be fraught with all the same perils and disadvantages as the possession of a woman. For in both cases, said Mr Wilkes, the posture was ridiculous, the pleasure uncertain, the expense beyond all reason, and the consequences often less agreeable in reality than in expectation.

For all that, the evening went off with great acclaim, and nothing was talked of in the town for several days following but the grandeur of this royal occasion. Yet the reports that were often given of the Prince's amiability were not always to be believed. With those who tried his patience too far, he could be as peevish as any man. During this same month, there came to Williamsburg Mr Wesley, the preacher, and his brother, who was something of a canting rhymester. They came for the purpose of vilifying, as was their custom, the Prince's great-uncle, Charles II, and had strong hopes from that of persuading the great-nephew to their own way of thinking.

Lord Hervey was present when the Prince and Mr Wesley were brought face to face at a levée in the Palace.

'I was', said Mr Wesley to the Prince, 'plucked by the hand of God, sir, from the burning of Epworth rectory that I might preach His Name to a great multitude in

173

many lands. Those who are chosen must answer the call, sir.'

The Prince, not much remarking the cant, replied familiarly, 'Why, Mr Wesley, and an't it a singular thing, that had you been burnt to a stick in your rectory, and not saved, you would not have thanked God for that, but rather complained of damned ill fortune?'

'We are to praise the chastisements of Providence, sir, as much as we do its mercies,' said Mr Wesley, pursing his lips.

'Damned stuff, sir!' said the Prince, after much more of this. 'There was never yet a man that set his hand upon a hot iron and then burst out a-praising!'

'Have you never read, sir,' said Mr Wesley softly, '*The Whole Duty of Man*, and the dreadful cautions therein upon profane swearing?'

'Saving your reverence, sir,' said the Prince, 'I may wager I have read as many and as good books as yourself.'

'And there are wholesome warnings against wagers in the same volume, sir,' added Mr Wesley, wagging his head in reproof.

'May I be damned!' exclaimed the Prince. 'This ranting does put one out of all patience!'

'Patience, too, sir, is commended as a virtue in those same pages,' resumed the preacher. But the Prince had turned upon his heel and gone.

'The more I am struck down, the more I am lift up,' said Mr Wesley to Lord Hervey. 'Was not that what Dr Burton said to the executioner?'

But Lord Hervey was not wise enough to instruct Mr Wesley in such a matter.

1761

The beginning of January, there arrived a messenger from Hampton, in dirty boots, who had been at sea three weeks and brought a letter from the Cardinal Duke of

York to Prince Charles Edward. It was very plain that this answer was *à propos* to the Prince's marriage, which was at that time being much canvassed.

During this same month, an affair of yet greater moment was brought on the tapis, the Court of Williamsburg learning for the first time that George II had died in October and that the territories of England and Hanover had been ruled by his grandson, as George III, all these weeks. The old King had died suddenly, just before he set out upon a day's hunting, and he who now wore the crown in his place was hardly more than a child.

The tumult this thunderclap provoked throughout Virginia is more easy to be imagined than described. They who a week before had preferred their old King to Prince Charles Edward now knew not whom to prefer, and were as little informed of the boy king, George III, as if he had been the Emperor of the Hottentots.

This state of affairs worked at first strongly in the interest of the Stuart Prince, for the planters were soon convinced that the government in England must henceforth be wholly in the hands of such men as Lord Townshend, Lord Mansfield, and the new King's uncle, the Duke of Cumberland. Nobody spoke much of the boy who was to occupy the throne, for they knew nothing of him to speak about. Thus it appeared that the old King's death gave Charles Edward the advantage in Virginia at a single stroke. Until this time there had been two contenders for the hearts of the people, one of whom now being dead the contest must needs go to the other by default, he seeming the very person of a prince.

As soon as the fact of the King's death was known, it was rumoured in the whole town, and suspected by some in the Palace as being true, that the Duke of Cumberland had sworn upon the coffin of his royal father to crush the Pretender's rebellion in America as surely as he had done at Culloden. Yet the Prince in Williamsburg behaved with great seeming unconcern, and even in private with unaccountable good temper. But this indifference and *sangfroid*, which bid such defiance to his former vanquisher, was believed by no one.

About this time, Mr Wilkes told Lord Hervey, 'As the devil will have it, the Prince has set his heart upon a Frenchwoman, one Antoinette Poisson, who was for a short while Lady of the Bedchamber to Queen Marie of France. And she would have been Lady of the Bedchamber to King Louis also, had the Queen permitted it.'

The uninterrupted kindness of the Prince to him, made Lord Hervey solicitous to discover the antecedents of the bride.

'Why,' said Mr Wilkes, 'Miss Fish (for so he would call Mademoiselle pleasantly) offered King Louis the sweetest lips to kiss, and the dearest bubbies to dine upon of any lady at their court. The Queen feared as much, and would have sent her packing in the name of outraged Virtue. But what Virtue failed to do was accomplished instead by Vice. The Comte de Maurepas, who held the fort of Louisberg for the French King, and the Comtesse d'Estrades, pretended friendship to the young woman. Yet this was only to bar Miss Fish's way to the King's bed, and to open an easier path thither for the Comtesse herself and the Marquise de Coislin, as Maurepas's *protégées*. Vice, sir, when clad in Virtue's armour, proved irresistible. Poor Miss Fish, whom our own Prince courted by back stairways when he fled to Paris, was sent on her way without so much as a *pourboire*. After so much shill-I, shall-I, she endured the greatest of all mortifications by leaving the presence of her royal admirer a perfect virgin.'

Yet the affair between Prince Charles Edward and this lady soon proceeded with such haste that Mr Wilkes at one time assured Lord Hervey of the Prince's actually having married Mademoiselle in Europe two years since. Lord Hervey said that such things were so often talked of and so often dropped again that he could not believe the Prince had already married her. It might have been that she knew of the design in America and had promised to come to him there as his consort, but that could not properly be construed as a marriage settlement.

As to the Prince's conduct at this time, he wrote her by every means of despatch. The Chevalier de Johnstone assured Lord Hervey that His Royal Highness's passion and tenderness in this correspondence must be incredible to anyone who did not see it. Whoever had read it, without knowing from whom it came or to whom it was addressed, would have concluded it written by some young gallant of twenty to his first mistress.

Notwithstanding this, much of the familiar talk in Virginia exhibited the Prince's bride as a royal whore and a frumpish old maid, though it hardly seemed reasonable that she could answer both descriptions. It would be too tedious to enumerate half the jokes, verbal and practical, that were put upon Mademoiselle, or the pleasant pasquinades upon the name of Miss Fish. There was hardly a tavern wag in Williamsburg who did not proclaim that 'a Fish by any other name must smell as sweet', and who did not claim the dusty jest for his own.

Lord Hervey was uneasy, from all that he could discover of Mademoiselle. Among the courtiers of Williamsburg she was spoken of generally with as little decency as affection, and all this made one wonder who she was that the Prince had sworn to marry. It was commonly said that she had been assured by a wise gypsy, at nine years old, that she must infallibly become a royal mistress, a tinker's tale which hardly disposed one in her favour. In the next place, she had been refused in marriage by the Sieur d'Étioles. Or, rather, she was refused by Monsieur's parents, who feared that the unchastity of Mademoiselle's mother might appear as strongly marked in the daughter. From this it would not have been surprising if the Prince's advisers had urged him to make some other match. He had, however, no great natural propensity to changing an opinion once he had conceived it.

The end of January, the veil was drawn from the enigma. Mademoiselle landed at Yorktown from the French ship which had conveyed her with all speed from the port of Nantes. The quantity of presents and possessions which accompanied her was so prodigious that it at first quite diverted the attention of the spectators from the poor young creature who was the object of so much curiosity. Besides enough furniture to fill three palaces the size of that at Williamsburg, there were elegant canvases upon which she was depicted as a pilgrim, a shepherdess and, with too little decency for a royal consort, as the goddess of love. There were ormolu lanterns, screens of amaranthus wood, Dresden candlesticks, figures in white Vincennes, a dove cote with pigeons on the roof, bouquets of flowers in Meissen porcelain, and so many dogs and birds in Vincennes china that they turned one sick to look at them.

All around the Palace, the little mall was thronged like a fairground, when the Prince escorted her from Yorktown to Williamsburg. Those who had made their jokes upon her, shouldered one another to catch a glimpse of her in the coach. Two footmen in blue and purple velvet rode upon the coach-box, when the whole cargo was driven at a full gallop through the Palace gates. She who was soon to be the Princesse de Virginie then stepped forth, followed by a turbaned negro page-boy who held a coral parasol above her. Out of prudence, she had dressed for riding, wearing skirts of coral taffeta, a coatee, and a small tricorne hat that tilted a little in a roguish manner towards her left eye.

The Prince, who used to be the centre of admiration for his handsome appearance and elegance of bearing, now found that he was quite overlooked, and saw all that admiration drawn to his Consort. She was above the average height, slender, supple in her carriage, and graceful in the least gesture. Her face was a perfect oval, crowned by hair of a dark gold, and illuminated by her large eyes, fine features, and the fairest skin in all the world. The infinite variety of her expressions and gestures never disturbed the grace and harmony of her person. They who had come to spy or to mock stayed to marvel and admire.

In her conversation she spoke sensibly and without affectation, not obtruding herself in any way. She had a very uncommon quickness in learning, spoke English, and Italian, as well as French; played upon the harpsichord and sang everything at sight, loved needlework and painting, and did both extremely well. She had little need to value herself upon her rank, because she had so many qualities besides her rank to pride herself upon.

She was a model of amiability, remarking, 'If one is to live in the world, one must be pleasant to everyone. For to confine oneself to people one esteems is to be deserted by almost the whole human race.'

To Lord Hervey, she once said, 'I have learnt that one can only be happy by aiming at whatever is not impossible.'

To which Lord Hervey replied that in her present situation she had already achieved that which was an impossibility to almost all her sex. At this, the Princess asked him, in a very grave manner, if such a marriage as hers, and in such circumstances, would be possible to two people who were not consumed by a mutual passion in the first place. Lord Hervey said, 'Lord, madam! In half a year all persons are alike. The figure of the body one's married to, like the prospect of the place one lives at, grows so familiar to one's eye that one looks at it mechanically, without regarding either the beauties or the deformities that strike a stranger.'

On the 16th of February, the Prince was married. The

whole ceremony was performed with great regularity and order, though not with such splendour and magnificence as might have been the case at St James's. The occasion was of a private kind, yet the chapel in the Palace was fitted up with extreme good taste, and as much finery as velvets, gold and silver tissue, galloons, fringes, tassels, gilt lustres, and sconces could give. They were married according to the service of the Church of England, though if Mr Wilkes was to be believed they had been joined two years earlier by the ceremonial of Rome, so that one way or another all parties must be satisfied. The Prince gave a necklace of diamonds to his bride, conferring upon her also those titles which, in the Jacobite view, were his to share with his wife, as Jeanne-Antoinette, Princesse de Virginie, Princess of Wales, Duchess of Cornwall, and Countess of Albany. The French Queen, out of lingering resentment at her, would at first not have it that the King should confer upon the Princess any title that belonged to France. Yet King Louis, being pressed also by the Cardinal Duke of York to recognise the marriage, relented so far from his own peevishness as to create her Madame La Marquise de Pompadour. With that she was to be satisfied as to a dowry, and yet for all her greater titles the one that came from her own country gave her a special pleasure. Lord Hervey observed that in private she would often refer to herself by that honour alone.

The night after the marriage there was a great *bal costumé* at the Palace, at which Madame La Princesse absolutely extinguished all the other women at the Court, although some were very beautiful. She appeared simply enough dressed in a cherry-coloured domino, needing no greater refinement of apparel, whose own loveliness was her true ornament. Her features and her marvellous complexion set off the brightest, the wittiest, the most sparkling eyes that could be imagined. Everything about

180

her seemed rounded, including her very gestures. The Prince squired her with that humour and gallantry of which his very enemies made acknowledgement, he being in the costume of his royal clan.

The Palace of Williamsburg was a mere toy palace beside St James's or Versailles. Yet every window was lit up, and the courtyard blazed with torches at midnight as though it had been noon. In the gardens, the light shone upon white statues of graces and nymphs. In the *salons*, the figures in Vincennes or Meissen looked down silently upon the pressing throng of guests. This press of people in their multitude of dresses, the sound of so many voices, the echoes of harps, flutes, and fiddles, is beyond all description. The ball room was so crammed with Harlequins, Pierrots, Scaramouches, Turks in their turbans, Persians in fine robes, that dancing was almost an impossibility. The planters of Virginia had left off their own dress to appear in that of their enemies, for they were now Indians, wizards, and friars, whose wives had become a hundred shepherdesses and nymphs.

Among the great mirrors and the pier-glasses, there hung the pictures which Madame La Princesse had brought from France, including that in which Monsieur La Tour had shown her as a shepherdess, and that by Monsieur Boucher, where she reclines upon a day-bed with a book in her hand. The other, which represented her in the costume of Mother Eve before the Fall, was hung in some private apartment, where the eyes of strangers might not fall upon it.

On the 21st of February, the whole world knowing that Lord Loudoun or some other commander might fall upon Virginia when the next campaigning season should begin, Mr Johnson, Mr Wilkes, and Lord Hervey resolved upon returning to England as soon as might be possible. Lord Hervey, having always been steady to his own party, had little wish to be looked upon now with suspicion for his undue dallying at the Pretender's Court. On the 23rd of February, Mr Wilkes came to Lord Hervey and desired him to ride to Yorktown, where a vessel was lying that would sail for Lisbon in a day or two more. By making their final passage from Lisbon to England, it might appear that none of the travellers had ever touched at Williamsburg.

'For', said Mr Wilkes to Lord Hervey, 'I fear much a warrant in London, signed by the pale Mansfield, beginning, *The King Against John Wilkes.*'

They stayed in town until the day following, and then went with Mr Johnson by coach to Yorktown. At the Prince's wish, they were accompanied by a dozen Scots foot guards. These were commanded by Colonel Lovat Fraser, a tall and light-complexioned man who spoke little but listened more eloquently than any person whom Lord Hervey had ever met.

Mr Wilkes hoped much that a sea voyage might be the means of recuperating from what he had at first thought to be St Anthony's Fire, but was obliged to conclude to be St Cythera's Pox.

'I hope', said Mr Wilkes to Lord Hervey, 'it will not go off in an obliging gonorrhea, which (from whom communicated I know not) is at present ravaging the constitution of Miss J., and playing the devil with your humble servant.'

On the 30th of March, after a tedious voyage of five weeks in most disagreeable circumstances, their ship entered a great fog. But presently the sailors found sand at a few fathoms, and the next day they reached Lisbon. By the latest despatches, Lord Hervey learnt that the Court and the Ministry in London had grown very outrageous against the Pretender's action in Virginia and thought only how speedily they might defeat his rebellion by means of the mighty power which lay at their call.

6

THE IDES OF MARCH

The entries in Lovat Fraser's journal resume on 24 February 1761, the very day on which he commanded the escort that accompanied Lord Hervey from Williamsburg to the ship at Yorktown. It is, of course, possible that Fraser made entries in his journal for the period September 1760–January 1761, and that these were somehow lost. However, with his eccentric habits of diary-keeping he may have allowed the entries to lapse for this period.

Having brought Bonnie Prince Charlie to Williamsburg, Fraser says nothing of how, following the departure of the Cardinal Duke of York, and the news of the death of George II, many Virginians, including members of the Council of the Province, and of the House of Burgesses, appeared ready to make their peace with the Prince who had ended the war against France. He says nothing either of the secret diplomacy during this period, by which Virginia sought to draw Maryland and Carolina into a Stuart alliance against Lord Loudoun's forces in New York.

It is a matter of record that during this winter Fraser was heavily occupied as Colonel of the 2nd Highland Regiment in the Prince's army. He may have felt that the drilling of his men, or the routine mustering of his regiment, hardly warranted mention in his journal. Yet by the end of February 1761 there were threats to the Prince and the Province, which only a few months earlier had seemed distant enough, that now became a growing reality.

It seemed evident that there were extreme republicans in Virginia itself who would stop at nothing to ensure that the Prince should never wear a crown in America. As soon as the euphoriai nduced by the French peace at Fredericksburg began to fade, these men set to work secretly but in earnest. A second and greater danger lay in the overwhelming power of the Hanoverian army which Lord Loudoun might soon assemble in the northern provinces of America. Both this force, and the still greater resources available in England, seemed to offer little hope that the Stuarts could hold Virginia against the armies of the young George III.

If Lovat Fraser had, indeed, allowed his diary-keeping to lapse for several months, he may have been prompted to return to his journal on 24 February 1761 by the certain knowledge that events in Virginia were now moving towards the great crisis which must decide for ever the fate of America and of the Royal House of Stuart.

24 February 1761. Coming at night from Yorktown to Williamsburg with a party of the Highland Regiment, I found the city as brightly lit as it has been every night of the winter. There was such an air of gaiety everywhere that it hardly seemed as if the season of Lent could have begun. From Candlemas until now nothing has been heard of at Court but masquerades and pleasure. The Prince must be amused by such entertainments, if only because he thinks them necessary to amuse Madame La Princesse. At the time of the marriage, no evening passed without some masquerade or *jeu du roi*, or some piece played before the royal pair. These diversions occupied so much of the night that Colonel Byrd confessed to me he had passed a whole week without ever seeing the day. There was universal relief when Ash Wednesday came. The courtiers remained for several days dead beat, and Colonel Ogilvie swore to me privately that he never expected to live beyond Shrove Tuesday.

To a soldier, such displays as these must seem like trumpery and gew-gaws. Yet to the people of Williamsburg it was the very stuff of royal splendour. It may work to our advantage here to permit them to see the Prince play as a prince in pleasure as well as in earnest. But it will do little to protect us from Lord Loudoun's regiments of redcoats.

As to Madame La Princesse, no fiddlers or dancing masters could improve upon her natural qualities. Her presence sets a pleasing fashion at Court, for the sweetness of her wit and her unexampled graces communicate these very qualities themselves to those who have them not. Besides her extreme goodness of heart, she wears wisdom easily, knowing many things thoroughly without ever wishing to appear as though she knew anything.

At the *bal costumé* I had some conversation with her and asked her, among other things, how she liked Virginia in all its simplicity, after the glories of France.

'Monsieur,' said the Princess, 'I know enough of the theatre to be certain that most women who dream of playing the great roles would indeed be happier playing the smaller.'

'Why, madame,' said I, 'the part you play here is not small!'

'It must be,' said she, 'for I have learnt that where a queen or a princess becomes a figure of great consequence there are always those who will use her as the means of shaping her husband's will to their own designs. Such attempts are the ruin of the state. No, sir, a prince and princess, or a king and a queen, must be two heads under one hat.'

All this was spoken with great firmness, and yet in a voice that seemed gentle and engaging. The strength of her mind may equal that of any man, yet in the softness of her womanly qualities she is without a rival among her entire sex.

28 February 1761. The departure of Lord Hervey and his friends from Yorktown, a few days since, proves how transient the world believes the Prince's regency to be. All those curious visitors, who came to Williamsburg as to a raree-show, are now prudently packing their effects and making haste to join the stronger side once more.

The 2nd Highland Regiment lies near the city, while the 1st Highland Regiment, with Colonel Ogilvie, defends Fredericksburg. The Irish Brigade, under General O'Sullivan, is deployed between Winchester and Fort Cumberland (that is now to be called Fort Charles). The ports of Norfolk, Hampton, and Yorktown are held by the Royal Americans under the command of Major Shaw, while Colonel Byrd has mustered the Virginia regiments of foot near Westover. So it turns out that Major Shaw must defend us from the sea, Colonel Byrd must turn a friendly gaze upon Carolina while Colonel Ogilvie is to deny Lord Loudoun a crossing on the Potomac from Maryland. General O'Sullivan's line is more extended but he faces the French and their Indian allies, who are not at the present our most likely enemies. The Chevalier commands for the Prince in Williamsburg, where two hundred horsemen of His Highness's Life Guards and Fitzjames's Horse, with two hundred more of the Virginia Cavalry, are ready to do business with any invader.

In conversation with the Chevalier, I urged that the 2nd Highland Regiment, now in camp close to the city, should be marched to Fredericksburg or Alexandria, where it might assist to deny Lord Loudoun the passage of the Potomac, and might also give heart to the Marylanders.

'No, sir,' said the Chevalier, 'not a man shall leave Williamsburg, neither the Highlanders nor the troops of horse. You have spoken, sir, of the enemy that would invade Virginia, but let us not forget the enemy that may already be among us. Consider what might be done by an insurrection of republicans and levellers if there were not five hundred Highlanders and the Prince's own guard in Williamsburg. Consider what must happen if Charles Edward be taken, or worse than taken, by the creatures of George III. No, sir, your regiment shall remain here, and the troopers of the Life Guards or Fitzjames's Horse shall ride with their Prince wherever he may go. They are loyal to a man, sir, for have they not given up all else for the honour of sharing exile with their true sovereign, King James, and the Prince, his son?'

This conversation happened three days since, the eve of the Prince's departure for Westover, where he was to hunt Colonel Byrd's country. The Royal Hunt met there upon the 26th of February, the Prince and Princess riding from Williamsburg in a fine carriage that bore the arms of England and France upon its side. Before and behind them rode two squadrons of horse, the whole expedition making so brave a sight that they were cheered the length of Duke of Gloucester Street.

Lord Elibank remained as the Prince's representative, and Sir John Randolph was his chief minister. The House of Burgesses, which adjourned last December, when so few of its members came to do business there, is fixed to meet upon the 15th of next month. There is, for the time being, little enough for the 2nd Highlanders to do, though it is impossible the regiment should be disbanded yet. The men are camped close to the race-field, a little way out of the town, in tents and the wooden huts they have built. One company is always in Williamsburg, where they mount guard over the Palace, the Capitol, and the powder magazine. The regularity of such duty, and the natural feeling they all have for a Stuart Prince, must contribute much to maintain discipline at present, under conditions of some hardship. The Prince has been with them often, commending them, and promising them that as soon as the business of war is done they shall all of them be his freeholders in the Kingdom of Virginia.

2 March 1761. For all the manly spirit of the High-landers, the gaiety that lit the winter season a few weeks ago grows daily more dank and cold. Two nights since, a journal that came from London through the port of Charlestown in Carolina was freely handed about in Williamsburg. It promises that we have not yet heard the last of the Elector of Hanover, who now offers a reward of £20,000 to any man who shall take the Prince alive or bring him in dead.

'Why, sir,' said the Prince, when the Chevalier told him of this, 'that is £10,000 less than was offered at Culloden. You may be sure, sir, we shall find this sham-king still more mean spirited than ever his grandfather was.'

Beyond this, His Royal Highness would make nothing of it. Yet at the Chevalier's insistence he was persuaded to draw up a plan for the safety of the Princess (for he scorned any that was for his own) to be put to good use if ever he was taken or killed. The design was to save the Princess and, what to the Chevalier and me must be of still greater importance, to guard any heir to the Stuart line that might then have been born or conceived.

A troop of the Life Guards, under the command of one Captain John Sobieski, a distant kinsman of the Prince, was to be the Guard of the Royal Household. These troopers were to be ready, in the event of some great reverse of fortune, to convey the Princess to Yorktown and then accompany her upon a waiting ship to such port in the Spanish province of Florida as might put her beyond the reach of Hanoverian barbarity. The Prince would not at first have the Princess told of this, but being assured that it might prove difficult of execution unless she were a full party in the knowledge of it he at last consented. However, he made it a joke with her, as though it could never happen in reality. Madame must have been truly alarmed that all might end in this manner, but she bore up bravely and wept only for love of him, at the prospect he painted.

What was worse than any of this, I have heard sedition preached in the playhouse itself, where I happened to be in a box last night with my kinsman, Simon Fraser. We had gone late, intending only to see the afterpiece, *Pasquin Turn'd Drawcansir* by Mr Macklin. The players had finished the main business and were about to raise the curtain upon this satyr play. It happened just then that I heard some commotion among our neighbours in the next box, whom we heard plainly enough although we could not see them. One of these wretches loudly wished damnation upon Prince Charles Edward and swore that his brother, the Cardinal Duke of York, would be sent from Rome to anoint him with the oil of kingship as the Pope's catamite. At this there was an exclamation from the other.

'May I be damned if Charles Stuart shall ever play the tyrant here! You may tell that royal pauper that the day of his coronation shall be the day of his death, for he shall find my dagger in his heart before the sun sets.'

There was an earnestness in the speaker's voice which bore ample witness to his intention. I was first upon my feet, opening the door of the box where we sat, and pushing my way into the passage outside. Unhappily, there was a great press of people, some of whom were making their way out after the main piece, while others were intent upon finding places to see Mr Macklin's little comedy. I had such trouble in making my way among them that by the time I could reach the next box the door of it was open and the seats empty. I questioned some of those who stood nearby but could not learn the identity of the men that had lately occupied the place, only that one of them was tall, thin, not yet of middle years, wore a red wig and appeared to be extremely out of humour.

The party that returned today with the Prince from Westover included Colonel Byrd, who has imparted a great passion to His Royal Highness for playing at billiards. Colonel Byrd assured me that this diversion occupied as much of the Prince's time at Westover as the pleasures of the chase, for the rain stopped, the ground froze hard, and all such sport was over after the first day. While they were both so engaged I took the Chevalier on one side and told him what I had overheard at the playhouse last night.

'Sir,' said he, 'there is much of this stuff that blows like the wind and will come to nothing. But take care, sir, that you discover the men if it can be done, for what the Elector of Hanover has lost he may take again without an army, if he can find a single man who is truly apt and cunning for such a bloody purpose as this is.'

3 March 1761. The words that appear against the Prince grow still more outrageous than they lately were. Bills, broadsheets, and daubs are common enough, and one cannot tell if they are the work of a few hands or many. The worst of it is that they have disturbed the minds of the people who now wonder whether the days of the Prince may not be numbered, and whether they themselves may not soon be called to account for any show of friendship towards him. They who drift with the tide and used to cheer his progress now stand silently, as if unwilling to act contrary to their neighbours. For all that, their neighbours have no idea what to act any more than themselves. How long it may be before these same fair-weather sailors begin to hoot and hiss at the Prince they so lately applauded is any man's conjecture.

The very walls of Williamsburg grow outrageous with the signs of disaffection. The Princess herself is not spared, for knowing that she played a little part in a court masque on Shrove Tuesday her detractors have daubed the town with their sentence, 'Women Actors Notorious Whores'. On the walls of the Capitol itself stand such sentiments as that 'All Hereditary Government Is Tyranny', and 'No King, No Bishop'. The sheets of stuff that are scattered about the town spare neither the Prince, his Princess, nor any of us. The indecency of such satires is almost beyond description. One, which came to my hands yesterday, speaks of the Prince in terms of the greatest scurrility.

'Now stinking with brandy and itching with lust,
This hopeful Pretender to all that is just,
Sits tight in his Palace with duns at the doors
To give places to Scotsmen and pox to his whores,
To take all our liberties from us, and bring
The Bishops, the Pope, and a Jacobite King.'

There was much more than this, but not half so decent. No one knows from where it comes or who does it, but its effect must be to make the world believe that Virginia is weary of Charles Edward and would willingly show itself worthy of the reward which the Elector of Hanover has offered to the murderer of our Prince.

5 March 1761. Last night there was a mournful sight at the playhouse, where the Prince and the Princess were in a box that was curtained in velvet and bore the arms of Stuart above it. On the way there, their carriage was accompanied the length of the mall and Duke of Gloucester Street by a company of the 2nd Highland Regiment, at whom several of the mob sang a verse to *Lillibullero*, which was sung when the Hanoverians barbarously hanged the Prince's soldiers after the '45.

'O Brother Sawney, hear you the news?
Twang 'em, we'll bang 'em, and
    Hang 'em up all!
An army's just coming without any shoes;
Twang 'em, we'll bang 'em, and
    Hang 'em up all!'

In the dark it was impossible to see who did this, and our men resolved not to notice the insult.

The piece that was played upon the stage happened to be the tragedy of *Julius Caesar*, which had been arranged some time before, but an unhappy enough choice as it was to be proved. Mr Pitch, who played the part of Caesar, had reached that scene where he was admonished by the soothsayer to 'beware the Ides of March', when there ran a murmur throughout the entire house, which was renewed when the words were repeated a moment later. The Prince seemed not to notice this restlessness but the Princess was much affected, though she would not show it.

The conferences of Brutus, Cassius, and their fellow conspirators, the tears of Calpurnia begging her dear Caesar to avoid the Senate House that day, all these seemed suddenly to afford a most unhappy parallel to the apparent state of affairs in Virginia. I was afterwards told by Lord Elibank that the Princess begged His Royal Highness that they might take their leave of this woeful piece before that scene should be acted in which the conspirators must let Caesar's blood. Yet he would not, and upon her asking a second time he spoke to her softly two of the lines from this same play.

'Cowards die many times before their deaths;
The valiant never taste of death but once.'

All this was done not to chide her but in an attempt to restore her spirits. The Prince believed that if he were to shun the exhibition of those things he most feared the courage of the Princess might begin to fail her (for, in truth, she has a great deal of it) and that the waverers, seeing him shrink, would act like dogs that turn their fangs upon whichever of their number gives ground.

Yet when that scene was acted, in which Caesar walking to the Senate House was met there by the conspirators, whose knives ringed him about and hacked him down, there was a sensation in the house as though some murder was indeed taking place. Many eyes were then turned upon the royal box. The Prince sat still and watched, as though it had been the tragedy of Hamlet, or the Moor of Venice, with no greater application to his own position. It is certain that the players themselves intended no satire upon his presence, for it was afterwards noticed that they had mounted the royal arms of his House above their stage, in proof that he had been their most gracious patron.

The sad parallel which Shakespeare's Roman history had suggested was not much spoken of among those at Court. Yet the Chevalier was quick to make light of the whole business.

'Why, sir,' said he, as though he were about to flourish a sword, 'he must be the most contemptible, lily-livered poltroon who would allow his resolution to weaken because a company of gallows-birds with wooden swords must needs mimic the roar of battle in their own feeble ranting!'

I objected that, however acted, the parallel was an unhappy one.

'Parallel?' said he. 'What parallel? I am reminded, sir, that Caesar was three times offered a crown and that he three times refused it. Now, you may be certain that Charles Edward will not be offered a crown three times, for on the very first occasion he will take it with both hands so soon as it is spoken of. Then, sir, what parallel is there? But if you mean that there are men, and great men too, who die by the sword, why that is such a commonplace as scarcely to be dignified with the high-sounding title of a parallel instance.'

And so he would have it, and not all the persuasion of which any man was capable would argue him out of his present mood. Yet the next morning, not four hours since, there came further evidence of what hatred must fester somewhere in Williamsburg, be it among never so few of the people. While the Princess rode back in her carriage from some little excursion she had made, a purse was thrown in through the very window of the coach itself. How this was contrived, no one knows. It proved to be a little bag of wash-leather containing two pence (rare enough in this Province, where so much of their trade is in kind) and with the two coins came a note, inscribed,

'Twopence for a good strong rope to bear the weight of the tyrant and his mistress.'

This caused a good deal of consternation, not only for the cunning with which it was delivered but more for the evidence that those who, in the literal sense, could throw their money in the street must be men of some consequence. Lord Elibank would even have it that there must be some plot against the Prince in the very Court itself. The worst of it is that in a little while more each man will look upon his neighbour as the enemy of us all. The news of the latest insult was soon known by the whole town, and daubs of 'Twopence for a rope' were found in two or three places.

Colonel Byrd, who knows the men of consequence in Virginia better than any other of the Prince's party, was for letting the matter drop. The Chevalier, however, insisted that a closer guard must be set upon the Palace, and that for the future a stricter guard must be kept by the escort that shall ride either with the Prince or the Princess. There is also to be a special watch kept about the gardens of the Palace whenever their Royal Highnesses shall walk there. Yet Charles Edward is the same Prince who, not a year since, walked alone into the city of Williamsburg, and trusted to the people who thronged about him, and was received by them with acclamation. I do not believe that Virginians are such a giddy rout that they can change their hearts so soon. Whatever the appearance may be, I shall continue to suppose that all the present discontent is the work of a fanatic minority, who hope by their displays of ill-feeling to herd other men's thoughts the way of their own. For, even while the latest insult was offered to the Princess, there were those among the onlookers who gave a huzza for Madame, and called God's blessing upon Her Royal Highness.

11 March 1761. After so much apprehension, almost a week passed in the most perfect calm imaginable. Though the Princess kept to the Palace, the Prince has been about his business, either without being so much noticed by the people, or else receiving amiable salutations from them. This I have heard for the most part at secondhand, for I was occupied much of the time with the 2nd Highlanders, who must be ready for campaigning as soon as the weather grows more kindly. A strange word 'kindly', for it might be kinder in the weather to keep arctic snows between Williamsburg and New York.

The Highland soldiers of the Prince's army lack much in their knowledge of the use of muskets, being accustomed to trust to their broadswords and their unadorned courage. Now they must learn that art, so despised in General Wolfe's army, of taking good aim when they fire. We have also practised how, by forming two lines, they may advance through one another, the first firing while the next loads its muskets, and then that second line coming through the spaces of the forward one to become, in a manner, the first line. By this practice, a double line of men might be always firing and always advancing. It is what cavalry are accustomed to do, in a different sense, when one squadron advances or retires through another that stands fast.

The Prince, who so distinguished himself with the Spanish army at the battle of Naples, as well as in the affair of the '45, was twice with the regiment lately. He was made much of by his Highlanders when he came to witness a field day, where the Life Guards, Fitzjames's Horse, and two squadrons of Virginia Cavalry made up the mounted troops. The Prince himself took the command of these.

A further sign of the general improvement is the assembling of the House of Burgesses in a few days' time. They are, for the most part, mild in their attitudes towards His Royal

Highness, provided that he allows them sufficient exercise of their powers without impediment. Some of them, like the Chevalier, Colonel Byrd, Sir John Randolph, Mr Wormeley Carter, and Fitzhugh of Marmion, are the Prince's men, who now begin to be called the Court Party. Others, like Colonel Landon Carter, are of the Constitutionalists and would assert the right of Parliament as the supreme consideration of any government. If the Prince will but submit to them, they make no objection to his living in Virginia as a private gentleman. Between these two factions are the men of independent view, among whom one may number Colonel Washington. They will never be of the Court Party, and if the Prince were to show himself any way arbitrary he would drive them into the company of the most extreme Constitutionalists. If he will only be patient, and guarantee men their liberty and their property (for one will not do without the other), Charles Edward may find his friends among the independent men, and even among the better sort of the Constitutionalists.

It is arranged that upon the 15th of March the Prince shall attend the meeting of the Council of the Province at the Capitol. The extreme Constitutionalists and the fanatic Whigs murmur that this savours too much of a king or a regent riding to the opening of his parliament. Such suppositions are all absurd. The House of Burgesses will not even meet that day, its session being held over until the day following. It is every man's interest that the Prince and the Council should meet and agree to be of one mind. Else there must be one government in the Capitol, held by Councillors and Burgesses, and another in the Palace, held by the Prince, his courtiers, and his army. There can then be no doubt but that one government must be rebels against the other, which will foment such civil war between us that shall endure until the Hanoverian army brings us to a terrible retribution. We who remember Culloden may assure Colonel Washington, and even

Colonel Carter, that in such a reckoning their heads as surely as our own will ornament the poles of London Bridge or the Tower.

15 March 1761. Had it not been for a sickness of the Princess's, they would both have driven to the Capitol. What it was that so affected her the women would not say, which gave rise at once to a story that she had miscarried. Indeed, one of her waiting-women swore that she spoke to another that had seen the abortion lying in a basin. Yet to conceive so aptly and come to labour so prematurely seems not to be in the nature of things. For all that, Madame was not herself. The Chevalier told me that he had seen her between a drawing-room and her own apartments, Lord Elibank pushing her from behind, while Lord Caryll and one of the women tugged her forward at the arms. For a moral certainty this will prove to be some trifling sickness and nothing more, however disagreeable it may be at present.

The Prince was with her some part of the morning and then retired with the Chevalier, Colonel Byrd and Lord Elibank to consider the meeting with the Council of Virginia that should take place in the afternoon. There was nothing decided between them but that the Prince should speak fair and reasonable words to the Councillors, swearing that he brought them no dowry but their independence of Hanover, and that neither he nor his father would impose upon them any measure which they would not themselves have chosen. In such a fair and open treaty any man might have a part who was not attached to the House of Hanover out of a purely natural and obstinate stupidity. It was thought among the Court that once the Prince had made his terms with the Council the Burgesses would not be long in following, for many of them had already resolved to part with the Elector of Hanover in the best way that they might.

It was a certainty that no man living was ever proof to

the charm and amiability of the Prince. In his middle years he has lost none of that quick spirit and movement which so distinguished him in youth. At almost 40 years old, he was met by men who would afterwards refer to him by such appellations as 'that good-natured boy'. At his setting out for his meeting with the Councillors, he made the same figure as always, his form sprightly, his profile noble, his head carried high, his wig neatly tied and powdered, his linen of the finest. Indeed, he walked with the step of a young lover who sets out to court his first mistress.

It should be recorded that he defied the Chevalier and rode to the Capitol on horseback, in order, as he said, that his people might better see him. He feared no man's hand against him and would not, he declared, skulk in the corner of a great coach, like some tyrant who dared not meet the eyes of his poor subjects. This was a true Prince, for he was more so in his mind than even in his figure!

Before he left the Palace, Charles Edward retired a little with his Chaplain, that Dr Shebbeare who is shortly to be consecrated Bishop of Williamsburg and, says Colonel Byrd, Archbishop of all Virginia. Some time later, the Prince came out and asked one of his attendants how the Princess did. On hearing that she was improved, he thanked God for that and went out with the commander of his escort to mount his white horse, Reynard.

It happened that the Chevalier and I were among the first at the Capitol of Williamsburg, for the Prince and his escort were a little delayed by the crowd of people in Duke of Gloucester Street. The Prince's coach, which was to be used to convey him back to the Palace afterwards in company with one or two of the Councillors, was driven empty a little way before his escort, though flanked by a dozen Life Guards. This I did not see, but heard it soon after from Lord Caryll who witnessed it.

Lord Elibank had objected to the Chevalier that the

Prince's riding upon horseback exposed him to every evil-doer who would level a pistol and despatch him in an instant. Charles Edward himself, overhearing this remark which was no way intended for his ears, only laughed and said, 'Why, who should complain that his way out of this vale of tears came so suddenly and with so little pain as that!'

Yet he was in a graver mood when he mounted his horse. Lord Caryll, who was close by, swears that he heard him say to Captain John Sobieski of his Life Guards, 'It matters nothing to me whether I live one day or twenty years. Yet it greatly concerns the people of Virginia. If I am killed, there may be such blood spilt in this place by the several factions, and such barbarous revenge exacted by the Hanoverians, that one would pity the man who shall live to see that day.'

The Burgesses, and their wives and dependents, some of whom had lately come to town, waited in the streets for their first sight of His Royal Highness. Yet there was not the crowd that there used to be when he first came back from the French Peace, for his presence in the city is not now the nine days' wonder it used to be then. Some of those who watched him now had not come to gape but rather because they had business with their Prince. Several threw their petitions into his empty carriage as it passed, supposing him to be riding in it. But one ran towards the Prince himself, bearing a paper in his hand and demanding His Royal Highness's intercession in a dispute which related to Lord Fairfax's ownership of a great tract of land in the Northern Neck of the Tidewater region.

This fellow seemed so importunate that the Prince reined in his horse and spoke with the petitioner, who knelt submissively and addressed Charles Edward as 'His Majesty'.

'Indeed, sir,' said the Prince, 'I am my father's Regent,

but I am no king, and never may be. Yet I will serve you, if I can.'

And with that he took the paper and entrusted it to Lord Caryll. His conduct in this incident seemed to please the spectators. His talk of serving his subjects was much commended by those who had otherwise feared that a Stuart knew nothing of serving but only of despotically commanding the obedience of his people.

While this encounter was occupying the Prince, it happened that the Chevalier and I had reached the Capitol and dismounted. The Capitol of Williamsburg is a pleasing building but of unusual construction. It is built of two wings, the east and the west, each ending in a rounded bay and at a height of three floors. They would be separate buildings but that a gallery, like a covered bridge, runs between them. This gallery has a clock tower above and an open arcade below it. Around this arcade, and at the approach to it, were clustered those Burgesses and others who had business at the Capitol, or else had gathered out of idleness to see the Prince and the brave show of his Life Guards.

The Prince was to meet the Council in the fine oval room on the first floor of the west wing, which served as the Council Chamber for the Province. The chairs were drawn up round the green baize table and the Councillors awaited His Highness, who was to come to them in company with Colonel Byrd and Sir John Randolph. The Chevalier and I were standing close to the panelled door of the Chamber when there was a sudden commotion, which we heard plainly enough although it came from the far end of the gallery that joined us to the east wing. It happened that Colonel Carter and several of those who had begun to call themselves Constitutionalists were in conversation together in one of the rooms of the east wing, and I thought at first that some difference must have occurred to excite the wrath of the choleric Colonel himself. Yet all too soon I heard what it was that caused such commotion among them. It was one man's voice, as he ran up the far stairway and towards them, shouting, 'Tyranny is dead! The farce of monarchy is over!'

The consternation these words put us into needs not to be described. We both ran towards the gallery that lay between us and the east wing. In the arcade below was a great shuffling of the crowd and voices loudly raised.

Across the archway, at the far end of the gallery, there ran a brightly complexioned young man, who shouted at us as he went, 'Tyranny is dead!'

What troubled me most, and what I hardly had breath to tell the Chevalier, was that I knew his voice, though I had never in my life seen his face before. His was one of the voices I had heard at the theatre, when one of those in the next box sneered at the Prince and his brother, while his companion promised that his knife should lie in Charles Edward's heart the day of his coronation. Which of them had worn the red wig, I could not tell, but this was the voice of the man who had first sneered at the royal brothers.

It was impossible that we should catch him quickly, for he disappeared almost at once into the other wing. Moreover, the Chevalier had one thought alone, as he afterwards confessed to me. Far from despising the parallel of this instance and the tragedy of Caesar, he now saw how a fanatic mind might seize upon the Prince's arrival at the Capitol of Williamsburg as the ancient conspirators had chosen for their time Caesar's coming to the Capitol of Rome.

'The 15th day of March, sir,' he muttered as he ran. 'The 15th day, sir, is the Ides of March!'

Half-way across the gallery, he took the window that stood beneath the clock-tower and wrenched it open with such force that it was half-torn from its hinge. A throng of a hundred and more men moved below us in a disordered pattern. The coach with the arms of England and France upon it stood empty to one side.

'The Prince!' cried the Chevalier to anyone who would listen. 'Where is the Prince, sir?'

I could see no more clearly than himself, and our voices were quite lost among the noise of the crowd below. I was in half a mind to set up a cry of murder there and then, but at that moment I saw to my astonishment the Prince, walking alone and unharmed towards the crowd that shouldered and jostled before the Capitol. He had dismounted from his horse at some distance and was as yet unaccompanied by any of the Life Guards. Colonel Byrd and Sir John Randolph were behind him, though much further off than I had expected. Whether this was their respect for the Prince, or whether he advanced at a pace that took them by surprise, I do not know. Soon there was a jostling in the gallery too, for Colonel Landon Carter and his little band of Constitutionalists were pressing hard around the Chevalier and me for a view of the events outside.

'It appears', said one of them with a laugh, 'that we were misled by that happy report just now. See, the farce of monarchy is still being played, and the groundlings still give audience to the principal comedian of the piece.'

At any other time, the Chevalier would have resented this insult and called the man out upon the field of honour, but here was no leisure for that. The Burgesses and the others below us were opening a path in the crowd for the Prince to walk through to the arcade of the Capitol. The afternoon was warm as midsummer, the spring sunlight glittering upon the windows of Williamsburg, and the heat rising from the earth again in a shimmering veil. The crowd was silent, hardly a man exchanging a word with Charles Edward as he passed, though he nodded a greeting here and there. He walked unhurriedly, his figure distinctive in the pale blue coat, ruffles, and tied wig. His progress, that seemed to take an hour, was hardly more than a minute. At the heart of the crowd, each step brought him closer to where Colonel Washington stood, and next to Colonel Washington a thin, youngish man in a red wig!

I knew not what to do. From our point of vantage we could see every movement, which those below us could not. Yet we were helpless to change the course of events ourselves, for there was no direct means of getting to where the Prince was. The man in the red wig seemed to stand a little aside, towards Colonel Washington, to give place to a common-looking fellow behind him, who now came forward on his other side. I saw this fellow draw his hand upward, and the sun glinted on what I knew full well was a steel blade.

The Prince drew level with Colonel Washington, acknowledging him as he passed, and then just noticed the thin man in the red wig, who was a perfect stranger to him. He was about to pass on to where the villainous-looking fellow stood with what appeared to be a sturdy knife in his hand. The Chevalier saw what I saw, and for the only time in my whole knowledge of him he stood spellbound as a hare before the hunter. Knowing not what else to do, I found my voice and cried out in what was no less than a ghastly shriek, 'Murder! Murder! Look to the Prince!'

At this, several of Colonel Carter's friends, who had not seen what I had seen, took the matter up as a jest, crying, 'Oh, aye! Murder! Murder! Anything you please, sir!'

Yet in the same second that I had cried out my warning, the assassin raised the knife clenched in his fist, no more than twelve inches from Charles Edward's breast. The hand that held the knife was shielded from the view of others by the red-wigged man. But Colonel Washington, with his great height, saw what was done and sprang to grasp the wrist that would soon drive home the blade. The red-wigged man moved to bar the Colonel's way, at which the Colonel fairly threw him into the side of the assassin, shouldering that man a little and giving the Prince time to turn and face his deadly enemy.

The Prince never raised a hand to defend himself, but keeping his eyes upon those of the villain he said softly, 'Did I save you from the French, sir, only that you might murder me?'

At this, the wretch paused hardly at all, but ran forward at His Royal Highness. So did Colonel Washington, and it may have appeared for a moment that they were confederates. Yet it seems the Colonel had determined that if the Prince would not save his own life another must do it for him. He was, as he said later, resolved only to throw Charles Edward so far that he should be out of harm's way for a little space. And thus it happened, the Colonel fairly wrestling with the Prince, though his own back was offered to the assassin's knife, and the murderer seeking only an opening through which to thrust at the body of His Royal Highness.

Then there was a scene of pandaemonium, while Burgesses and others ran this way and that, leaving a sort of arena in which the murderer, the Colonel and the Prince were combatants. Yet at that very moment Captain John Sobieski, his helmet gone and rolling in the dust, his sword drawn and its scabbard half tripping him, ran forward from the arcade where he had just appeared. The assassin's answer was to present a pistol, which he carried in his coat, so that it was cocked and aimed at the Captain's breast. He might have used this against the Prince, had he not thought it easier to find the heart with a knife.

Sobieski never flinched, but walked towards him, his sword held out directly before him, commanding him to surrender in the name of the Prince. The murderer held fire until the Captain was not two yards from him and then let fly in an explosion that rang across the courtyard of the Capitol. The ball tore a most terrible wound in the breast of the brave soldier, yet he only faltered a little and then walked on till his own sharp sword entered the ribs of his enemy and, with his dead weight behind it, scraped horridly against the bones it touched before its point came out of the back with a little jerking movement. They who had fought as enemies fell united in death, the murderer quite senseless already, and John Sobieski mortally wounded, so that he could hardly live out the hour.

The Prince never left his side, and wept for one who was in a manner a cousin to him. He gave his assurance that the children of the brave Captain should want for nothing, and that he would care for them as if they were indeed his own. Captain Sobieski lived until about sunset and then died, though he had lain unconscious the greater part of that time.

In all the confusion of the attempt upon the Prince's life, every man in the crowd seemed only to fear that his neighbour might be one of the assassins and so it happened that each took care of himself. They scattered in every direction, except for those like Colonel Washington who had enough of the soldier in them to stand and face the enemy. Yet, when some account was to be given of the whole affair, no trace could be found of the thin man in the red wig, who was suspected to be the accomplice of the assassin and who, from what I saw with my own eyes, seemed so to a moral certainty. Nor could any further account be given of the young man who had run hither and thither, shouting that tyranny was dead and that the farce of monarchy (as he called it) was ended in Virginia. Thank God he made such a proclamation, for otherwise neither the Chevalier nor I would have been where we were in the gallery. It seems this youthful traitor mistook some signal from his confederates, or mistimed the Prince's arrival, or else hoped that the Constitutionalists might be got to mingle with the crowd and take the assassin for their hero. Whatever the reason, it is a mercy to us all that he played his part too soon.

Who they were or where they have gone is yet to be

discovered. The town buzzes with the story, and with other stories which never happened. It is already said that Colonel Washington was one of the conspirators, for was he not seen to set briskly about the Prince in front of a crowd of the most unimpeachable witnesses? Even if this had been thought, which it never was by His Royal Highness, both the Chevalier and I would vindicate the Colonel's part in the affair. The Colonel himself is in a quandary, for he never sought to be any kind of hero to the Stuarts. He swears that he went to the Prince's aid, not as he was a Prince and still less as he was a Stuart, but because murder must not be done. Like every sensible man in Williamsburg, the Colonel knows that, whatever ill-opinion he may hold of Charles Edward, his bloody assassination must open the way to the breakdown of all civil order and the coming of the most horrid anarchy and murder. If that were to happen, there would be little hope for the Colonel's own estates at Mount Vernon, or for the many other comfortable homes of the Province, most of them not one hundredth as grand as his.

28 March 1761. Today there was a splendid service of thanksgiving for the Prince's deliverance from the late attempt upon his royal life two weeks since. It was not a time for any sort of jubilation, as after some great triumph of arms, but rather a serious and devout acknowledgement, which His Royal Highness was the first to make, of the great goodness of Almighty Providence towards him. The Princess, who is now quite herself again, was his companion upon this solemn occasion.

Yet we might have rejoiced a little, for all that. There is no further sign here of the two conspirators. Which is not to be wondered at, since we hear that they have made their way to New York where they are to be pampered up by Lord Loudoun. They were not Hanoverians, by all accounts, but downright republicans and levellers who were prevented by no consideration at all from shedding the blood of him who stood in the path of their ambitions. For all that, they may now go to New York and be made much of, on the presumption that they did what they did out of love for the Elector of Hanover.

The identity of the dead conspirator is not known and perhaps never will be. Yet it was not long before the residence of the two fugitives was discovered, together with many of their effects. They it was who were the main instruments of vituperation against the Prince and Princess, and who were so outrageous that one would have thought Williamsburg contained a whole regiment of sedition. They left behind them such broadsides as that Caesar had had his Brutus, Charles I had had his Cromwell, and Charles Edward must be made to profit by the precedent.

There was much more in the same vein, all of it tending to show that the murder of kings and princes was the only true way to greatness, and preaching up popularity as the sole virtue of the commonweal. Government of whatever kind is denounced as a fraud and an hypocrisy. It is so far from commonsense that I do not know the man who could understand it. It is certain that the Elector of Hanover will no more welcome such ranting than would King James III. In Virginia, Colonel Landon Carter and his Constitutionalists will have no more part of it than will the most devout believer in the divine right of kings and the Stuart cause.

One of the two fugitives is a young Hanoverian exciseman, Paine, who was brought to Virginia not a year since when it was proposed to take from the pockets of our people whatever was necessary to fight the Elector of Hanover's wars. The news of his occupation, added to the disgust which is universally felt at the attempt to murder the Prince, has quite undone the effects of the daubs and the ill-natured lampoons. The other fugitive, one Henry, was a tradesman in a small way of business whose affairs had not prospered as they might have done. He, with his red wig, may have been the verier fanatic of the two.

It is to be expected that they do not confess their parts in the murderous conspiracy. Both of them claim that they had no part in the attempt and never before saw the man who made it, though they gladly admit to being peaceful advocates against Charles Edward and the Stuart cause. They swear that the cry of 'Tyranny is dead' was only a greeting to say that while the Constitutionalists met in the capital the victorious spirit of parliamentary liberty must triumph. They vow that their presence at the Capitol that day was no more a sign of their guilt than the presence of a hundred other men should make any of them to be murderers either. They repeat, who the villain was that killed John Sobieski and was finally killed by him they do not know, as he was a perfect stranger to them. They boast that they fled to New York only out of fear of what terrible deeds should be done to men of conscience in Virginia who would not bow to a Stuart tyrant. In their pleading they talk much of the rack and the thumbscrews that would have been prepared for such innocent men as themselves in a new Court of Star Chamber at Williamsburg. Believe this who can. What I heard and saw I have set down and will stand by every word of it against any man's opinion.

Yet what proves them to be poor judges of men and events is the manner in which the people of the Province and the Prince now greet one another with amity and consideration. They do not want his blood, and never did! He does not want to tyrannise over them, and never did! This is now plainly shown on both sides.

'Sir,' said the Chevalier to me this evening, 'the attempt upon the Prince's life has more firmly established him in his people's hearts than ten years' residence in the Palace of Williamsburg might have done. Why, even the independent men, who will never be of the Court Party, are now too sensible not to see that the evils which must follow such a dastardly murder far outweigh whatever grievances they may presently feel.'

And so it seems to be, for the people who filled the Church of Bruton Parish at the thanksgiving, and those who greeted the Prince and the Princess as they passed along the way, bore ample witness to the Chevalier's words. The dangers that threaten us from without, as soon as the campaigning weather shall come, are enough to unstring all but the most resolute minds. Our little army is a toy by comparison with the might of the Hanoverians and all their mercenaries. Yet, if we fight, we fight for our lives and our homes, not for any man's hire. To know that the Prince is a Prince indeed to his Virginian subjects, and to feel faith and loyalty to the good old cause growing here as it did in the Highlands, is to believe for a moment that we might face the whole world in arms, and bravely bear ourselves under the standard of that Bonnie Prince Charles for whom the clans at Culloden fought and fell.

7

ANNAPOLIS

Following the events of March 1761, the next set of entries in Lovat Fraser's journal begins some six weeks later, with the famous meeting between Prince Charles Edward and the Chiefs of the Nottoway, Tuscarora, and Cherokee tribes in the Blue Ridge Mountains. It was during this parley, by which the Prince intended to establish friendship between his European and Indian subjects, that the most dramatic crisis of his life was announced.

12 May 1761. Lagging somewhat behind the rest of the Prince's party, Colonel Ogilvie and I lodged last night at a Mohawk Indian's house, who offered me his sister and Ogilvie his daughter to sleep with us, as is their custom in these tribes. We were obliged to accept, so that this morning my bedfellow was very fond of me and wished to go with me. Yet I think that this cannot be.

Coming up with the Prince's party, some ten miles further on, we were later entertained by the King of the tribe, who lives in a very poor house with no emblem of majesty or royalty about him. He was an old man, shabbily dressed but very kindly. He called me his good friend and hoped that I should be kind to that Indian squaw whom he heard I had enlisted last summer on the road to

Fredericksburg. I promised him that I would be a model of manhood towards her in all things.

14 May 1761. So many tribes from such a great distance are gathered for the treaty that one would suppose it to be the occasion of some great celebration. This afternoon we were guests at the Indians' games, where the young men shot with arrows, and the girls ran races. At night, the Prince with Ogilvie and me were at the royal feast and saw their Indian dances to celebrate peace between their nations and the representatives of King James III, who lies sick at Rome.

In one of the Indian dances, the Prince was pleased to insist that I should have a part. My squaw divested me of all my clothes but for breech-clout and leggings, and then artfully painted me in the most elegant manner. We danced round the fire with little order, whooping and hollowing in a most frightful manner, being just drunk enough to care nothing for who heard us. Like the Indian braves, I had got strings of deers' hooves tied round my ankles and knees, with gourds containing shot or pebbles in my hands, that I might rattle them boldly. My little squaw and her girls wore bells and thimbles at their ankles and wrists.

The Prince and the rest of our party were overcome with mirth at the sight of Colonel Ogilvie and me so disporting ourselves. Yet one singular circumstance I noticed. General O'Sullivan and certain nice gentlemen of his kind professed to find nothing good in such a barbaric people. Yet these fastidious gentlemen were the very same whose ruffles and linen showed guilty signs of the red with which Indian ladies paint their copper-coloured bodies.

At last we retired to our beds, which were only clean rugs laid over hurdles in the Indian manner. My squaw insisted on painting in war colours what decency forbids I should name. Despite my weariness this brought to

211

perfection such a damned noble tarse that she must needs throw herself at it and make such a whooping that I should not wonder if everyone else at the treaty heard her. A knowing wench, but a warm heart and loins.

15 May 1761. This morning there came news indeed! Before daybreak, Hugh Mercer (who is made a General officer, as Colonel Byrd is to be, for his long experience) dashed with an escort into our settlement and ordered the picket guard to wake the Prince at once. No sooner had His Highness received them than Ogilvie and I were summoned, who seemed hardly to have got to our beds.

'Here is business for us all, gentlemen,' said the Prince, holding in his hand a sheet of paper. 'General Mercer comes from Williamsburg with this despatch from General Johnstone and Colonel Byrd. Four captains of vessels from Hampton and Norfolk have sighted an English fleet, no more than two days' distance from Chesapeake Bay. They describe twelve or fifteen ships of war and a score of transports carrying an army. They are too far south to meet the French in New England. It is we, gentlemen, who are to be honoured with their company. Make no mistake, gentlemen, their Elector of Hanover, who called himself George II may be dead six months or more, yet the Duke of Cumberland thinks to win a victory in the name of his new master, who styles himself George III. We shall see.'

It was some comfort that the Chevalier and Colonel Byrd were in Williamsburg, already rallying our forces, but Ogilvie and I feared that the great armada would land before the Prince could be there to lead his men. Charles Edward went to the Indians at once, pledging us as their friends and promising on his own authority to give a dowry to any of his subjects who should marry an Indian girl. This, he maintained, was the sweetest and the noblest way of conquest. The Indians, for their part, expressed honest indignation that he should be so basely betrayed by his white brothers across the sea, while he was engaged in a mission of peace, and they promised to be his firm allies in the struggle.

While it was still early, the Prince's party (of which I was to be a member) rode out of the Indian town and galloped towards Williamsburg as if all hell was howling at their heels.

17 May 1761. Yesterday, much of last night, and today we rode, managing to reach Fredericksburg at night by changing horses. The news of the English armada seems well known here. The citizens, the most loyal of any to the Prince who saved them from the French, are cleaning their arms and making cartouches for the coming battle. Charles Edward, whom nothing seemed to fatigue, spent much of the night giving orders for the building of beacons in the area between here and Williamsburg for signals to warn of an invasion. We hear that the fifteen warships have already sailed into Chesapeake Bay, but cannot tell if this is true. John Cameron was told that six of them have entered the mouth of the James River, off Hampton. It may be so.

18 May 1761. A despatch from the Chevalier this morning confirms that several men-of-war have sailed within the Cape but have come no closer. He also reports that as many as ten thousand English soldiers have landed on the other side of Chesapeake Bay but cannot swear to this. If this is so, they must march southwards upon us, from the direction of Maryland. As soon as he was in receipt of this news, the Prince ordered his party to prepare for the ride to Williamsburg, where we almost expect to find the Duke of Cumberland installed in the Palace. Indeed, it is the rumour of this same Duke of Cumberland's accompanying the fleet which has won so many of the uncertain Virginians to support Prince Charles. For they recall what mercy the Duke's men showed to Scotland after Culloden and they fear that if he is victorious here the same fate will overtake the men, women and children of Virginia. 'Better to die by the blade during battle than be butchered by the swordsman after defeat' is the motto of them all. Some of our people swear that they will train their black slaves to bear arms against the Hanoverian army.

19 May 1761. Upon our arrival in Williamsburg, we found a great calm over the city, for all that Cumberland's warships are cruising almost within sight of our shore, and no more than ten miles out to sea. The truth is that men of different persuasions have gathered behind the Prince in the face of the invasion. In the eyes of young George III and his uncle Cumberland, we are all traitors and our only hope lies in being victorious.

Trees and flowers everywhere are in full bloom and the heat of the Virginian summer already lies heavy on the town. The nuisance of dust and flies comes early this year. This is felt most where our army is assembling, a little way from the city, on the road to the Potomac. It was proposed that those Irish and Highland soldiers who followed their Prince should be given land close to the Ohio River, but by great fortune the regiments were held intact during last winter, as a precaution against other dangers, and are still at our disposal. The Virginia militia and Colonel Byrd's two Virginia regiments are camped near them, as are two battalions of Royal Americans and the Life Guards of the Prince. We may now muster some 5,000 foot soldiers and, perhaps, 500 cavalry, though this is little enough against such a force as Cumberland may bring. We also have Colonel Byrd's 600 Cherokee warriors and might, I believe, have called upon others from those tribes who lately entertained us with such a show of friendship.

22 May 1761. Soon after breakfast Colonel Ogilvie came back to Tazewell Hall, where he and I are both guests of

Sir John Randolph, the Prince's Attorney-General. His face was composed with great satisfaction, like a man who might speak great things if he chose to. I asked what news there was of the English armada.

'Oh, little enough,' said he, 'except that 10,000 English soldiers have landed in Maryland and seized the city of Annapolis. The ladies of Annapolis are much taken with the fine manners of Cumberland's officers.'

'And what of Cumberland himself?'

'He has taken Tulip Hill as his residence,' said Ogilvie. 'A fine enough house built a little way out of the city. It seems that they have no lack of men or supplies but we believe that the hearts of the Marylanders are with the Prince and the army of Virginia.'

When dinner was done, Ogilvie and I attended a council of war at the Capitol in Williamsburg. We were sent up to the fine oval room where the Council of the Province used to meet, and found the Prince himself, the Chevalier, General O'Sullivan (with a perfumed handkerchief to his nose), General Mercer and Sir John Randolph sitting round the green baize table. For all their perfidy towards his father and grandfather, the Prince had given no command for the removal of the two fine portraits of his royal aunts, Queen Mary and Queen Anne, which hung in the chamber.

'Twenty years ago,' said His Highness, 'I was persuaded to turn back from victory at Derby. Had we marched on only as far as Oxford, my father would now occupy the Palace of St James.'

'We are all subject to Fortune's will, sir,' said General O'Sullivan, taking his nose out of his perfumed handkerchief.

'Fortune is a whore, sir,' said the Prince impatiently, 'and she must be used accordingly. I shall not wait until Fortune chooses to bring the Duke of Cumberland to me. My army shall cross the Potomac into Maryland and seize him by the throat while he still thinks himself secure.'

General O'Sullivan protested a little that we should take a great chance in being so far separated from our supplies and our own people.

'Make no mistake,' said His Highness, 'if this battle is lost, it will be lost as easily in Virginia as in Maryland. If we would win it, we must win quickly, for our supplies will not sustain a long campaign. Yet, won or lost, I am determined to be where the battle is fought. The Governorship of Virginia shall be in the hands of Lord Elibank with Sir John Randolph as his attorney. Lord Caryll and Sir Robert Wormeley Carter shall be my representatives in Norfolk and Hampton. Colonel Simon Fraser shall hold Fredericksburg for us and guard our supply route.'

To all this there was general assent. The Prince then went on to name the Chevalier as his aide-de-camp, while Colonel Byrd, with the rank of General officer, was to command the Virginian troops and General O'Sullivan the Irish. The Highlanders, with whom both Ogilvie and I were to serve as commanders of regiments, were to be placed under General Hugh Mercer. These would have fallen, perhaps, to the command of the great Lord George Murray, who had fought so valiantly for his Prince in Scotland and who crossed the seas to Virginia last year as soon as he heard news of our victory. Yet it was only to lay his bones in an honoured tomb.

'As for the command of the army,' said His Highness, 'I will be my own commander, for I will be where the battle is. If that battle is to be lost, I would as soon die there by the sword of my enemies as live to see the surrender of power and the destruction of our state.'

Many protested loyally at this, General O'Sullivan faintly and the Chevalier with great force, for the danger in which the Prince must be placed. Yet he only turned it off with a joke, saying, 'Come, General Johnstone, I am afraid that we may be beaten by Cumberland. You are only afraid that we may win and my being there will oblige you to share the honour of victory with one more guest.'

And so the matter was decided.

26 May 1761. Last night our army camped in Virginia, close to the bank of the Potomac, where we saw before us the wooded slopes of Maryland beyond the water. This morning the two hundred horsemen of the Prince's Life Guards and Fitzjames's Horse, with an equal number of Virginia Cavalry, crossed the stream first, their mounts breasting the current with heads held high. The High-landers were next, pulling themselves by ropes to which their rafts were attached. Then the Virginia regiments and the Irish soldiers followed with General Byrd's six hundred Cherokee warriors coming over last.

When the crossing was completed, our scouts were told at once to discover what movements of the Duke of Cumberland's army there might have been. It was not more than three o'clock in the afternoon when we were halted by a message that the Duke's army had left Annapolis this same day and was marching in our direc-tion. We could not tell whether they knew of our river crossing.

The Prince, the Chevalier, Ogilvie and I were parleying on horseback in the shade of the trees, for it was oppres-sively hot.

'We and they are on the same road, sir,' said the Chevalier, 'and must now meet for a certainty. They have taken the road to cross the Potomac into Virginia, as we have crossed it into Maryland. If we continue our march, we may meet them before dusk and must blunder into a battle that would be better delayed until tomorrow.'

General Byrd, coming up at this moment, urged that we should march on.

'I believe, sir,' said he, 'our Cherokee warriors might do their business for them if we were to fall upon them in the dark. Yet if we postpone the battle until tomorrow we shall have to fight all through the day in such a damnably unwelcome heat as this is.'

For all that, it was resolved to call a halt and prepare our men against the battle which must be fought tomorrow. The ground is dismal and flattish, though with small hills here and there, an area of land some twenty miles to the south-west of Annapolis, which we have for the present christened Golgotha, or the place of dead skulls.

27 May 1761. By dawn today His Royal Highness had made his disposition for the battle. Our line lies at a right angle to the bank of the Potomac, which is too wide here for the enemy to cross downstream. In a line from the river bank, forming our right wing, is the Irish brigade under General O'Sullivan. In the centre are the two Virginia regiments and two regiments of militia, the whole commanded by General William Byrd III. The left wing, where the ground rises in a small bluff, consists of our two Highland regiments with several of our field pieces on the slight eminence, commanding a field of fire across the whole terrain. Here it is General Mercer who commands, the youngest of all the general officers, and Colonel Ogilvie and I who command regiments. We are supported by a company of foot soldiers raised from English Jacobite gentlemen in exile. In reserve, to be used as the Prince may command, are a hundred men of His Royal Highness's Life Guards, one hundred more of Fitzjames's Horse, and our two hundred Virginian Cavalry. With them are our Cherokee warriors and a regiment of Royal Americans, the other regiment of Americans having been left to secure the river crossing.

The whole formation made a brave sight in the dawn sun, for the Prince has dressed his army in royal blue to distinguish them from the redcoats of the British, though the Highlanders retain their tartan. General O'Sullivan, whose advice was sought, has arranged the line so that our men may make use of as many broken walls and fences as possible, for cover when firing on the enemy. This makes our line a little irregular and causes it to curve back somewhat towards the Highlanders at the end. From the little hill on which our clansmen stood I could look down across our army and upon the space of green behind it, where the reserves of cavalry and infantry were grouped with the Prince, his staff, and the baggage wagons. It was hardly light and the sun only just shining, when the Royal Standard of the House of Stuart broke bravely by the Prince's horse and proudly unfolded in the breeze from the Potomac.

At some distance behind us there were a few groves of pine trees but they were too few to afford us cover if we should have to withdraw. At a distance of some hundred yards or more before us there was a slight rise in the ground which just hid our enemies from us and we from them. Yet it was the Prince's judgment that to have drawn up our army precisely on that rise would have exposed us too early to the Duke of Cumberland.

At seven o'clock our scouts brought us word that Cumberland's army with an immense train of baggage wagons (a score of which carried the personal effects of the Duke and his whore) was marching towards us at a distance of some three miles. It was to be expected that their own scouts must by now have seen our formation. Our men stood to, their muskets primed, and each soldier issued with such rations as would last him for three days. I saw several parties of Cherokee despatched as scouts and some of the Royal Americans with two small field pieces marched out of the reserves towards a hill that lay about a mile to our front and rather on the left. From where I stood, I could later make out through my glass that they had formed a line behind fences on this knoll to harass the right flank of Cumberland's advance. This, I afterwards heard, caused some consternation among the English army who were unused to such unannounced cannonades. Yet it served the Prince's purpose by bringing his adversary up short and forcing him to draw up his line at a distance from our own.

I saw with some dismay, a little after nine o'clock, our advance party coming back with one of their field pieces lost and Cumberland's bully boys in red coats hard at their heels. I feared it might prove the beginning of a general rout for there followed two or three thousand of Cumberland's foot soldiers, marching in two ranks on a front a mile wide, their muskets at the ready and their drummers keeping the step. There was no doubt that they knew the position of our army, yet the Prince's calculation was as good as theirs. At his signal, our own first line, still hidden from the redcoats by the slight rise in the ground between them, marched forward to meet the attack.

It seemed that our formations moved less steadily than the English, yet on coming to the rising ground our line of blue threw themselves down (as they had been taught in our winter preparations) and opened fire with their muskets upon the redcoats. Some of Cumberland's first rank fell. Others still came on, halting at a little distance as they raised their muskets and returned our volley. Their place was taken by the second English rank who fired upon our men at a distance of sixty or seventy yards, killing several and causing the others to fall back to their first position. We left behind some thirty or forty dead upon the rising ground, as far as I could count, and they lost about the same number. It was now that the Chevalier, who had left the Prince in the centre, rode over to our left wing on its slight hill.

'General Mercer! Colonel Fraser!' he called out. 'You must scatter your men a little! Scatter them, sir!'

'Scatter them?' said I, coming up to him in some dismay.

'Yes, sir,' said the Chevalier, 'for do you not see how the enemy foot soldiers are drawing back?'

And so they were, for the rising ground which they had taken from our own advance parties was emptying as the redcoats stole away to their own lines.

'Cannon music, Colonel Fraser!' said the Chevalier. 'Cannon music, sir! They are being drawn back so that Cumberland's artillery may play upon us more freely.'

Orders were quickly given by Colonel Ogilvie and me to the men of our regiments to carry out the manœuvre which we had practised last winter in Virginia in expectation of such a moment as this. Of every four men in our line, the first was to stand fast, the second to take ten paces backwards, the third twenty paces, and the fourth thirty paces. By this means they were less packed and an enemy salvo would be unlikely to kill more than one man, at the most. Yet the line might be formed again in no more time than it took for the fourth man to come forward his thirty paces. For several minutes, as the summer sun grew warm upon our hillock, the air was heavy with our officers shouting, 'First man stand fast! Second man ten paces to the rear! Third man twenty paces to the rear! Fourth man thirty paces to the rear! March! Quick time!'

As our men crouched in their diagonal formation behind the broken walls and fences, the host of Cumberland's army came in sight on a downward slope less than a mile before us. There were ten thousand of them at the very least, English, Hanoverians or Hessians, Brunswickers, all that Captain-General Cumberland could muster. It was small wonder if our own men looked doubtfully at the motley array of Fraser's Highlanders, O'Sullivan's Irish, the Virginia regiments, the Stuart Life Guards, and General William Byrd III's six hundred Cherokee Indians. We seemed not half the number of the English, nor so well appointed.

At half a mile's distance, the army of Cumberland

halted and stood before us like the red and white rampart of a human fortress. Then, a little after ten o'clock, their masters of ordnance opened fire upon our formation, some from their line of battle and others from prepared positions further off. There was a groaning and howling of cannon shot in the air and the deadly whisper of musket shot. The slopes and the adjacent hills smoked as though on fire and echoed terribly with the bursting of the shells. Where their salvoes landed there was smoke and flame, the grass on our hillock being set alight in several places, though we endeavoured to extinguish it. Veils of smoke descending upon us from time to time blotted out the sunlight. The enemy sent grape and canister among us but, by a great mercy, it had little effect on our Highlanders, who were well separated and lay close to the earth, like men already dead.

Our own cannonade replied to them, though our gunners were fewer and the range of our field pieces less certain. Indeed it was common with our artillery to give their feebler guns too great an elevation when attempting to increase their range, so that they shot over the enemy's head. One of the first English shells that came our way landed not a dozen feet from me, showering me with earth. Then their guns played rapidly upon us, so that the remnants of the walls and the fences were soon smashed down and torn to fragments. Some of our men were killed and their bodies grievously mangled by the explosions. How many were killed, I could not tell, for all our regiment lay as if dead upon the ground. Only the two six pounders on our little hill maintained their fire upon the enemy and, though several times in great danger, they lost only one gunner in this action.

So thick was the fire that I could not help thinking anxiously of the fate of the Prince. Curling breakers of smoke engulfed parts of our line as the shells burst, so that I could see nothing of where His Royal Highness might be.

Yet, if a mere chance shot were to do his business for him, then we and our cause must be irretrievably lost, for there is no other leader.

Through all this inferno, a party of artillery appeared suddenly on the rear side of our little knoll, dragging a heavy twelve-pounder which had been somehow wrested from a Hanoverian party who thought to march round us and fire upon our left flank. It was now to be used against its former masters. The field carriage had sunk half-way to its axle in the sandy soil, so that I and some of our men (including Sergeant Innes) were obliged to run through the smoke of bursting shells to aid the young officer of artillery, whose men then brought the gun to the top with much spirit. He was a slender and fair-haired youth whom I at once knew for Lieutenant Louis de Johnstone, son of the Chevalier. As the gun was being trained upon the Duke of Cumberland's lines and the fury of their salvoes burst all about us, young Lieutenant Louis (who stood upright on the crest in view of all the enemy) turned to me as coolly as a dandy at an assembly ball and said, 'Oblige me, sir, by consulting your watch and telling me the time of day. For may I be damned if my confounded time-piece has not stopped at five minutes before eleven.'

'It *is* five minutes before eleven, sir,' said I with some spirit, not caring to pass the time of day in this manner.

'God's blood, who would have thought it!' said he calmly. 'Has one ever known time pass so deucedly slow? You are right, sir, however, for when the guns pause I believe I can hear the piece ticking.'

With this he strode over to the twelve-pounder and began to give orders for its elevation and sighting, in the voice of one born to command.

Just before noon the English cannonading stopped and our weary men lifted their heads. Much of the turf around us resembled a field that had been ploughed over by their shells. The extent of our losses was uncertain but of the nine hundred men of the Highlanders I calculated that a hundred would never fight again. Indeed, if our soldiers had not been so widely spaced, we might by this time have lost half our army.

A number of the English skirmishers closed on either side of us and one of them came within thirty yards of our baggage, where he concealed himself behind the stump of a tree and might almost have fired upon the Prince. The Chevalier ordered several of our Royal American marksmen in the reserves to shoot the man. Yet at the sound of their muskets the rest of our line, having endured the enemy's fire till they were maddened by it, rose and discharged their muskets wildly at the skirmishers or, what was even less to the purpose, at the main line of the English, which was too far distant to be fired on with any effect.

This loss to our store of powder was grave. While our men reloaded their muskets, the enemy skirmishers ran helter skelter for their own line, having successfully provoked such a waste of our ammunition. I had seen no sign of the Prince by his standard but discovered that he was riding the length of our line, encouraging and cheering his men, for he now approached his loyal Highland regiments. The clansmen in their plaid clustered round him as he dismounted, like children round their father.

'You have done bravely, my boys,' said His Royal Highness. 'The enemy has tried his worst with you and you have defied him. Now your turn is come, for he must soon resort to his foot soldiers. When they come to meet you, you will know how to greet them.'

These words put great heart into our soldiers. For all the danger to his royal person, I am sure that to have the Prince among us during the battle is worth five thousand men.

Hardly had His Highness left us when the English guns began to fire again, though it was a slighter cannonade and aimed rather over our heads. Indeed, we saw that it was only the covering bombardment for the advance of their massed foot soldiers, who strode towards us determinedly, some five thousand strong and more. The greatest force of their attack was along the bank of the Potomac, where General O'Sullivan's Irish met them. If the General and his men were once swept away, we should lose the line of the river, which was the anchor or mainstay of our whole position.

Their other regiments advanced upon the Virginian soldiers in the centre and upon our left flank of Highlanders. On came their double line, the redcoats holding their muskets at an angle before them and stepping out at seventy or eighty paces to the minute, according to the beat of their drums. Our Highlanders took shelter behind such walls and fences as were left, which were few enough. On coming up the rising ground, the English halted at a hundred yards' distance and discharged a volley. Under General Mercer's instruction, Colonel Ogilvie and I had ordered our soldiers to hold their fire. Now we gave the signal, and a ragged volley tore into the first line of Cumberland's infantry, just as they loosed off a second fusillade at us. Then their first line fell down and their second line fired twice upon us, while our men could only reply once, being then obliged to pause and reload.

Some eight hundred of our men held the bluff, and had what little advantage remained in the ruins of fences for their cover. Yet the English foot soldiers who faced us numbered sixteen or seventeen hundred and were able to pour volley after volley into our ranks. Our Highlanders and the little company of English gentlemen exiles fired back as bravely as they might, yet it was no equal contest. General Mercer summoned Ogilvie and me.

'There is nothing for it but to fall back a little,' said the General. 'Not two hundred yards behind us there are more ruins of walls and fences, which will give our men better protection. The ground slopes downward on the other side, and if our men are looking over the brow towards the enemy they will be better covered against his fire.'

'Indeed, sir,' said Ogilvie gruffly, 'but what of the flank of our army? Our retreat to that line pulls us round even more towards the Prince's centre and opens a possible road for Cumberland's men to march round this flank and take our entire position from the rear.'

'I have considered, sir,' said General Mercer, frowning, 'and shall request that the Royal Americans or some others be sent to close the way.'

With the crash of musket volleys, reek of smoke, and cries of the wounded all around us, it was no place to argue the matter further. Yet, as the General left us, Ogilvie shook his head.

'What three hundred Royal Americans may do against such thousands as Cumberland might send, I do not know,' said he. 'Indeed, the army we see before us now is not all his force, for he may have 10,000 men more in Annapolis. If we are victorious here, we must fight his other army next.'

At that moment a musket ball came so close that I could swear it passed between us, and we both cowered down before recollecting ourselves and returning to our commands. I gave instructions to Major Cameron and Captain Douglas that our men were to fall back to the last fences, while Colonel Ogilvie's men stood fast and delivered a double volley to the English line to secure our retreat. My own Highlanders then turned about and ran as they were ordered, while Ogilvie's volleys cracked out behind us, rolling us in a cloud of smoke. The English soldiers discharged their muskets at the backsides of our regiment till we were behind the wooden rails and turned about to cover the withdrawal of Ogilvie's men.

No sooner had Ogilvie and the 1st Highland Regiment turned, than the entire English line, where it opposed us, gave a sharp roar and charged our position with their bayonets. Seeing Ogilvie's men move, they had concluded that the whole Highland Brigade was fleeing the field of battle. Our men could hardly discharge a last volley before the mass of the English infantry was upon us, and men fought hand to hand for possession of the hillock.

It was now past two o'clock, and the day grew oppressive under a dull but sweltering sky. For half a mile across the rising ground a mass of redcoats and Highlanders, locked in a scrimmage, swayed to and fro, their officers on horseback urging them on. All around there rose cries, shrieks, and the groans of wounded or dying men, who slipped to the ground and were trodden over by the others. The English soldiers thrust over the fences and through them with their bayonets, while our men struck back bravely with their dirks in close combat or, when space allowed, swung at the enemy with their broadswords. It seemed less a battle than a mob in riot, where sheer weight on one side would push the defeated from their ground. The muskets of the English soldiers were useless, and their artillery had fallen silent now that the two lines were so mingled. Seeing Cumberland's soldiers at such close hand, I was struck by the apparent youthfulness of so many of them, who seemed little more than drummer-boys. Though they held superiority over us in numbers, a great proportion of them seemed new to battle. Some of our Highlanders had known Falkirk and Culloden, while almost all had endured the ordeals of Louisberg, the heights of Montmorency, and the Plains of Abraham. To such men, battle and death were familiar enough to be regarded with less terror.

The two armies broke apart a little from sheer weariness, and I heard Ogilvie's voice.

'Fraser! For God's sake look down there!'

Pinned as we were by the weight of Cumberland's numbers, I now saw what we had all the time feared. A great body of men, perhaps a thousand foot soldiers and a troop of cavalry, were preparing to march out of his lines and make their way round us on our left flank, so that they might destroy our army from the rear. Though our regiments were nearest to them, we could not have stopped them for hardly a man of us could free himself from the scrimmage with the English regiments. At General Mercer's orders, Colonel Ogilvie took the General's own horse and galloped through the musket fire to take down to the Prince the news of what we had just seen. Elsewhere along our line I observed little to bring us comfort. The Virginia regiments in the centre had brought the English attack to a halt but General O'Sullivan's Irish brigade had lost ground on the bank of the Potomac and could fall back no further without our line being broken.

For what seemed like half an hour longer, the battle raged on our entire front, and upon our hillock, which we were soon to know as Prince Charlie's Bluff, the line of redcoats came again and again, like a wave, charging at the fencing that marked our position and then falling back, leaving our dead and theirs behind them. Our clansmen showed their immense strength in this close combat but, for all that, the numbers of the English and their own losses began to bear them down.

I saw Colonel Ogilvie riding back, behind the lines of the Virginia regiments. There, in the centre, things had gone a little better for us and the English attackers had fallen back fifty yards or more under the accurate fire of our Virginian marksmen. General William Byrd's Cherokee warriors were also directing their fire into these English troops, as were the Royal Americans. Our centre was secure but certain destruction threatened us on either flank with not a regiment to spare for General O'Sullivan nor a force to meet the Duke of Cumberland's new expedition round our left wing.

Colonel Ogilvie had almost reached us and I was making my way across to the end of the fencing where he would arrive, when he threw himself back on his horse with a cry, falling so that the beast dragged him some little way through the smoke and the struggle before coming to rest. With Sergeant Innes, I ran to my friend, whose eyes were still open but whose face was pale as if drained of all blood. An English ball had laid open his breast to the bone and to the lungs. The Sergeant raised his head a little and with the blood on his lips, as well as on his breast, Ogilvie said softly, 'It is all over with me, Fraser. Only tell General Mercer that his message is delivered. God save us all.'

And with those words there died that gentle friend who had been my companion ever since we had sailed with General Wolfe. I could have shed many tears for him but this was no time for sorrow. Indeed, Ogilvie's men fought like tigers to revenge their lost leader. General Mercer and I anxiously watched the English column that prepared to march round our flank and destroy us from the rear. Its men were assembled in ranks three abreast and in two regiments.

For no apparent reason, the fighting along the whole length of the line began to slacken and the mass of men drew a little apart, as if feeling the exhaustion of their struggle. Then all eyes on our side began to turn towards the centre where our last reserves, the Prince's Life Guards and the Virginia Cavalry, were drawn up. The men were mounted and the whole formation appeared as a dark blue phalanx tipped with steel. At the sound of the bugle, all the foot soldiers on both sides forgot their own battle and watched the horsemen. There was a roar from our line as the glittering mass began to move, gathering speed as it passed between the Virginia regiments and General O'Sullivan's Irish brigade. The earth itself seemed to shake under the pounding hooves of their great horses, while the strong Virginian sunlight flashed on their helmets and sabres. As they cleared our regiments, the column of cavalry spread out like the opening of a fan. The entire mass streamed across the flat grassland, the Chevalier on a grey horse at their head. General Hugh Mercer, who had so far stood speechless at my side, looked down towards our centre and then spoke in a voice that was hushed with fear.

'By God, sir! Where is His Royal Highness?'

We both looked again at the centre, where the Royal Standard of the Stuart kings hung limp in the warm air. Then, with one common thought we turned our glasses upon the streaming blue squadrons of our cavalry. The Chevalier was there, but he rode a little behind the leader. It was Prince Charles Edward himself who had done what he had threatened to do at Culloden and now led his hard-pressed army in a desperate attack. The Prince and his Life Guards smashed through the centre of the English line, where it had advanced so close to our own, scattering their soldiers like leaves upon the wind. Then there was a flash, like a halo of steel above them, as the Life Guards and the Virginia Cavalry drew their sabres and followed the Prince, like a thunderbolt launched from heaven, against the main position of the Duke of Cumberland.

Glittering in the sun, they swept onwards in all the pride and splendour of war. Yet at a distance of quarter of a mile the English artillery opened fire, belching forth smoke and flame and filling the air with the deadly hiss of cannon balls. The ground beneath the Prince's men began to erupt with the explosion of their salvoes and we saw many a brave horseman and his mount blown aside. At the second salvo, there were several gaps in the ranks of our cavalry but the riders closed up and the whole mass charged forward. Bodies of men and carcasses of horses were scattered in the path of the advance, while wounded and riderless horses ran wild beside our cavalry. The English gunners fired again and it seemed as if the first rank of our horsemen was destroyed in an instant, while the second rank closed up to take their place.

General Mercer sat upon the ground, his head in his hands, yet it now became apparent to me that the gunners of Cumberland's army had not the time to defend themselves further against our horsemen. The Prince's men flew into the smoke of the batteries with a cheer that was heard from where we stood, their swords flashing as they fell upon the gunners.

We waited anxiously, unable to see them for the smoke and not knowing which of them might be alive or dead. Yet those who lay dead or dying upon the plain had not fallen for nothing, since we could now hear that the whole of Cumberland's artillery had been silenced. That column which had been about to outflank us had been obliged to turn about and face the charge. A hundred or more of our horsemen emerged from the drifting smoke and flew upon this force, scattering them here and there. Yet almost at once they were engulfed by a mass of Cumberland's men.

Having done their duty, the few Life Guards and Virginians who remained alive and unwounded heard the trumpeters sound their recall. From the entire length of the English line, which was in a turmoil, single horsemen of our army, or men in groups of three or four, broke free and rode hard for our own line. The English artillery had been silenced but their foot soldiers sent volleys of musket shot after our retreating cavalry. The courage of our riders is some consolation for the number of our losses, since of the four hundred who set out no more than eighty or ninety returned. The Prince, in company with the Chevalier on a borrowed horse, came safe back in a party of five or six men. It was a miracle that His Highness was not hurt, beyond a cut which he received at the guns. Yet it is said that he was recognised and orders were given by

Cumberland that he should not be fired upon but, rather, taken alive. The Chevalier's horse, which rode almost next to the Prince's, was shot from under him as they reached the guns and it was only by mounting another, whose rider had been pulled down and murdered by the English, that the Chevalier came safe home.

By four o'clock, only the dead and the dying lay before the English guns. Yet our losses have not been in vain. The English column, which was to have outflanked us, was scattered and had suffered considerable destruction. The power of their artillery is broken, for many of the gunners were killed and a number of their field pieces rendered useless. As our cavalry went forward, the Virginian foot soldiers in the centre poured after them and fell upon the broken advance line of the English, whose men fled in some confusion. General Byrd's warriors and the Royal Americans turned into the flank of that English force which pressed so hard upon General O'Sullivan at the river bank. Here too the enemy fell back, though with most of his units intact. Only on our hillock, which we called Prince Charlie's Bluff, was there an uncertain pause. This General Mercer resolved to put an end to. Seeing their comrades fall back, the English foot soldiers who faced us felt themselves in danger of being cut off. They expected an order for retreat and showed little stomach for a further conflict. Our Highlanders being rested, the command was therefore given them to charge upon the English soldiers with their broadswords. The sight of these wild clansmen leaping towards them with strange cries, their great swords raised, unmanned many of the young English soldiers who fled precipitately, leaving the entire hill in our hands once again. Most of our Highlanders we had taught, by long training, to pursue the enemy only as far as was prudent. Nonetheless, a dozen or more followed the English close to their own lines and were shot down by their marksmen.

Our losses today have been more than we feared. Our comfort must be that the enemy who came against us is driven back at all points. The Duke of Cumberland, who thought so little of the 'Jacobite rabble' at Culloden, may now nurse his bloodied nose and consider his own boastfulness. The greatest concern among the Prince and his generals is that we cannot sustain many more attacks of this kind, yet we have hardly the strength to carry the war into the English camp.

By the late afternoon the sun was setting behind us and shining into the eyes of Cumberland's men, which made them unwilling to try us again. Our men rested on the ground where they had fought while the Prince and his officers computed our losses. Colonel Ogilvie is dead. Poor General O'Sullivan, who had always sworn to die in his bed, was doing so from a wound received when an unlucky shot struck him as the day's fighting was almost done. More than three hundred cavalry and twice that number of our infantry are lost. With the remainder of our army, which is less than four thousand foot soldiers and no more than a hundred cavalry, we must face the superior power of the Duke of Cumberland in front of us and whatever garrison he may hold in reserve at Annapolis.

28 May 1761. Last night, after I had recollected my thoughts upon the day, I was with General Mercer, the Chevalier, and General Byrd in the Prince's tent. Like our few other tents this is pitched a little way back from the line of battle. Yet the Prince lives in no grander a manner than the rest of us, having for his council chamber only the canvas walls and grass floor with a bare trestle table set upon it.

'We must make the best use of this night, gentlemen,' said His Highness, 'for at dawn the weight of their army will be thrown against us once more. It cannot be otherwise. I fear that whatever garrison they have in Annapolis may march to Virginia by another route while we are still held here. There will be none but the Virginia militia and General Simon Fraser's little force at Fredericksburg to stop them.'

'Our spies report that the Duke of Cumberland is still here with his army, sir,' said the Chevalier, whose face down one side was bruised from a blow inflicted by the butt of an English musket.

'Why then,' said the Prince, 'it must be so. The Duke is of too fair a size and bright a complexion to be mistaken for any other man.'

Indeed, there was a great contrast between the fat and gouty Duke, his face and body corrupted by luxury and whoredom, and our own Prince, who seemed as fine a man in dress and manners as he had been at Culloden.

'Sir,' said General Byrd, 'I believe we must face a new danger tomorrow. The English navy is at Annapolis and they will surely send a pair of sloops up the river to bombard our flank with all their might. Now, I have a chart of the river, sir, and I have known the Potomac all my life. Let two boatloads of my men drift downstream in the darkness and alter the position of certain buoys. May I never win a wager again, sir, if we do not lead their ships from the true navigation channel and ground them where they will block the river most conveniently.'

The Prince gave his consent to this and General Byrd performed an extravagant bow.

'Moreover,' said the Prince, 'a party of your Indian braves must harass the English camp on every side until dawn.'

General Byrd bowed even lower than at first, and His Highness turned to me.

'Colonel Fraser, I would have you take a party of twenty of your own best men and twenty Virginian soldiers who are useful scouts. You will form a mounted patrol to assist our Indian skirmishers in reaching the enemy's powder magazines and baggage train. Destroy what you can. See if we may by any means get round his army and block his supplies. Do whatever you can to diminish the force of his attack tomorrow. Today, gentlemen, it was a victory not to be defeated, but tomorrow we must win or die. If Cumberland should have us dancing attendance upon him still, he may send another force to Williamsburg and we cannot move a man to stop him.'

Our plans were made and I was curious to find that the score of Virginians, who joined my Highlanders, were under the command of Lieutenant Louis de Johnstone. Whether this was done by the Chevalier's means, or whether the young man had done it in spite of his father, I could not discover.

Before we left upon our patrol, there was great anger throughout our camp at the fate of Captain Jonathan Fitzroy of the Prince's Life Guards, who had fallen a captive to the Duke of Cumberland after the charge of our cavalry. Contrary to all the usages of war, this gentleman was at once condemned by the Duke as a traitor to George III of England for having gone with his true Prince. A cart was procured and a rope and gallows set up. Fitzroy would have spoken something to the Hanoverian soldiers but their drums were played to drown his words. Coolly enough he examined the halter and told the hangman that the rope was not strong enough, he being a heavy man. The knot was adjusted, the rope slipped over his head, and he was swung off instantly. For all that, the rope snapped and he fell to the ground, by which he was much bruised. He calmly reascended the ladder, saying, 'I told you the rope was not strong enough. Do get a stronger one.'

Another rope being procured he was then launched into eternity. Such barbarous execution of a prisoner has brought more shame upon the Duke of Cumberland than any other deed in the entire battle.

General Byrd's warriors left our camp as soon as it was dark. Our party, which was to take a wider sweep round the English army, mounted and left almost directly afterwards, Lieutenant Louis de Johnstone leading my Virginians and Captain John Drummond leading the Highlanders under my command. The moon had not yet risen as our men rode in a single file across the grassland, while General Byrd's warriors invested the woods behind which Cumberland's front line had withdrawn for the night.

We chose as our redoubt a pine grove some half a mile beyond the right flank of the English picket line, which was the furthest from the river. From here, several of our Virginian scouts went forward on foot and returned shortly with news that the greater part of the English baggage train and their powder kegs were not a mile from us, by the road that ran to Annapolis. They had also seen three men, who appeared to be prisoners from our army, bound hand and foot to the wheels of one of the wagons. I resolved to release these captives, if it should prove possible.

I employed ten Highlanders and an equal number of Virginians, including Lieutenant Louis de Johnstone, who would not be denied, and moved forward to within sight of the fires of Cumberland's army. Sergeant Borrow of the Virginians and two private soldiers crawled forward close to where the three prisoners had been. The picket guard, never expecting that our motley army would trouble them much before morning, had given little attention to this part of their line, where only one or two men were posted. One of our Virginians slid forward with his knife in his teeth, Indian style, and rising behind one of the guards soon did his business for him. Meanwhile, Sergeant Borrow and the other Virginian private sought for the three captives. Away to the front of the army we could hear the occasional whooping and calling of General Byrd's warriors, who intended that Cumberland's men should have little sleep before the next battle.

I heard, rather than saw, our three scouts returning through the grass. They brought two men with them, for the third had been mortally wounded, though nonetheless barbarously chained to the wagon wheel, and was already dead. We withdrew a little and I discovered that one of the men was of the Virginia Cavalry, while the other was a Marylander, seized as a traitor by Cumberland and awaiting execution as soon as the sun should rise.

'Sir,' said the Marylander, whose name was James Walters, 'I congratulate you upon your victory.'

'Upon what victory?' said I.

'Why,' said Walters, 'Annapolis is yours, as the people's hearts have always been.'

'Let alone their hearts, sir,' said Lieutenant Louis de Johnstone facetiously, 'the Duke of Cumberland's army holds Annapolis with several regiments.'

'He has several regiments, sir,' said Walters, 'but they do not hold it.'

I feared at once that Cumberland's regiments had marched out of Annapolis and were got behind us on the road to Williamsburg.

'There is no time for riddles, man,' said I shortly. 'Tell us plainly what you mean.'

'Why then, you do not know?' said Walters with astonishment, 'You do not know why Cumberland has only his 6,000 men here, and why most of the rest of his army will never fight again?'

'Only tell us, sir,' said Lieutenant Louis patiently.

'Have you never heard of the gaol fever?' asked Walters.

'Indeed,' said I, 'it is reported that Cumberland himself lost as many as four hundred men from it during the march to Inverness in 1745, because he had two gallows birds with it among his men.'

'So he did,' said Walters, 'and five years later London lost most of its judges and jurors when the fever came to court. Now this same Cumberland has scoured the gaols for soldiers to make up yet another army. Many were taken from Newgate where the fever is rife and where more murderers perish from it than ever live to be hanged. When Cumberland's felons were battened under hatches on the transports, they soon favoured their comrades with the same fever. We hear that Cumberland would have brought 10,000 men from England but two of his transports could not sail and the plague broke out on five more during the voyage. He brought to Annapolis only 8,000 or 9,000 men of whom as many as a thousand have died on the ships or in camp. All who could march, but for one regiment, were brought with him to this place.'

'Then who holds Annapolis, sir?' I asked.

'There may be a thousand of Cumberland's soldiers sick of fever on the transports, but there is hardly half a regiment of his in the city. There is, perhaps, a regiment of Marylanders in addition but their loyalty to the Duke is so uncertain that their officers have all been replaced by his men. Indeed, sir, Tulip Hill, where the Duke was lodged, is held only by Marylanders with one or two English officers.'

Here was news indeed! The army of 5,000 which we feared had marched to Virginia behind us was no more than a thousand or so sick of the gaol fever, and three or four hundred Marylanders who wanted only the right opportunity to change sides and join the Prince. Yet to what purpose was this when Cumberland's men faced our little army with such superior numbers?

From where we stood, a good horseman might reach Annapolis in an hour. Yet our orders were only to destroy as much of Cumberland's supplies as might be. If Cumberland were left with power to destroy the Prince's army, it mattered little who was in Annapolis. Our scouts reported that there were some thirty horses tethered near the baggage wagons, whom we might release and drive off. There were also kegs of powder and two field pieces close by. It seemed that we had located their powder magazine.

Six of our Virginians crept forward to untether the horses, while two parties of Highlanders attempted if by any means they could spike the two field pieces. The remainder of our force, about two dozen men prepared to open fire upon those kegs which our scouts thought to be a magazine.

The Virginians reached the horses unobserved and we heard the hooves of the beasts on the soft earth as they were driven off. Then our marksmen fired upon the kegs, at first with no result, yet in a moment there was a great roar and the field around us was light as day, for a keg of powder had blown up, and then another seemed to shoot skywards in a spout of flame. For all that, it was not their magazine but only two or three kegs which had been carelessly disposed. One of our Highland parties was fortunate enough to find and spike a twelve-pounder gun while the gunners slept, yet the other party found itself face to face with the enemy and we lost two men killed to no purpose.

By this time their whole camp was awake and soon discovered that they had lost twenty or thirty horses, two kegs of powder, one field piece, and a picket guard, to say nothing of two prisoners. From their front, General Byrd's Cherokee warriors fired irregularly upon them, so that if their losses were not great we nonetheless fulfilled our vow that they should not rest easily upon the eve of the final battle.

As soon as we had withdrawn to our rendezvous at the

pine trees, where our horses were left, I sent Lieutenant Louis de Johnstone himself with our Marylander, James Walters, to the Prince's camp. Lieutenant Louis carried my message urging that our Highlanders (who were unused to much riding) should be replaced by Virginians and that our party of forty men should then make a reconnaissance by dark to Annapolis.

Our answer came at midnight with another score of Virginia militia on horseback. The Highlanders were to return to the Prince's camp under Captain John Drummond; only Sergeant Innes, whom I had known and trusted since the time of Quebec, was to remain. With Lieutenant Louis de Johnstone and the forty Virginians we were to make for Annapolis with all possible speed. Our other companion was James Walters, who had been the Duke of Cumberland's prisoner. Under his directions we rode hard towards the city and a little before two o'clock approached the handsome brick mansion of Tulip Hill, where the Duke of Cumberland had lately lodged. Walters, with Lieutenant Louis at his side, went forward and approached the two guards at the entrance, one of whom slept.

Both men proved to be Marylanders with little enough love for Cumberland, which they assured us was true of all the men who garrisoned the house. There were twenty or thirty militia there with two English officers and they would hardly have been a match for our force even if they had been inclined to dispute the matter. They and several others found horses and joined us, yet we did not raise the household, for fear that there might be some there who would give warning of our approach to the city.

We entered the town unchallenged for, indeed, the place seemed almost uninhabited, and we rode at a steady pace down one of the principal streets with fine houses and capacious gardens on either side. All their roads appear to radiate from a central point, on which is built the parliament house, a structure somewhat smaller than the Capitol in Williamsburg. Just as we passed St Anne's Church, two sentries on either side of the road stepped into our path and three mounted soldiers approached us from the front. These were the first Hanoverian troops to cross our path, which made me think that Walters spoke the truth and that there were indeed few of Cumberland's soldiers in the town.

'Stand forward, sir, and be recognised!' called one of the horsemen.

'Lovat Fraser, Colonel of the Highland Regiment in the army of Prince Charles Edward, who claims Annapolis as Regent for his royal father, King James III.'

There was a moment of profound silence as this intelligence made itself felt. The Hanoverians were astounded to find themselves the prisoners of a squadron of the Prince's cavalry in the centre of Annapolis. It was Sergeant Innes who ended the silence in his loud Scots voice.

'God bless His Majesty King Jamie, and all his Royal House!'

'Come, sir,' said one of the English officers, 'the Jacobite army is twenty miles from here, begging mercy from the Duke of Cumberland.'

'As to that, sir,' said I, 'it is the Duke's army which is lost, particularly after such a night attack as it has now endured. But that is not my concern, sir, for you must surely know that the Prince has two armies in the field and that it is our second force which now marches upon Annapolis and whose main body will be in the city tomorrow.'

There was a further silence, they not wishing to believe such a story and yet seeing us with their own eyes as apparent proof of it. I had not spoken the entire truth, yet I wonder if my subterfuge was any worse than that of General Wolfe, who suborned me to speak in French to Montcalm's guards at Quebec?

'I shall not make you my prisoners, gentlemen,' said I, 'for the Prince's army will take Annapolis tomorrow, whether you be captive or free, and so you may tell all the Duke of Cumberland's men.'

With that we rode on toward the parliament house, and had almost reached it when we heard several riders spurring hard behind us. It was a sergeant of the Maryland militia and his companions, who greeted us with the news that the Marylanders at Tulip Hill had seized their two English officers and were now holding the house against the Duke of Cumberland. Moreover, they were able to take twenty of their men and obstruct the road by which supplies were sent every morning to the Duke's army at the Potomac. So we had won a score of Marylanders to our allegiance. They were few enough in number but their example might serve us well.

The sergeant and his companions volunteered to accompany us in our plan to seize and fortify the parliament house in the centre of the city. I mentioned that this might more readily be done if we could acquire a supply of powder and weapons. He informed me that there was much powder and arms stored in the Treasury Building near the parliament, which Cumberland's army had turned into a sort of magazine and from which their force on the Potomac was supplied.

As we approached the centre of the city, the body of our men broke into the parliament house and secured it. Our Marylanders and nine or ten of our own men approached the Treasury. Several of the Maryland militia who guarded it yielded to our challenge, while a dozen of Cumberland's men fled after a sharp engagement. For a full hour, parties of our Virginians and half a dozen Marylanders brought powder and weapons into the parliament house, even fetching two small brass field pieces of such ancient design that Cumberland had neglected to take them on his campaign. An hour before dawn our men had made loopholes at the windows of the council chambers and passageways, the two brass three-pounders being directed down the avenue to St Anne's Church, the way we had come. I sent two pairs of riders by separate routes to carry news to the Prince of our occupation of the place, instructing each pair to divide at the approach of danger so that one, at least, might safely reach His Royal Highness.

Some thirty of our men and the six Marylanders positioned themselves with muskets at the loopholes to await the first light of day, while six more manned the small field pieces. Even before daybreak, we heard the shouting of orders and the marching of men at some little distance, but who they were we could not see. Then a single horseman rode up close and hailed us under a flag of truce, calling to us that Colonel James Brice and Dr Charles Carroll would speak with us on behalf of the citizens. I replied that these two gentlemen might come forward and parley. But just then, the sky growing light, there came such a volley of musketry from all sides as assured us that we were surrounded by the soldiers of Cumberland's regiment. The horseman, whoever he may have been, fell dead from his saddle, and the horse cantered away towards St Anne's Church. The fire of the muskets came from that direction, and also from the opposite side, where the road ran towards Spa Creek and the harbour.

The flashing of the flames from their English muskets lit the morning twilight, and then the rolling smoke seemed to bring night back upon the dawning day. We suffered no great harm from their first volleys, and since we could see little enough of them I gave instructions that every one of our men was to hold his fire. This made the red-coats feel more secure, and they began to appear at a

243

distance on the road to St Anne's. I gave a command that our gunners should open a toy bombardment upon them with the two small field pieces. Soon I heard Lieutenant Louis, who alone among us was expert in the business, calling out his orders.

'Powder! Ram! Make ready! Fire!'

In the enclosed space of the parliament house even the discharge of a small piece sounded like a thunderbolt from Jove. I watched the ball shoot out in a long arc, seeming to move most slowly. Yet it struck a glancing blow on a building a hundred yards from us, smashing to fragments the stout door and lintel. The English redcoats on that side seemed dismayed that we had a troop of artillery(for they had no notion how slight our 'artillery' was) and they fell back a little to both sides of the street.

Our triumph was blemished by the news which Sergeant Innes then brought me, that our second little field piece was so defective as to be more dangerous to ourselves than to the enemy if we should attempt to fire it. It had been neither kept nor cleaned with that care which such weapons require.

From every side, the redcoats advanced upon us. The parliament house, which we had made our fortress, was an oblong building with a bay at either end. A dozen of our sharpshooters fired from their loopholes along each side, and six more from each bay. The English came at us in four sections, from the points of the compass, fifty of them on each side, in two ranks. The first ranks fired their muskets and dropped to their knees to reload, while the second ranks discharged a volley over them. This was repeated two or three times, so that a storm of shot beat upon the brick walls of the building. A score of their bullets smashed through the windows and buzzed like a swarm of bees over our heads.

By the very rapidity of their firing, rather than by any accuracy, they hit some of our men, killing three before they were sixty yards from us. Our soldiers, goaded by this, longed to return their fire, and despite my orders several of them did so. Yet the remainder held back, and must therefore have given the enemy a very incorrect estimate of our numbers (there seeming to be only four or five soldiers firing from the building). When the burly redcoats with their black hats and white gaiters were no more than twenty yards from us, our muskets spoke. Each of our men had a weapon in his hand and another, ready primed, close by his side. In the face of four volleys discharged at such a range, three of the squadrons of redcoats, who had come on so bravely, broke up. A dozen fell dead or dying, some of the rest dropped to their knees to fire, and others sought shelter to fire from. Our men fired again, and all the English fusiliers who were able fled precipitately. I counted thirty men whom they left behind them on the ground.

Yet their fourth squadron had come close enough to take up positions behind the Treasury building. From that point they kept up a galling fire upon us, killing or maiming four of our twelve Virginia militia who manned the loopholes at that side of the parliament house. To counter this, I ordered our little cannon to be brought to where there was a door that looked out upon the Treasury, for we had left several kegs of powder in that one-storey building.

When all was ready, the door was opened and the cannon manhandled forward. Yet to load the piece it was now necessary that one man should stand in full view of the enemy to ladle a pound or so of powder and the shot into the barrel. While the redcoat musket balls pitched and struck furiously around the doorway, Lieutenant Louis de Johnstone took the ladle and stepped into their view. This young man, whom I could ill spare, calmly poured the powder into the barrel (as he might have ladled rum punch at his own table), rammed it home with a wooden plunger and added a three-pound ball. Before he could ram this home, he was thrown aside as if by some invisible and mighty hand, and lay writhing upon the path outside with the cloth torn from his back and blood upon his flesh. Sergeant Borrow of the Virginia militia, as soon as he saw the unlucky shot hit Lieutenant Louis, seized the ram and drove the ball home. Then, at great risk to his own life, he pulled the Lieutenant behind the shelter of the door.

I could not see the nature of the wound exactly, only that Lieutenant Louis, with the aid of Sergeant Borrow, was struggling to his feet, as though there was one last deed expected of him. He waved back the gunner, who was about to put his flaming linstock to the touch hole. Then, with his left arm hanging limp as a dead man's, he took a carpenter's square in his right and coolly sighted the gun, ordering first a little more elevation, then a little less, then somewhat more again. He seemed not to hear the volleys of their muskets and the deadly hiss of the bullets in the air.

At length, two of our men carried him away where they might lay him on his face and endeavour to staunch the flow of his blood. The gunner put the flame of the linstock to the touch hole and the ball was shot forward with a roar of flame. The field piece recoiled with great force, causing our men to scatter from its path. Yet the ball, which I imagined would hit the brick wall of the Treasury building, seemed to miscarry. It rose too high, breaking the roof instead and falling inside. In the silence that followed I concluded that our plan to destroy the building had come to nothing. I had almost turned away to attend to Lieutenant Louis, when there was such an explosion as made the earth tremble under our feet. The walls and roof of the Treasury blew outwards in a most fearful ball of fire, the fragments being thrown with unimaginable force in every direction. The glass was blown from all the windows on that side of the parliament building and had our soldiers not concealed themselves they might have been sorely wounded by it. An immense cloud of smoke, like a great fog, blotted out the day around us. When it cleared, there was neither sign of the Treasury (but for a few scattered remains of bricks and planks) nor of the redcoats who had used it as their fortress.

For that moment we were as astonished by the unexpected devastation of our attack as any of the English might have been. Lieutenant Louis, who was conscious all this time, said softly, 'The roof, sir. It must be the roof, for the thickness of their walls might withstand our three-pounder and they would not give us time to fire again.'

I wondered at his accomplishment as a master of ordnance and concluded that, if he and the rest of us were to live this day, he might prove such a son as befitted the Chevalier.

The English soldiers were dismayed by the arts of irregular warfare and now fell back from our sight. Yet we heard in the distance the thunder of a cannonade, in no way directed against us, and guessed from its direction that the Marylanders at Tulip Hill had indeed engaged the Hanoverian army. Our thoughts were also with the Prince's men who must by now have engaged Cumberland once more at the place of Dead Skulls. If Charles Edward were defeated, our loss would have no consequence. Yet it was to his advantage that Cumberland could call not a man nor any supplies from Annapolis. A second battle was even then obscurely beginning in the city.

By ten o'clock in the morning there was still no sight of the redcoats who had withdrawn from our range. In the parliament house we had eight dead and thirty-four living, of whom Lieutenant Louis and two others were grievously wounded. We knew our skirmish could not be over, for if the English did not approach us nor did those Marylanders who might be our friends. In Scotland, we had learnt the bitter mercy of the Duke of Cumberland after our battle. In Maryland, however, the people had been condemned as 'traitors' before any battle commenced. The Duke and his men favoured them with the usual harshness of military tyranny and summary execution. Small wonder that the Maryland militia, when they saw their people treated as traitors, resolved that there was no more to be lost by living up to that title.

A little before eleven, Sergeant Innes told me that a party of English sailors was manhandling a ship's gun on a carriage across the road to St Anne's Church. Sergeant Borrow then reported that a second party was training a naval gun upon us on the other side.

Their first gun was still slewed across the street more than a hundred yards off. Our soldiers manning the three-pounder were instructed by Lieutenant Louis, whose face was white as pork and who was supported by two troopers. Ignoring the tumult, he gave orders for adjusting the elevation of the gun and then commanded the gunners to fire. The gun lurched back and the ball sped low towards the English sailors, landing in a spout of dirt and stones a little way beyond them. Lieutenant Louis gave further instructions for mopping the barrel, loading and firing. This time the ball threw up such a cloud that we could not for the moment see the result. Yet as the air grew calmer our men gave a great cheer, for the carriage on which the English gun lay was broken and turned on its side, while the iron gun itself lay uselessly in the road with two of its artificers beside it.

Their other gun, however, was in position and soon fired upon us. The first shot fell short, throwing up earth from the remains of the Treasury. A second salvo cried over our heads and landed on the far side. Our men kept up a fire upon the gun with their muskets and swore they hit two of the sailors, but the range was too great and we had no field piece to spare for that side. Soon after eleven, the English gunners fired a third shot, which tore open the parliament roof and came rushing down in a torrent of bricks and plaster. The whole interior was filled with a fog of dust, so that our men choked for their breath.

By great fortune, none of us was killed then. Yet in ten minutes the building was struck a second time. Part of the outer wall, where it faced their gun, was brought down, killing three of our Virginian soldiers and injuring two others. Under Lieutenant Louis's skill, our field piece frustrated all their attempts on the road to St Anne's, but on the other side they brought up a second naval gun. Not long before noon we were hit twice, the first shot bringing down another part of the south wall, so that daylight shone brightly among the broken beams, while the second hit started a fire in the opposite end of the building.

I had hoped that we might take and hold this point in the centre of Annapolis until the issue of the Prince's battle was decided, for it had never been possible that we could hold it longer against superior numbers. Yet under this bombardment we had lost a dozen of our men, ten more were disabled, and the score of us who still fought must soon be destroyed if we remained mere defenders. The fire at one end of the building sent billows of smoke across our front and I decided that several men must make the best of their way through it and outflank the English guns. This method of forcing the enemy from his position was one in which the army of Virginia excelled, being skilled in irregular warfare. If we could but seize the ground for a while, we and our wounded might reinforce the defenders of Tulip Hill.

Six of our Virginians crept forward through the smoke, while twelve able-bodied soldiers opened a fire to cover them. They soon disappeared from our sight and we waited with great apprehension to see the outcome of the sortie. In a few minutes we heard the crackling of musket shots and, on one side, saw the English sailors draw back from their gun. Then the sound of muskets spread like a fire and seemed to come from every side. I concluded the English soldiers had seen our men and were doing their business for them.

Knowing the cruelties of the Duke of Cumberland towards the vanquished, I knew not whether to attempt honourable terms for our soldiers and our wounded or whether to fight on until a dozen of us had sold our lives at the highest rate. Then Sergeant Innes, as stout a companion as a man could wish for in this sort of action, came to me and reported that the other English sailors had left their gun and that one of our Virginia militia was sitting astride its carriage, waving his musket. I was at first angry at so foolish a display, when our little band was hard pressed and when the loss of a single man more might be the loss of us all.

Then a group of men, whom I first took to be English soldiers with their red coats removed, marched boldly up the road towards us under a flag of truce. Seeing that neither of the English guns was now manned, I ordered their three leaders to be admitted. We met in the shattered remains of the parliament house vestibule, our Virginian soldiers looking as wild and dishevelled as any of General Byrd's Cherokee warriors. Their most senior officer, a man of middle years, broadly built and with very dark brows, was the first to speak.

'Colonel Brice, sir, of the Maryland militia.'

'Lovat Fraser, sir,' said I, 'Colonel of the 2nd Regiment of Fraser's Highlanders in the army of His Royal Highness Prince Charles Edward, Regent of Virginia.'

'I am deeply honoured to make your acquaintance, sir,' said Colonel Brice with a bow.

'Your servant, sir,' said I.

When these civilities were closed, Colonel Brice informed me that the muskets firing all about us were, for the most part, those of the Maryland militia, who had chosen this moment to rid their city of the two hundred of Cumberland's men who remained in it. Indeed forty or fifty of these had been disabled by our own men, so that the Marylanders in the city and at Tulip Hill were only lightly opposed. Cumberland's other men were confined to the transports in the river, where the fever raged.

'And would you declare for the Prince, sir?' I asked.

The Colonel shook his head slowly.

'As to that, Colonel Fraser, sir, I cannot say. It is not my privilege to do such a thing on my own authority. But this I will say, sir. If you would rid Annapolis of the Duke of Cumberland, why then we are your men for the business.'

There is a certain guile in Colonel Brice, for he must know that whoever defeats the Duke of Cumberland will give the victory to Prince Charles. Yet we gladly accepted this alliance. Our men came out cautiously from the smouldering parliament building, bringing with them their wounded, to whom the Marylanders gave prompt and humane attention. The firing in the streets around us grew less, and presently a sergeant of the Marylanders brought word to Colonel Brice that the English soldiers in the town had withdrawn to the neighbourhood of the harbour, and that it was the guns of the ships themselves that were now trained upon Annapolis.

Yet before any cannonade could begin there was a mighty roar, and a great cloud of white smoke rose above the glittering water of the river and drifted across the hot Maryland sky. To the perfect astonishment of all, the 64-gun *Centurion* had blown up. Masts, spars, and rigging were thrown far and wide, for a party of patriots had ferried a bum-boat across the harbour, under pretext of provisioning the vessel, and had moored it close to the ship's magazine. The barrels on the bum-boat contained little salt pork but a great deal of gunpowder. The fuse was just of a length for the plotters to swim to safety before the great explosion was set off.

There was consternation among their fleet, and no less among the hundred or more of their foot soldiers who remained ashore. These men were instructed to wait until Cumberland's commanders should disembark such a force as would retake the city of Annapolis and establish his rule there. Yet the whole regiment of Maryland militia was now in arms and any soldiers who would come ashore from the fleet must pass under the very spouts of their muskets. The English also lacked twelve of their officers, who had been put to command the Marylanders but were now under close guard in the Reynolds Tavern on the other side of the town.

Our friends agreed that we must speedily inform the Prince of what had occurred. I was accompanied by twelve of our Virginia militia, Sergeant Borrow, Sergeant Innes, and no fewer than seventy Marylanders under Colonel Brice's officers, who insisted on being our escort. Half-way along our road we were caught up by a dozen more riders, who vowed that they longed for nothing so much as to offer their services to the Prince. Whether this is because they foresaw victory on his side I cannot tell.

Close on four o'clock we saw that the road ahead of us was impassable, for two lines of wagons had approached each other from opposite directions and were at a deadlock. A score of wagons from Annapolis bore the women of Cumberland's army who were in flight from Annapolis to the supposed safety of the Duke's camp. On the other side were wagons bearing the English wounded and the possessions of the English officers from the dangers of the battlefield to the imagined security of Annapolis. In the confusion, the women on one side appeared to find consolation in looting the possessions of the other. At our appearance, there was a general rout, all who could do so leapt from the baggage train and sought shelter among the trees. A young, though ill-favoured, wench jumped from a carriage whose door carried the emblem of the House of Hanover and then scurried for the trees, carrying several objects under her arm.

We had little enough time for these fugitives but left the road, made our way round the *impasse*, and hurried forward to within sight of the rear of Cumberland's camp. Here it was that two of our Virginians, scouting ahead, came up with one of their fellow countrymen in charge of a party of General William Byrd III's Cherokee warriors. We learnt that the battle had been as bloody today as yesterday, both armies suffering great losses. Making our way to some higher ground, we observed a scene of great confusion. The Prince's men fought bravely as ever but under the weight of Hanoverian numbers the line had been forced back and the only ground still securely held appeared to be Prince Charlie's Bluff and its surrounding slope. In an attempt to turn the flank of the Duke of Cumberland's army and bring some relief to the Prince's line, General William Byrd III and his entire Indian party, with a score of Virginian officers, had made a great march round the north of the place where we met them.

From where we were grouped, to the right and some-what to the rear of the English force, the ground was clear for an assault upon an undefended quarter of Cumberland's army. A hundred mounted men, or somewhat less, and a regiment of Indian warriors might do great damage at that point. Cumberland's guards might take some of us to be Marylanders under English command, but there was no mistaking General Byrd, who led his Cherokee braves riding on a white horse and wearing a royal blue uniform trimmed with gold lace.

With our horsemen at the head and the Indians follow-ing, we bore down upon the English camp. The sight of this force bursting through the trees upon the rear of their position, which they had thought secure, unmanned many of the English soldiers. As our horses bore us over the ground, the Cherokee following with the speed of Highlanders, I crouched a little over my charger and saw some of Cumberland's guards level their muskets at us. Yet they hardly had time for a single volley before we tore between their ranks and the Cherokee fell upon them. Their gunners, whose field pieces all pointed towards the front and away from us, fled at the approach of our irregular cavalry, and our men rendered useless every piece of artillery that came our way. While some of the Cherokee overturned the gun carriages, others set linstocks to the powder barrels, which went up with a great flame, while the rest fought the English foot guards with knife and fist.

That part of the English camp which lay farthest from the river was soon in turmoil and Cumberland's men were running towards the river bank, where they still had time to form a new defence. Fire and smoke swept across the rear of their position in the wind from the Potomac. In all this confusion it seemed as if they were driving off horses and hauling their wagons to that left flank of their army, where they were to draw up a formation on three sides with their backs to the river. They went, taking what they could and seeming to care nothing for what they left behind, which was a great part of their supplies and all but two or three field pieces.

Our Virginian and Maryland horsemen rode across the burning camp, where flames were spread by exploding powder kegs and where the grass itself was on fire. As we crossed the flat land towards the Prince's line several musket shots sped us on, yet the English bugles were calling their men back. Before us, I saw the redcoats retreating from the escarpments of Prince Charlie's Bluff, and the clansmen leaping down the slopes in great strides, their broadswords swinging in the dying sun. Though Cumberland's men had seemed invincible, we little knew how far their strength and courage had been spent.

As our irregular troop of horse, under General Byrd's command, rode in through the Prince's line, the second Virginia Regiment gave us a lusty enough cheer. Yet everywhere we saw men in blood-stained tunics, hungry, begrimed with dust, and unshaven. Those who had fought and still lived fell exhausted next to the bodies of their fellows who died for their Prince. His Royal Highness had given up his tent to the surgeons and stood with the Chevalier among the general disorder. His face was pinched and wan, while his uniform seemed a faded blue under the dust of the conflict. Yet one of our messengers had reached him with the first news from Annapolis. To this I could now add that the city was in the hands of our Maryland allies with no more than a hundred of Cumberland's men left to oppose them.

There was great rejoicing at this, for the day had gone hard enough with our army and several times the line had been almost overwhelmed. Just before three o'clock in the afternoon, the peril had been so great that the Chevalier had urged the Prince to retire with several of his Life Guards to a position where he might yet have room for escape. Yet Charles Edward would have none of it, staying to rally the Highlanders himself as their position on Prince Charlie's Bluff was almost cut off from the rest of the army. In reply to this news from the Chevalier, I informed him of Lieutenant Louis's injuries, which news he bore in a soldierly manner, wishing only that he himself might have borne some part in the battle of the parliament house at Annapolis.

Scanning the enemy before us, I observed a little way down the river an English sloop stranded upon the mudflats in consequence of the alteration of the buoys by General Byrd's force the night before. Yet what was more

255

remarkable was the great movement now going on within the English camp, from which smoke and fire poured upwards as the flames lit by our Cherokee braves reached more of the powder kegs. Cumberland's men had pulled back from this destruction of their supplies and drew up in a new formation by the bank of the river.

As the dusk began to close in, the Prince ordered our own line forward until we enclosed the three sides of Cumberland's force. Irish, Virginians, and Highlanders formed our three brigades. In the gathering darkness we loosed two or three volleys of musket fire against them with hardly any reply. Then, under General Byrd's direction, half a regiment of Cherokee made a sortie and broke through their line in two places. Before they could regroup, our marksmen had sent another volley into Cumberland's ranks. Our own supply of powder was little enough but we did not then know that our destruction of their kegs, here and in Annapolis, had left them with hardly a round for each musket.

I was in conversation with the Prince and the Chevalier when an officer of Cumberland's army with an escort was brought through our lines under a flag of truce. To our surprise it was Lord Loudoun, who had been sent to ask for terms. There was astonishment in our ranks at this sudden submission, for we little knew how badly things had gone with them, having neither powder nor serviceable field pieces, and finding the gaol fever come as their companion from Annapolis. Indeed, in the warmth of the Maryland summer the fever spread with a terrible speed. The lower reaches of the Potomac were cluttered with the bodies of those who died on the transports and, having been buried with too little weight, were brought ashore by every tide.

We afterwards heard that, until our attack this afternoon upon the rear of his position, the Duke of Cumberland had no news of his loss of Annapolis. Thereupon he called a council of war and received the bitter advice from his senior officers that no victory could be achieved while his own army diminished and the Marylanders swelled the ranks of our own. If he would fight on, it must be by the banks of the Potomac, in a hostile land, without supplies, surrounded on three sides by his enemies and with the river on his fourth side. The whole of his army (which might otherwise serve to keep the French from New England) must be lost. Having it in his power to lose both the northern and southern provinces of America for his master, the Duke wisely chose only to abandon the south.

Lord Loudoun, a bluff and honest soldier in his way, was brought into the presence of that Prince whom he had hunted and harried in Scotland, and had but lately confronted in Williamsburg. Now his lordship knelt courteously and, with equal courtesy, the Prince bade him rise and be seated. Terms were then given him.

'Sir,' said His Royal Highness, 'you may tell the son of the late Elector of Hanover that I will be kinder to him than he ever was to my people in Scotland. His soldiers, who come here as rebels against the government of my royal father, King James III, will ground their arms and remain in their camp. When the articles of surrender are agreed and signed, they will march out with colours cased and without any music being played. The ships of war that brought them here shall await them at Annapolis and, with the transports, shall carry them at once to England. Yet there is one thing more. Before any soldier leaves Maryland, he is to be given a free choice, either for returning to England or for staying in Maryland or Virginia as a loyal subject of my father. Those are my terms, sir. If they are to be accepted, I shall expect that acceptance to be conveyed to me here by your commander himself before midnight.'

This last requirement caused some dismay to honest

old Loudoun, who then retired to the English camp. A little while after, it being now ten o'clock, a message was brought that the Duke of Cumberland was with the fleet and could not appear in person, but that Loudoun had been authorised as his deputy in all matters.

'He cannot be with the fleet yet,' said the Prince at once. 'He has fled the field of battle, that is all. Colonel Fraser, you know the road to Annapolis well enough by now. Find him and bring him to me.'

Weary though I was, having slept only for two short spells since the battle began, I set off with Sergeant Innes and a troop of the Life Guards on the road to Annapolis. We rode several miles, finding disorder everywhere with many stragglers on foot and carts piled high with baggage. Yet there was no sign of anyone resembling the Duke of Cumberland. We had gone fully four or five miles towards the city when we saw in the middle of the road a coach, the very one I had seen in the afternoon on our returning from Annapolis. Its doors were open and it was deserted. From the trees by the roadside I heard an obscure scuffle, and I guessed from the royal arms of Hanover on the door of the coach what this must mean. By the light of our lanterns we saw a poor old man in a shift, sitting against a tree in terror, while a boy prepared to fire a pistol at him and a young woman looked on.

'Pray, sir,' begged the old man of me, 'save me from this boy!'

I could not at first credit what I saw. Yet this was the Duke of Cumberland who had fled the confusion of the defeated army in his nightshirt and had hoped to find sanctuary with the fleet. How had he been betrayed by his whore and his coachboy, who seemed to be his only escort!

We gave him surety of safe-conduct and treated him as humanely as we might. The whore and the coachboy were taken to Annapolis, where both were subsequently stripped and whipped, in the sight of the citizens, for their unexampled cruelty. Our little party rode back to the Prince's tent by the Potomac. The Duke of Cumberland rode in his coach, in company with Sergeant Innes, the Duke speaking not a word and the Sergeant, from time to time, saying in a voice for all to hear, 'God bless King Jamie and the bonnie Prince, his son.'

At the Prince's tent the Duke was brought to His Royal Highness, who looked in amazement at such a sight. The Duke's appearance is gross, his face fat and enraged, his eyes staring as they habitually do. His body, which was all too evident in his nightshirt, bore the outline of a vast and loathsome corpulence. At the appearance of the Prince, whom he was accustomed to sneer at as 'the Pretender's boy', the Duke seemed not to know where to put himself. The Prince before whom he stood was to him both Prince and traitor, rebel and conqueror. He might have knelt or bowed, or done nothing, but he inclined his head in a sort of bow and said, 'Your servant, sir,' in a gruff voice which indicated that he considered himself to be no man's servant.

'Will you not be seated, sir?' said the Prince mildly.

'No sir, I will not.'

'Oh come, sir, pray be seated,' said the Prince, 'for I do not care that my guests should stand upon ceremony.'

How the Duke expected to be treated I cannot tell, but the two men of royal blood acted together as ordinary gentlemen. The Prince insisted that clothes be brought for his prisoner and these were acquired, though of an ill fit, for the only officer among us who approached the Duke's bulk was a Virginian captain of artillery. Yet the clothes of an officer in the Stuart army were better than a nightshirt.

Prince Charles Edward repeated his terms for the conclusion of peace. Cumberland became sulky and did not care, and would not listen, but finally did listen and agreed to all that was demanded, saying, 'Very well, sir. If it must be so, it shall be so. I wish you joy of this infernal swamp and the savages who live among it. You shall have your terms, sir.'

'I am glad to find Your Grace so amenable,' said the Prince, doing the Duke the courtesy of allowing him his Hanoverian title. 'My Life Guards shall see you safe to your own camp.'

'No, sir,' said Cumberland testily, 'I would go to the fleet, to Annapolis.'

'So you may, sir,' said the Prince. 'My Life Guards shall escort you there.'

Cumberland stumped over to the door of the tent. Neither man, though they had twice been one another's adversaries, spoke a word of Culloden and its terrible history. Yet at the door of the tent the Duke of Cumberland turned to look for a last time upon the Prince whom he had defeated in Scotland but who had escaped him then, and whose prisoner the Duke now was.

'You have been lucky, sir,' said Cumberland gruffly. 'Damnably lucky, sir. On two occasions, then and now. You know you have been lucky, sir. But I tell you this, sir, that you shall not be lucky another time!'

And with that he parted from us. His carriage bore him away to Annapolis, where he was taken aboard his fleet in the ill-tailored uniform of a Jacobite captain of artillery. I afterwards heard that two sailors upon the flagship, who were witnesses of this, were flogged for laughing.

9 June 1761. For the better part of two weeks the camps of the Prince and the Hanoverian army have faced one another with no shot fired. The arms of Cumberland's men are grounded, their guns spiked, and they pass the time by calling out to our men, though forbidden to do so. It is believed that two or three hundred of them may remain here as the Prince's subjects.

This morning the articles of surrender were signed by the Prince, for his father King James III, and by Lord

Loudoun. The Duke of Cumberland remains on board his flagship with some indisposition. Both the Prince and the Chevalier signed on our part and I was happy that the brave young Lieutenant Louis de Johnstone was sufficiently recovered from his wound to witness this, though he has lost the entire use of his left arm.

Early in the afternoon the English soldiers, who were camped close to Annapolis last night, marched out of their camp, having grounded their arms. They passed down the road to the harbour between two lines of Virginian, Maryland, Highland and Irish soldiers. It was a sad spectacle, though a necessary one. Their colours were cased, their drums silent, and many of their men limped or shuffled rather than marched. There were no fewer than 4,000 or 5,000 of them in three files, almost a mile in length. They were marched on to their transports and a little after one o'clock the first of the English merchantmen swung slowly from her anchorage and sailed towards Chesapeake Bay and the open sea. Beyond Cape Charles their men of war awaited them. A dozen of their transports were loaded during the afternoon and, one by one, turned out into the stream.

The Prince, who had attended a solemn *Te Deum* in St Anne's Church, was seen by the citizens of Annapolis for almost the first time when he left the building. He was cheered by his own soldiers and by the people of the town as he rode on his horse, with the Chevalier and General Byrd, to witness the departure of the last of the enemy force. The church bells pealed and above the ruined shell of the parliament house, where the bricks were blackened by fire, there flew the standard which bore the Prince of Wales's feathers and the motto 'Charles P.R.' in gold, signifying his Regency for his royal father. All eyes turned to him as the very emblem of our future, for by the light of the setting sun the last English ships were already hull down upon the horizon.

8

ABDICATION AND SUCCESSION

*Following the victory at Annapolis, two further entries occur
in the journal of Lovat Fraser. They were made in September
1761, three months after the battle. The first was written at the
beginning of the month, and the second towards its end.*

1 September 1761. The Cardinal Prince, Henry of York,
is come again. He appears as a private gentleman, though
one who bears a most solemn message. Yet to the most
tender consciences of Williamsburg the marriage of
Prince Charles Edward and the prospect of a direct line
of inheritance takes away much of the sting otherwise
imparted by the presence of his brother, the Cardinal
Prince. So he, the Duke of York, comes here as the envoy
of King James III, who lies so sick at Rome that he
could not survive a journey from there to Westminster
to be crowned, much less an ocean voyage of many weeks
to Williamsburg. This is a sorrow to many of our people,
for the world never knew so gentle a man nor so noble a
king.

To many of his subjects, the first news of the King's
message was its reading in the form of a proclamation.
This was done before the Palace, the Capitol and the

Courthouse of Williamsburg. It was read also in Fredericksburg, Winchester, Norfolk, Hampton, Yorktown, and several other considerable towns of the Province. It was read too in Annapolis and Charlestown, that the people of Maryland and Carolina might hear their Sovereign's will. It might have been read in London, Edinburgh and Dublin, for it belonged as much there as here.

The people stood silent before the Capitol of Williamsburg as the proclamation was read in English, French and Latin by the Athlone King-of-Arms.

We, James Francis Edward, by the Grace of God, of Great Britain, France, and the Americas, King, Defender of the Faith, do solemnly enjoin Our loyal subjects to witness this, Our Instrument of Abdication.

Let all men know that We do henceforth resign Our Crown and Our Exercise of Kingship to Our Well-Beloved Son, Charles Edward Louis Casimir, Prince of Wales, Regent of the Americas, Duke of Cornwall, and Earl of Albany, Knight of the Most Noble Order of the Garter.

All those powers which God entrusted to Us, We do now convey to him. All powers, titles, and dignities whatsoever belonging to Us are henceforward his, entailed to his heirs in perpetuity. All lands, territories, and kingdoms which, by Divine decree and the laws of men were Ours, shall now be his. All loyalty paid to Us shall now be due to him.

Given under Our Royal Seal at Our Court in Rome, upon the Festival of St Dominick, in the Year of Our Lord One Thousand Seven Hundred and Sixty-One.
JAMES R.
God Save the King!

In that moment, how many thoughts among the Highlanders, who were now freeholders in the land of Virginia, must have turned to the battles fought by their clans for the old cause, and for the dying King who lay at the Palazzo Muti in the heat of the Roman summer.

And then, as 'God Save the King!' was proclaimed once more, it was not King James but King Charles III of Virginia for whom proclamation was made. A little afterwards the new King drove from the Palace to the Capitol to receive oaths of allegiance from his principal ministers of state and, the length of Duke of Gloucester Street, the crowds cheered for him and for Queen Antoinette (as Madame La Princesse must now be called) who sat beside him in the carriage. To have a king in London, or even in Rome, is one thing. But to have a king in Williamsburg, where the people may see him, and where he may smile upon them and call them his own dear subjects, is quite another consideration. The natural grace and amiability of Charles Edward have now won all but the most adamantine hearts.

23 September 1761. This was the day chosen for the Coronation of the Prince as his father's successor. From early morning the streets of Williamsburg were crowded as for a May fair. The Burgesses from all the counties of Virginia, as well as those from the other Stuart provinces of Maryland and Carolina, have brought their wives and all their dependants to see the procession and the ceremonial. The great houses are decked with flowers and with bunting, seeming as busy as they might be at the height of the season.

The sun shone brilliantly, and by eight o'clock there was such an appearance of midsummer that men were sent to lay the dust by watering the streets the procession was to follow between the Palace and Bruton Church. There was never such a parade of bonnets and dresses, or such a traffic of coaches and carriages, as the great men and ladies of the Stuart Kingdom, attended by their black servants in livery, wheeled here and there, the spokes glittering in the strong light.

The Prince rose early the day of his Coronation and retired a little before breakfast with Dr Shebbeare who was to perform the ceremony. The Reverend Doctor suffered long in England for the cause of his true King, roundly and bravely condemning the malignant star of Hanoverian politics. For this, the usurpers set him in the pillory and mocked him, not three years since. Yet he bid defiance to them all and swore loyalty to King James alone. He was pressed to abjure his beliefs and run with that herd of clerks that cringed about the Elector of Hanover, but he would not. Twelve months since, he crossed secretly into France and thence to Virginia, where the Prince received him with honour. This same Dr Shebbeare is now consecrated, by the wish of His Royal Highness, Bishop of Williamsburg and Primate of all Virginia.

Having prayed some time with the Bishop, the Prince next received his brother, the Cardinal Duke of York. Though there was some misgiving on the Cardinal's part that the ceremony of crowning was not to be performed according to the Roman faith, they met lovingly as brothers. Some time since, the Prince explained to his brother York that he would have the ceremony done according to the religion as by law established. For, though in his conscience he might keep a place for the Bishop of Rome, yet here he was Prince of all the people and must be crowned in the most public manner for all of them by the Bishop of Williamsburg. Yet to show himself brotherly he wished today to create the Cardinal Duke the Prince of Maryland, an honour standing only less in America than the title of Charles Edward himself and his own progeny. It was done, also, that the Cardinal Duke might move a little away from Williamsburg to a province where the great number of Papists would make him a welcome protector.

I am assured by the Chevalier that, in truth, the Cardinal Prince will never determine to settle here or in Maryland.

'Mark me, sir,' said the Chevalier, 'Prince Henry will shortly take ship and return to Rome. I have known him a dozen years and I promise you that he has too strong a taste for that Holy City ever to settle in so worldly a Kingdom as ours.'

A little after this, Charles Edward went to his Queen and greeted her tenderly, she being prepared at this time to accompany him to the place of the Coronation. I had gone to the Palace with the Chevalier a little before this hour and saw Her Majesty in a fine silk robe. The radiance of her eyes, the perfect oval of her face, and the beauty of her hair so chestnut brown, held such loveliness that, though a man had seen her a thousand times, yet he would be seized by her appearance as upon the first occasion. She has that perfection which makes every man think that, if he could choose a mistress, he would have her of no other pattern than this. There never was a Queen who combined with such a liveliness of mind so complete a presence as this. By her, the Prince's dominion over his people will not be so much added to but rather multiplied an hundredfold.

For all that I knew of her and of the Prince, there was something in her manner today which was quite new to me and which I could not explain. In the presence of the Prince they both seemed more loving and more pleased with one another in a fashion which was much at variance with the great solemnity that the day required. Her eyes played upon him, as his upon hers, so as to suggest that in their mutual affection they were for the time being indifferent to the world and all its honours. A fine enough game for a shepherd and his shepherdess, but no sport for a king upon the day of his crowning! I recollected then the Prince's telling me that he was never happier than when living with his few followers in the Highlands after the '45, while the Hanoverian army hunted him for his life. Yet now he must break himself of such fond imaginings as this, and train his mind to matters of policy and to the great affairs of government. I did not, of course, know this morning what the Chevalier was later to make me acquainted with.

As seems the custom here, the crowds along the way remained almost silent until the Prince himself appeared. The people of Virginia make one feel that they may either like or dislike the hero of the hour and that they have not yet made up their minds whether to do one or the other. Then, at a few minutes after eleven o'clock, there was the thunder of a single cannon to show that the procession had begun to pass out through the gates of the Palace. A squadron of Life Guards in royal blue with bronze helmets, the sun through the leaves dappling their tunics with splashes of light, led the triumphal procession that rode down the broad mall and entered the main highway. Though the church of Bruton Parish lies only a little way from the Palace, the Prince had given orders that the procession was to make a circuit of the town, so that all who wished to see him might do so.

Behind the Prince's Life Guards, there came first the royal carriage with the arms of the House of Stuart upon its sides. The Prince and his Queen sat together, a picture of grace and harmony, the footmen in livery standing behind them as they rode. The carriages which followed them bore the Cardinal Prince, Henry of Maryland and York; the Secretaries of State, Lord Byrd and Sir John Randolph; Fitzhugh of Marmion, and the Athlone King-of-Arms; the envoys of France, Spain, Portugal, and Rome; the Commander of the Virginian Army, Lord de Johnstone (whom I shall never learn to call other than the Chevalier), and those who made up their Majesties' royal household. I rode with the Chevalier, being now Secretary of the Army under his command, while Captain Louis de Johnstone, who will never have the use of his left arm again, rode as Equerry to the Prince.

At every window there was bunting and a great waving of handkerchiefs. At every moment the cheers of the people were so loud that, if all the church bells of the land had pealed together in Williamsburg, I do not suppose that we should have heard them. I thought of Annapolis, and of Ogilvie, my friend who had fallen there. I thought of Quebec, and the terrible judgment that overtook the Hanoverian army there. I thought, too, of an April day sixteen years ago, when I and my kinsman, Archibald Fraser, and Mackintosh of Farr, and the young Laird of Inshes, had played truant from our tutor at Petty to lie all night in the heather upon the verge of Drummossie Moor. There in the morning light we had seen the clans forming their line of battle, and heard the pipes that played in the dawning of Culloden. The Master of Lovat and the Clan Fraser took their places there against the mighty army of the Duke of Cumberland, swearing either to see King James III wear the crown that was his by every right, or else to die there as his champions. It seems now as though it were all a story, the clans charging into the rain of English shot, the Prince vowing to lead his beaten men in a last and glorious attack upon the Hanoverian victors.

Who would have thought then to see him wear a crown? And who would have thought that it would be placed upon his head in a new continent, which none of us had ever seen, not two hundred miles from the territory of savage tribes and a great unexplored wilderness? I thought of the Chevalier's words after Quebec, and his promise to restore the House of Stuart to a Kingdom greater than any that the Elector of Hanover possessed. What had then seemed a vain fancy, even after the defeat of General Wolfe, now appeared almost a probability. I even thought that I, who had seen the murder at Culloden, might live to see this great Kingdom built in the new world.

After the brilliance of the late morning sun, the light inside Bruton Church seemed little enough. There were candles in a great array, and sconces, whose softer glow fell upon the robes of the kneeling Peers, Councillors and Burgesses loyal to their Prince. The church of Bruton Parish is smaller than an abbey, and yet it was large enough to contain within its pews some hundreds of the greatest citizens of the new world, and some of the best of the old. Opposite to the pulpit, on the other side of the chancel, stood what had once been the throne of the Governor of the Province, and which was now become the throne of the Prince himself, under a red silk canopy.

At the entrance of the Prince, his Queen and the whole company of us, the choristers of the College of William and Mary began their gentle anthem, 'O Where Shall Wisdom Be Found', the work of Dr Boyce, whom the Prince wished he might have for his Master of Music. By the chancel steps, the Bishop of Williamsburg and his attendant clergy received Charles Edward and accompanied him to the throne. A little apart from us, I saw that the Cardinal Duke of York observed the proceedings in a plain habit, which had been chosen so that he should not easily be distinguished among the congregation. He seemed not to notice the ceremony much but was content to pray from a little book of his own, which no doubt contained such prayers as were consonant with the faith of a Prince of the Church.

The Peers, Councillors, and Burgesses who were present wore robes of scarlet silk, which were simpler than might have been the style at either Westminster or St Germain. Yet, in such numbers as were there, they made a brave display. I was close to the Chevalier as the liturgy of the

Coronation began. He seemed to be much occupied in seeking out who, among the Burgesses and others, had come to be present with us, and who had not. He would mutter to me from time to time that such an one was present, or that another had chosen to slight his Prince by refusing to attend. Soon I was playing at the same game, and after a time I thought I detected some who were absent.

'I do not see Colonel Carter, sir, nor his son,' I said softly to the Chevalier.

'No, sir,' muttered he, 'but neither is of much consequence. They will huff and puff at one another until they are of no account to any other man.'

With that we gave our attention to the ceremonial for a little while.

'Colonel Washington is not here either,' said I.

'No, sir,' said the Chevalier, 'Colonel Washington is not here. But mark my words, sir, he is likely to be heard from again. Why, was he not the instrument of Charles Edward's greatest victory a few months since?'

'Why,' said I, 'Colonel Washington was not within a hundred miles of Annapolis that day.'

The Chevalier dropped his voice still further and favoured me with a significant glance.

'A greater victory than Annapolis,' said he. 'To put it more plainly, sir, the Prince and his Queen are like a pair of love-struck calves. Sir, *la Reine est enceinte*. There will be no Cardinal Prince ruling Virginia. There will never be King Henry IX. God willing, in five months more King Charles will have an heir. No battle, sir, will so secure the hearts of his American subjects as the first inheritor of our old dominions to be born in this new continent. Imagine, sir, what an American king might do!'

'And Colonel Washington?' said I.

'Why, sir,' said the Chevalier with some impatience,

'was not all this in pursuit of the very advice that Colonel Washington gave His Highness in Fredericksburg at the time of the French treaty? Annapolis taught him to win a Kingdom, sir, and Colonel Washington has taught him how to keep it!'

Several of those nearby were by now looking curiously at the Chevalier. We both fell silent. The news of the Queen's pregnancy explained all her closeness with the King that morning. The idea so seized my mind that I could only think what effect it must have in the ears of the Cardinal Prince, the courtiers of Williamsburg in their scarlet robes, and the silent crowds that waited in the sunlit streets outside to greet their new, undoubted King.

When I looked again, a stronger light falling through the windows of the nave lit that chaplet of gold which Dr Shebbeare's hands now lowered towards the temples of the kneeling Prince. The din of the trumpets on either side at once proclaimed to the world, Charles Edward, by the Grace of God, of Virginia and Great Britain, King, Defender of the Faith. The brazen triumph faded, and from the scarlet ranks around him burst the loyal shout that drowned the trumpets' dying echo.

'Vivat!'
'Vivat!'
'Vivat!'

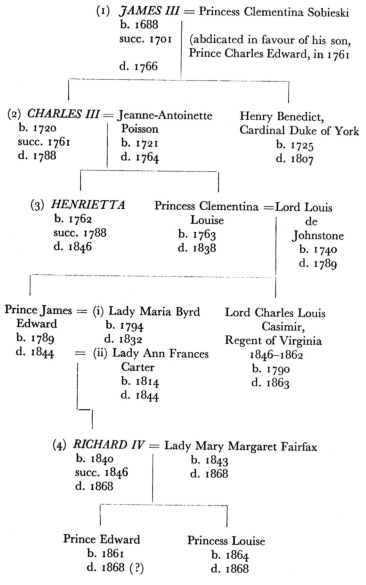

(1) *JAMES III* = Princess Clementina Sobieski
b. 1688
succ. 1701   (abdicated in favour of his son,
Prince Charles Edward, in 1761
d. 1766

(2) *CHARLES III* = Jeanne-Antoinette   Henry Benedict,
b. 1720   Poisson   Cardinal Duke of York
succ. 1761   b. 1721   b. 1725
d. 1788   d. 1764   d. 1807

(3) *HENRIETTA*   Princess Clementina =Lord Louis
b. 1762   Louise   de
succ. 1788   b. 1763   Johnstone
d. 1846   d. 1838   b. 1740
                                                  d. 1789

Prince James = (i) Lady Maria Byrd   Lord Charles Louis
Edward   b. 1794   Casimir,
b. 1789   d. 1832   Regent of Virginia
d. 1844   = (ii) Lady Ann Frances   1846–1862
                     Carter   b. 1790
                     b. 1814   d. 1863
                     d. 1844

(4) *RICHARD IV* = Lady Mary Margaret Fairfax
b. 1840   b. 1843
succ. 1846   d. 1868
d. 1868

Prince Edward   Princess Louise
b. 1861   b. 1864
d. 1868 (?)   d. 1868

HISTORICAL NOTE TO

PRINCE CHARLIE'S BLUFF

At the time of the American Revolutionary War, it was rumoured that certain Virginian gentlemen, distrusting both rule from London and American republicanism, had invited Prince Charles Edward to become ruler of the province of Virginia. Such men were, presumably, anti-republican Tories of the stamp of William Byrd III or John Randolph. The Prince, over fifty years old and much the worse for drink, declined the offer.

The assumption of *Prince Charlie's Bluff* is that the offer was made under more favourable political and military circumstances, when the Prince was 38 or 39, and that he accepted it.

Though this novel alters particular events, it does not alter the most important underlying situations. The epigraph is, of course, a straight quotation. Facts and quotations given on pages 13 and 14 are authentic.

In 1758, Wolfe did break off the attack on Louisberg, resuming it only when he saw that some of his men were already ashore. The restrictions placed upon Fraser's Highlanders and the manner of their disposal was, in outline, as described on page 16.

Wolfe's remarks on Scots and Americans, his ill-health,

his enmity with Brigadier Townshend and his quarrels with his other brigadiers were as reported here. The blunder at Montmorency took place as described. It was expected by such men as Horace Walpole that Wolfe would fail to take Quebec. Bougainville and his force arrived before the city on the day of the battle, though not until the British had routed the French infantry. In this novel his arrival is some three hours earlier.

The Chevalier de Johnstone was aide-de-camp to Prince Charles at Culloden and, as a Jacobite exile, to Montcalm at Quebec. The interception of British despatches, to which he refers on page 65, took place.

Among later characters in this first book, Colonel William Byrd III, Colonel Landon Carter, Robert Wormeley Carter, Lord Loudoun and others of less importance had the general dispositions described here. The role of the Scots in Virginia, particularly of men like Hugh Mercer (who survived Culloden to die as one of Washington's generals in the Revolutionary War) was much as described. The forces available to Prince Charles, Scots, Irish, Virginians and Cherokee, would have been of about the numbers given. The details of gaol fever, at the battle of Annapolis, are taken from contemporary accounts. The outbreak of this fever on English transports was said to have reduced considerably the effectiveness of the army which went to fight in the Revolutionary War.

BIOGRAPHICAL NOTES

Since the events described in Lovat Fraser's journal differ considerably from the versions given in other sources, it may be useful to summarise the lives of certain characters as recorded in hitherto received history. Lovat Fraser, of course, occurs nowhere but in his own journal.

BYRD, William (1728–1777). Grandson of William Byrd, Stuart courtier and emigrant to Virginia; only son of William Byrd II, colonial legislator and diarist. William Byrd III was a staunch Royalist and Tory, who inherited the great house at Westover, Virginia, and other estates on the James River. He was Colonel of the 2nd Virginia regiment, held the allegiance of Cherokee warriors, and like Washington served against the French and their Indian allies in the Seven Years War of 1756–1763. He lost much of his family fortune by horse-racing and gambling. Encumbered by debts and depressed by the coming victory of the rebel colonists against the British Crown, he took his own life in 1777. The house at West-over contained one of the finest collections of books and furniture to be found in Colonial America.

CHARLES III, Charles Edward Stuart (1720–1788). Elder son of 'The Old Pretender,' James III and grandson of the deposed James II. Prince of Wales; Prince Regent of Great Britain, 1745–1746; succeeded his father as Charles III on 1 January 1766. Known to the Hanoverians as 'The Young Pretender.' Commander of the Stuart army in Scotland and England, 1745–1746. After landing in the Hebrides with a handful of supporters in 1745, he gathered an army of Highlanders and marched south to Edinburgh. James III was proclaimed King in the Scottish capital, Charles Edward being his Prince Regent and Prince of Wales. After defeating the Hanoverian army at Prestonpans, Prince Charles advanced as far south as Derby, and seemed on the brink of victory. But even when the royal yacht was waiting to carry George II to the safety of Hanover, the Prince's generals advised him to withdraw to the safety of the Highlands. Though he defeated another Hanoverian army at Falkirk, he was himself defeated by the Duke of Cumberland (q.v.) at Culloden, near Inverness, on 16 April 1746. After being hunted by the Duke's army for several months, with a price of £30,000 on his head (which induced no one to betray him) he was taken off from the western coast of Scotland in a French ship. It is said that he travelled incognito to visit his supporters in London at various times between 1750 and 1760, but the invasion of Britain by the Stuarts was never again seriously contemplated. In 1772 he married Louise, Princesse de Stolberg, but had no children by her. His only child was an illegitimate daughter, Charlotte, Countess of Albany, whose mother was Clementina Walkinshaw. He was succeeded by his younger brother as Henry IX (q.v.).

CUMBERLAND, William Augustus, Duke of (1721–1765). 2nd son of George II. Commanded British left against the French at Dettingen, 1743; commander of combined allied army at Fontenoy, 1745. Recalled from the Flanders campaign upon the landing of Prince Charles Edward in Scotland, 1745. Commander of the Hanoverian army at Culloden, 16 April 1746. Known as 'The Butcher' for his brutal hunting and killing of the defeated Jacobite soldiers and their families. Defeated by the Duc de Richelieu in 1757; obliged to surrender at Closterseven and evacuate Hanover. His popularity having declined steadily since Culloden, he then retired into private life.

FRASER, Simon, 12th Baron Fraser of Lovat (1667–1747). 2nd son of Thomas, Lord Lovat. A leader of the Clan Fraser and follower of the House of Stuart, though sometimes alleged to have worked for both the Stuarts and the Hanoverians. Military adviser to James III at the court of St Germain, 1702–1704. Secret mission to Scotland, 1704. Imprisoned in the castle of Angoulême on suspicion of betraying information to the English court, 1704–1714. Returned to his Highland estates, 1714–1745. Despatched the Fraser Highlanders under his eldest son, Simon, the Master of Lovat (q.v.) to join Prince Charles Edward, 1745. Castle Dounie, the seat of the Frasers, was destroyed by English troops after Culloden. Lord Lovat was captured by Cumberland's soldiers on an island in Loch Morar, tried for treason, and executed, 9 April 1747.

FRASER Simon (1726–1782). Eldest son of Simon, Lord Fraser of Lovat. Master of Lovat. Colonel of the Fraser Highlanders in the army of Prince Charles Edward, 1745–1746. Captured and imprisoned after Culloden. Pardoned, 1750. Raised 1,800 clansmen as part of the army of General Wolfe (q.v.) for the campaign against Louisberg and Quebec, 1757. Colonel of the Highlanders at the capture of Quebec, 1759. Brigadier-General of the British army in the Portugal campaign, 1762.

HENRY IX, Henry Benedict Stuart (1725–1807). Younger son of James III. Duke of York; Cardinal Bishop of Ostia, Tusculum, and Velletri; Cardinal Bishop of Frascati. Succeeded his brother as Henry IX on 31 January 1788. His acceptance of a Cardinal's hat in May 1747 contributed to the extinction of the House of Stuart and to an immediate alienation of support.

HERVEY, John, 1st Baron Hervey (1696–1743). Son of John, 1st Earl of Bristol. Court favourite of George II and Queen Caroline. Whig M.P. for Bury St Edmunds, 1725; Vice-Chamberlain to the royal family, 1730; created 1st Baron Hervey, 1733; Lord Privy Seal in Sir Robert Walpole's ministry, 1740–1742. Author of *Memoirs of the Reign of George II*, published in an expurgated edition in 1848; new edition, 1931. Satirised as 'Sporus' and 'Lord Fanny' in Pope's *Imitations of Horace*. Lady Mary Wortley Montagu divided mankind into three sexes, 'men, women, and Herveys.'

JOHNSON, Samuel (1709–1784). Conversationalist, poet, novelist, critic. Subject of James Boswell's *Journal of a Tour to the Hebrides*, 1785, and his *Life of Samuel Johnson*, 1791. Johnson's principal works include the verse tragedy *Irene*, 1749; *The Vanity of Human Wishes*, 1749; *A Dictionary of the English Language*, 1755; *Rasselas, Prince of Abyssinia*, 1759; *Lives of the English Poets*, 1779–1781. He was the principal contributor to the *Rambler*, 1750–1752, and to the *Idler*, 1758–1760. His literary achievement was eclipsed by his reputation as a talker, following the foundation of the Literary Club at the Turk's Head, Gerrard Street, London, in 1764. Among his fellow members were Sir Joshua Reynolds, Edmund Burke, Oliver Goldsmith, David Garrick, and Charles James Fox. Johnson was an ardent Tory, and a Jacobite supporter, until it seemed that all hope of restoring the Stuart Kings was lost.

JOHNSTONE, James, Chevalier de (1719–c.1800). Only son of an Edinburgh merchant. Captain in the army of Prince Charles Edward (Duke of Perth's regiment), 1745–1746. Aide-de-camp to Lord George Murray; aide-de-camp to Prince Charles Edward. After escaping from Culloden, joined the French army as the Chevalier de Johnstone. Aide-de-camp to Montcalm at Quebec,

1759. Created Chevalier de Saint-Louis, 1762. Author of *Memoirs of the Rebellion, 1745–1746*, published in 1820.

POISSON, Jeanne-Antoinette, Marquise de Pompadour (1721–1764). *Maîtresse en titre* of Louis XV after 1745. Patroness of Voltaire and Crébillon, among writers, and of Boucher and Greuze, among painters. In later years she thwarted her rivals for royal favour by personally supervising the entertainments of the court and by procuring less ambitious young women for the King. She gave her name to a fine artificiality in the decoration and style of life at Versailles. In politics, she influenced the appointment of the King's ministers, and endeavoured to destroy the alliance with Germany in favour of a new treaty with Austria. This was a contributing cause of the Seven Years War of 1756–1763.

WALPOLE, Horace, 4th Earl of Orford (1717–1797). 4th son of Sir Robert Walpole. Creator of Strawberry Hill, Twickenham; author of *The Castle of Otranto*, 1764, and *Historic Doubts on Richard III*, 1768. His volumes of correspondence with Sir Horace Mann and others, between 1732 and 1797, offer one of the most intimate and detailed pictures of English society and politics in the eighteenth century.

WASHINGTON, George (1732–1799). Aide-de-camp to General Braddock in the campaign of 1755 against the French and the Indians. Retired from the British army in 1758 in order to attend to his family estates at Mount Vernon, Virginia. Appointed Commander-in-Chief of the American forces in the Revolutionary War, 1775; President of the American Convention, 1787; first President of the United States, 1789. He appears as a Colonel in the army of George II in Thackeray's novel, *The Virginians*.

WILKES, John (1727–1797). Rake, wit, and political satirist. With Sir Francis Dashwood and Bubb Doddington, became a leader of the notorious Hellfire Club. M.P. for Aylesbury, 1757. Editor of the *North Briton*, 1762.

Prosecuted in 1763 for a libel on Lord Bute, the Prime Minister, and for an *Essay on Woman*, an obscene parody of Pope's *Essay on Man*. Fled to Paris, outlawed, returned to England, 1768. M.P. for Middlesex, 1768; expelled from the House of Commons for libel, 1769; re-elected three times for Middlesex before being allowed to take his seat. Lord Mayor of London, 1774. Famous for his ripostes: when told by Lord Sandwich that he would die either on the gallows or of the pox, Wilkes is said to have replied, 'That depends, my Lord, on whether I embrace your lordship's principles or your lordship's mistress.'

WOLFE, James (1727–1759). Ensign, 12th regiment of foot, 1741. Present at the battle of Dettingen as adjutant of the regiment, 1743. Captain, 4th regiment of foot, 1744. Present at battles of Falkirk and Culloden, 1746. Major, 1749; Lieutenant-Colonel, 1750; Brigadier-General, 1758. Commander of Cape Breton expedition, 1758. Capture of Louisberg, 1758. Commander of Quebec expedition, 1759. Mortally wounded in the successful assault upon the city, 13 September 1759.